JAMES BOND

the history of the illustrated 007

Alan J. Porter

HERMES PRESS

neshannock, pennsylvania

Copyright ©2008 Alan J. Porter
No part of this book may be reproduced in any form without written permission from the publisher

Published by Hermes Press
2100 Wilmington Road
Neshannock, Pennsylvania 16105
(724) 652-0511
www.HermesPress.com; info@hermespress.com

Cover artwork: Bob Peak
Cover and book design by Daniel Herman
Cover and book design ©2008 Hermes Press
First printing, 2008

LCCN 2008935001
ISBN 1-932563-18-0
Image and digital corrections by H + G Media; Louise Geer, Editor; Margaret Sopkovich, proofreading
From Dan, Louise, Sabrina, and D'zur for Gort and Maya

Portions of this text have previously appeared in different formats in the following publications: Back Issue Magazine (TwoMorrows, ISSN 1932-6904), Comicopia – The International Comics APA (Savage Enterprises Publishing, ISSN 1480-9508), James Bond: Death Wing (Titan Books, ISBN 1-84576-517-6), James Bond: Shark Bait (Titan Books, ISBN 1-84576-591-5), James Bond: The Paradise Plot (Titan Books, ISBN 1-84576-716-0)

The publishers have made every effort to credit the artists and/or copyright holders whose work has been reproduced in this book. We apologize for any omissions, which will be corrected in future editions.

All DC Comics, Marvel Comics and other comic book companies' material, illustration, titles, characters, related logos and other distinguishing marks remain the trademark and copyright of their respective copyright holders and are reproduced here for the purposes of historical and scholarly study. All illustrations used in this book that show trademarked material have been reproduced from copies in the private collections of Alan J. Porter, Daniel Herman, Johnny Oreskov, and Anders Frejdh and are included for illustrative purposes only.

This work is not authorized or endorsed by either Ian Fleming Publications Limited (formerly known as Glidrose Publications Limited), or EON Productions.

The 007 gun symbol logo is © Danjaq S.A. and United Artists Company.
The Bond silhouette logo is © Danjaq S.A. and United Artists Company

Dedication
For Gill, Meggan and Erin. Without you, the world would not be enough.

Publisher's Note

For those of us who grew up in the 1960s, James Bond, The Beatles, President Kennedy, the Civil Rights movement, and the Vietnam war were indelible parts of that era. James Bond was hardly the most significant aspect of those times but the series of films which came to fruition starting in 1962, and which inspired countless imitators, have come to typify, at least in part, what was "cool" and "hip" in the swinging 1960s. One aspect of the Bond series which preceded the 1960s and which continues to this day, James Bond's appearances in comic strips and comic books, has up until now has never been properly documented. This situation has now been rectified by the excellent scholarship of Alan J. Porter which you now hold in your hands.

— *Daniel Herman*, Publisher

Printed in Hong Kong

introduction	James Bond and Me	4
chapter 1	James Bond — A Comics History	10
chapter 2	The Series	32
chapter 3	The Missions	46
chapter 4	Talking Bond	156
chapter 5	A Bibliography and the Films	168
acknowledgments		172
afterword		174

contents

JAMES BOND
AGENT 007

Nr. 1 - Pris kr. 1,85

HØJT SPIL I MONTE CARLO

introduction
James Bond and Me

It began with plastic frogmen. The year was 1966. My friend Geoff had been given the *Thunderball* board game for his birthday. We played it incessantly. Every chance we got, after school, on weekends. Whenever we could we would immerse ourselves in the world of James Bond. The thing was, no-one in our circle of friends really knew who James Bond was. Sure the name was familiar in our seven year-old world, but in the same way that names heard on TV or seen in the newspapers permeated our consciousness. But, this game with its plastic frogmen and the cool looking hero figure seemed to hint at even greater adventure.

I guess my conversation at home must have been littered with mentions of Bond, for that Christmas among my stack of presents there was a Corgi model Aston Martin DB5 complete with ejector seat, and a James Bond hardback annual. The stories, articles, and above all photographs in that annual added whole new layers to the fascinating world of this Secret Agent.

Cover from a Danish James Bond comic book adaptation of *Casino Royale*, 1965.

The photographs were stills from *Goldfinger* and *Thunderball*. They made the world of secret agents seem cool and glamorous. I was determined to find out more. But with the fickleness of youth, my resolve lasted less than a few weeks before something else caught my attention – the arrival of American comics in my local newsagents.

A few years later I entered a competition in the local newspaper, and for the first (and so far only) time in my life I won. My prize, free tickets to the local cinema to see *On Her Majesty's Secret Service*. My first exposure to the cinematic Bond, but who was this guy playing 007? It wasn't the same one from the photographs in that well thumbed annual, which still sat on the bookcase in my bedroom. In the end it really didn't matter. The car chases, explosions and bad guy being eaten by the snow plow soon drove that problem from my mind. This was high adventure - better than anything my young mind had dreamt up.

As we exited the theater my parents and I discovered that our car had been broken into and the radio stolen. Full of juvenile bravado and the spirit of 007 I vowed to track the miscreants down and bring them to justice, Bond style. Unfortunately there was a definite dearth of snow plows in northern England at that time, and I doubt the local authorities would have condoned a ten year old with a license to kill, so we just reported it to the police and my father filed his insurance claim. Not as exciting as my plan, but eminently more practical.

A few months later with our in-car entertainment restored we set of for a vacation to nearby Wales, where we rented a cottage for a week of rest and relaxation. That meant a good chance to spend lots of time doing what I loved most, reading. Tucked away in one of the cottage's bookcases was a volume of the *Readers Digest Condensed Books* series apparently left behind by a previous vacationer.

The second story in this particular volume was by some guy called Ian Fleming and was entitled *The Man With The Golden Gun*. I ended up rereading the tale of Bond's encounter with master assassin Scaramanga three times during that vacation week. Discovering Fleming added a whole new layer to the character of Bond.

Unfortunately, the children's section of the local library didn't stock his Bond novels (although I did discover Fleming's *Chitty Chitty Bang Bang* well before Dick Van Dyke and his appalling accent flew across the movie screen). However I soon got into the habit of picking up any Bond books I came across in second hand book stores (a habit I still have). Each adventure would be read and reread until the pages fell out. As the years progressed each rereading brought new layers of understanding and appreciation of Fleming's skill as a storyteller.

During my second year at Grammar School some enterprising sixth-formers decided to start a school film society. The first film shown was a 16mm copy of *You Only Live Twice*, in fact for the first two months of the film society's existence it was the only film shown. It played in the common room every Thursday after school and I was there for every single showing.

After that I got into the habit of hanging out in the school library before school started and checking out the daily newspapers. While I glanced through the *Times* and the *Daily Telegraph* trying to fool myself that I understood what they were going on about, my real target was the *Daily Express* for my daily dose of Bond via the comic strip adaptations. This was my Bond, the seemingly perfect blend between the cinematic and literary.

So that's me, but what's the universal appeal of Bond?

Like all the great pop culture figures Bond resonates on a primal iconic level, a combination of fantasy, wish fulfillment, and fear. A man who operates outside societies' normal conventions yet at the same time is its protector.

Fleming's Bond is very much a character of his time and place in history. The idea of Bond transcends cultures and eras. The movie Bond, the continuation novels, and the various comics adaptations all show that 007 works best when placed in a contemporary setting. Bond is not an historical character, he is always of the present. While Fleming wasn't the first to develop the idea of the secret agent in popular fiction, he was perhaps the first to give it character and present it in a way that gave hope to the reader: with the right training and practice, I could be that guy.

And maybe that is the underlying appeal of Bond, the wish fulfillment. The desire to be a hero. It's a sure bet that everyone reading this book has at one time or another struck a pose and practiced muttering the immortal movie introduction, "Bond, James Bond."

The cinematic Bond is fun to watch with his almost superhuman levels of physical abilities and endurance. Not to mention the smug way he delivers his expository encyclopedic knowledge (something that reached the levels of the absurd during the Roger Moore era). The cinematic Bond is an almost mythical creature, while the literary Bond reveals the man behind the mask.

Opposite page: British 30 x 40 inch movie poster for *Dr. No*, 1962. Right: poster for the James Bond newspaper strip in the *Daily Express*.

introduction

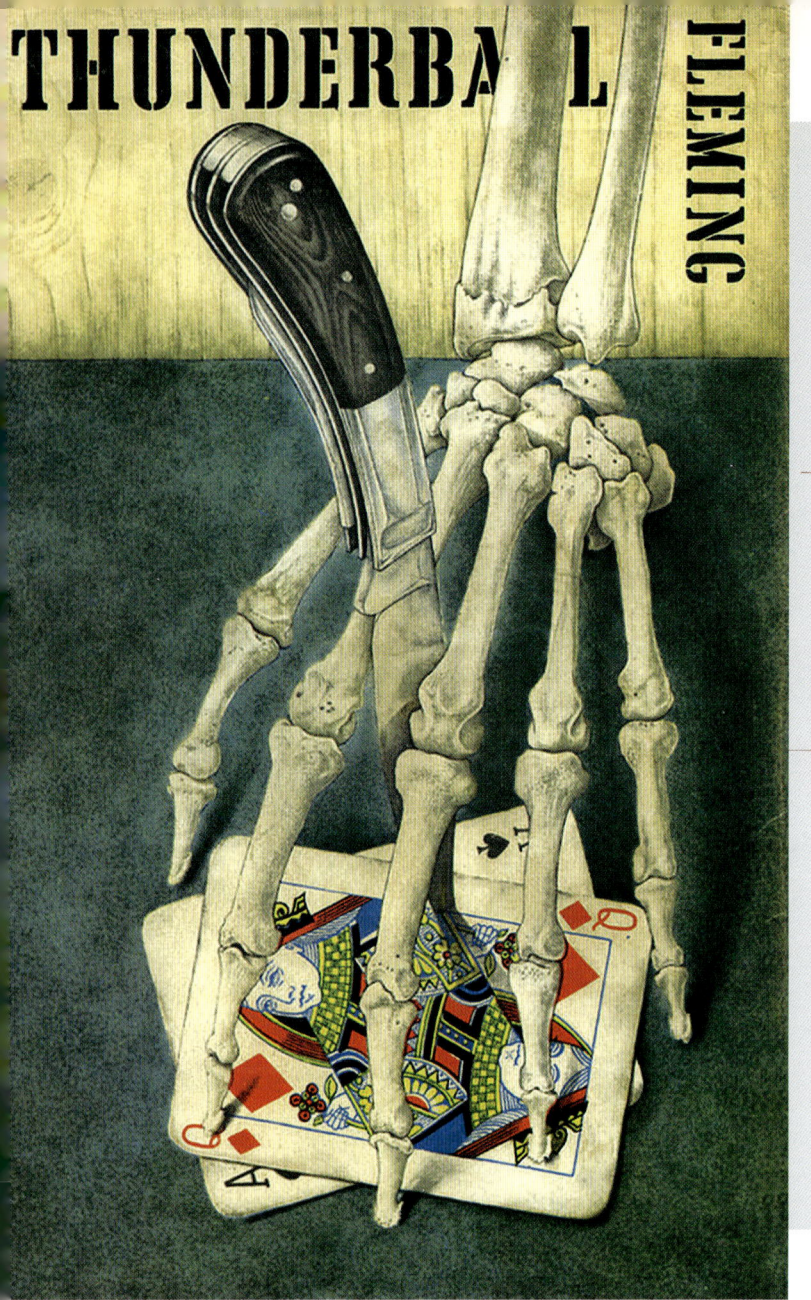

Here is a man who makes mistakes, gets hurt (both emotionally and physically), and who has to learn. Rereading all the Bond novels as part of the preparation for writing this book I was struck by how often Ian Fleming's Bond went on training courses, had to read instruction books and do his own background research before setting off on an assignment. In other words just like you and I with our day jobs. While he was naturally skilled in a lot of areas, he wasn't perfect and recognized the need to learn from others. The line in *Moonraker* where Fleming explains that Bond had "dabbled in the fringes of motor racing" had a particular resonance for me. I could say the same thing about my occasional forays into competitive driving. So maybe in that area I had comparable skills and experience to 007. It made him just that bit more human.

Perhaps writer Kingsley Amis said it best in *The James Bond Dossier* when he describes Fleming's Bond as "a simple pro forma we can all fit ourselves into. We don't want to have Bond to dinner or go golfing with Bond. We don't want to talk to Bond. We want to be Bond."

Above left: dustjacket from the first edition of Ian Fleming's novel *Thunderball*. Right: cover from the Titan newspaper strip reprint of "Dr. No." Opposite page: interior page from the ZigZag "Dr. No" comic book.

the history of the illustrated 007

| BOND CONOCÍA MUY BIEN AQUEL INSECTO. LO HABÍA VISTO UNA VEZ EN UN MUSEO. SU PICADURA ERA MORTAL SI ALCANZABA ALGUNA ARTERIA. EL AGENTE SE QUEDÓ INMÓVIL, MIENTRAS EL CIEMPIÉS SUBÍA POR SU CUERPO... | TRAS VARIOS MINUTOS DE INCREÍBLE AGONÍA PARA BOND, EL INSECTO INICIÓ SU CAMINO HACIA LA CABEZA... |

EL HORRIBLE BICHO SE DETUVO SOBRE LA FRENTE. 007 SINTIÓ EL ROCE DE LA ÁSPERA CABEZA... ¡EL CIEMPIÉS **ESTABA BEBIENDO**! BEBÍA LA TRANSPIRACIÓN QUE CUBRÍA SU CARA. AQUELLO ERA DEMASIADO, BOND SE SINTIÓ DESFALLECER...

LUEGO SINTIÓ QUE EL INSECTO SE INTERNABA ENTRE SUS CABELLOS. BOND HABÍA COMENZADO A TEMBLAR LIGERAMENTE. ESO ANTICIPABA LA CRISIS DE NERVIOS QUE LE SOBREVENDRÍA EN CUALQUIER MOMENTO. PENSÓ CON TERROR EN SI PODRÍA CONTROLARSE...

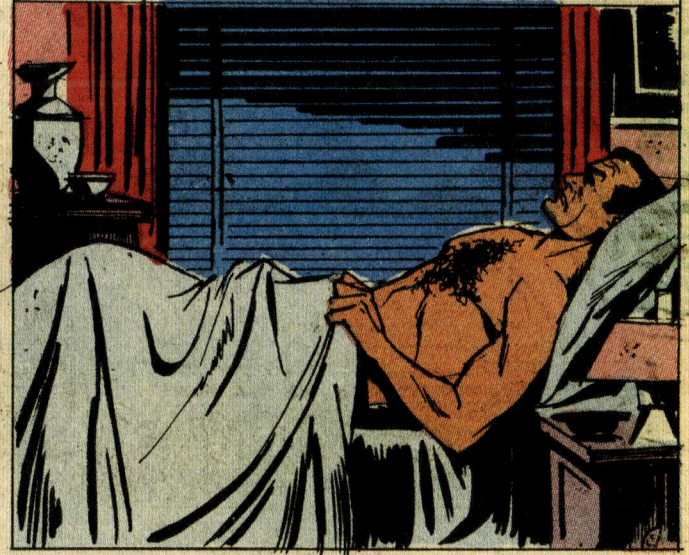

PASARON OTROS MINUTOS DE INDECIBLE ANGUSTIA, HASTA QUE POR FIN EL CIEMPIÉS SE ESCURRIÓ HASTA LA ALMOHADA. BOND DIO UN SUSPIRO DE ALIVIO...

ENTONCES REACCIONÓ PRESTAMENTE...

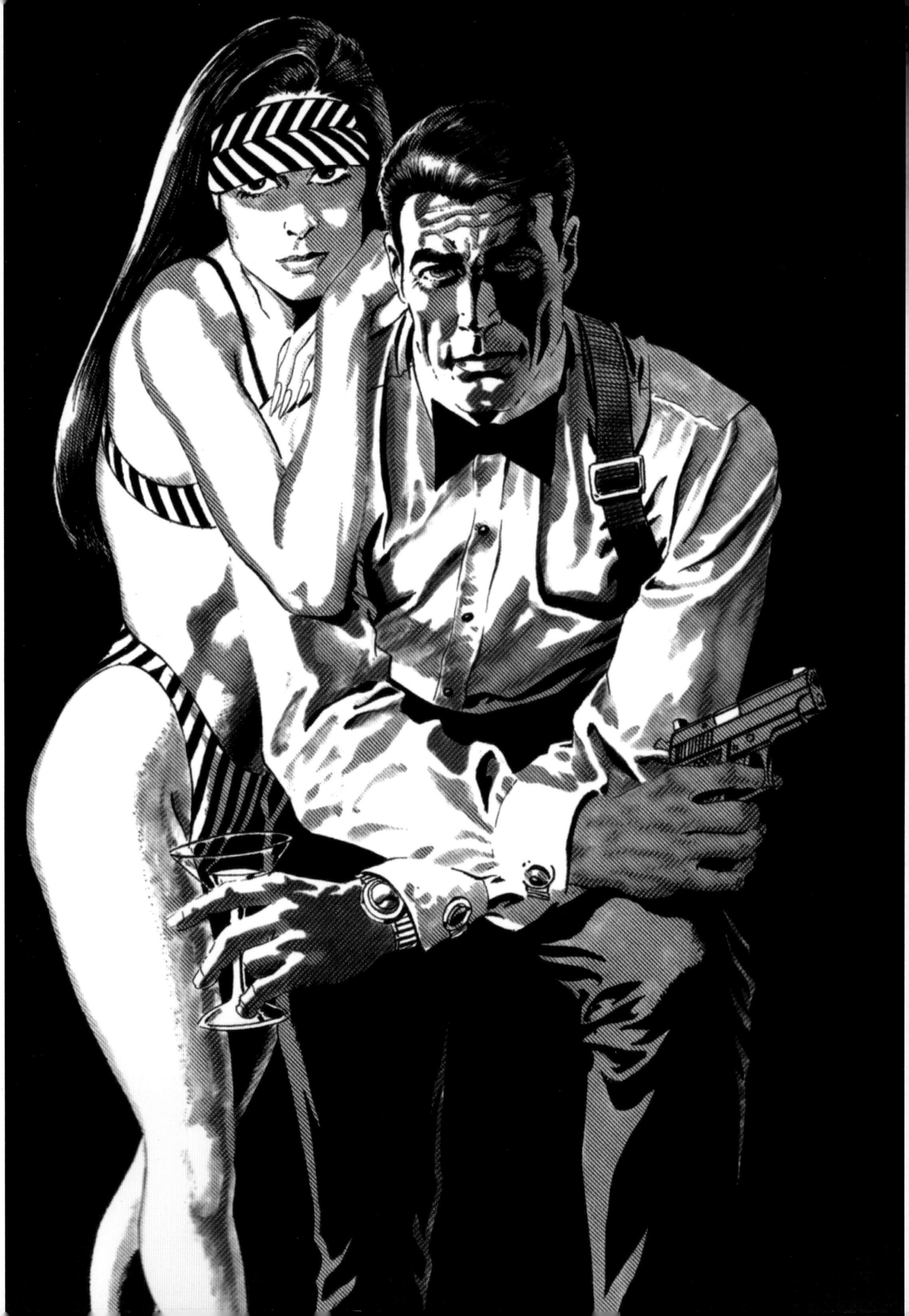

chapter 1
James Bond — A Comics History

Bond, James Bond. The world's greatest super spy. Idolized by millions, star of thirty plus novels and over twenty movies, his is the longest running franchise in cinema history. Yet despite his immense popularity Ian Fleming's creation has had a checkered career when it comes to the funny books.

The story of Bond in comics starts not with comic books, but with newspaper strips. In 1957 the managing editor of the British newspaper, the *Daily Express*, which had already serialized a couple of Bond short stories, approached Ian Fleming with the proposal to develop a daily comic strip starring Bond. Fleming was at first extremely reluctant, exhibiting a common prejudice against the comics medium by stating his concern that such an adaptation would "lower the perceived literary quality" of his novels, and even worse it might tempt Fleming himself to "'lower the standards" of any future Bond stories. To counter Fleming's objections the *Express* editors let it be known that the proposed adaptations would be written by Anthony Hern, the paper's literary editor who had been responsible for the earlier prose serializations. Fleming had approved of Hern's work and this, backed up by a promise from the paper's editor, Edward Pickering, that they would deliver a "Rolls Royce" of a job, persuaded Fleming to grant his permission. The £1,500 per story fee, and a share in future syndication rights also probably helped sweeten the deal.

To "assist" the *Daily Express* team, Fleming commissioned an artist (whose name has been lost) to produce a sketch of Bond based on Fleming's descriptions. This one-off sketch is the first visual representation of James Bond ever produced. It is obvious from the sketch that Fleming's view of his hero was very much set in a pre-war sensibility.

The artist assigned to the series, John McLusky, decided that Fleming's Bond was too old and outdated. He redesigned the character with a rougher and more contemporary feel. McLusky gave *Daily Express* readers their first look at Bond "in the flesh," years before Sean Connery became synonymous with the role.

Original artwork by Mike Grell of James Bond and one of his signature "Bond" girls.

Bond made his comics debut on 7th July, 1958 in "Casino Royale." The James Bond of the "Casino Royale" comic strip is subtly different from the Bond of the novels. In order to produce a strip that was accessible, and suitable, to a wider audience, possibly including children, some of the novel's edgier and harsher scenes, were toned down or restaged so that the action took place off panel. Another major change from the novels was that the *Express* editors dictated a three panel strip with each day ending with a "hook" sufficient to bring readers back the next day. Another editorial request was that each story run a specific number of weeks, in some cases this lead to very protracted plots which could run for weeks, with two stories eventually running over six months worth of daily papers.

The script was well received by both Fleming and the readers and the decision was made to continue adapting the Fleming novels in publication order. For the second strip, "Live and Let Die," the writing assignment was switched to Henry Gammidge, who introduced the idea of having Bond narrate the story. While this worked in places, in others it presented Bond as an "omniscient" narrator with knowledge of events he shouldn't have, ruining any sense of tension or mystery. In the next strip, "Moonraker," Gammidge took the device even further by having Bond break the fourth wall and address the readers directly. As if beginning to sense the limitations of this story telling technique it was scaled back in "Diamonds Are Forever" and used for the last time in "From Russia With Love." The adaptation of the next book in the Fleming canon, *Doctor No*, was handled by Peter O'Donnell, better known as the creator of that other British super spy, Modesty Blaise.

Henry Gammidge returned for "Goldfinger," a strip notable for the first signs of overt censorship as the infamous gold paint death of Jill Masterson is never shown or even described. The comic script simply states "she died." Also Bond's fight with Odd Job is shown as little more than a shoving match, yet when the strip was reprinted in Germany it became clear that the original art showed the two engaged in a knife fight. The next three strips were faithful adaptations of Fleming short stories, and then came "Thunderball."

It was 1962 and James Bond was about to explode on the silver screen, but before Sean Connery had the chance to utter his famous introduction for the first time, his comic strip counterpart was about to face a peril far greater than any of his colorful villains, the wrath of a publisher scorned. Just as "Thunderball" started to appear in the *Daily Express*, rival

Above: original artwork by James Bond daily newspaper strip artist John McLusky. Opposite page: cover from the Swedish comic book movie adaptation of *Dr. No*.

the history of the illustrated 007

DOKTOR NO

DETEKTIV SERIEN

NR. 6 KR. 1,75

Ian Fleming

newspaper the *Sunday Times* approached Ian Fleming asking for his assistance with the launch of a new color magazine. As Fleming often cited the *Times* as Bond's favorite reading material in the novels, he agreed and gave them permission to print "The Living Daylights." Lord Beaverbrook, the publisher of the *Express* group of papers, who believed he had a first refusal agreement with Fleming on any new Bond stories was furious and ordered that the Bond comic strip be withdrawn, immediately. The result on the "Thunderball" strip was that the last two thirds of the plot are basically reduced to just a few panels. The central character of Domino never appears and the climatic undersea battle between SPECTRE and the US Marines is shown in a single panel.

Just as Bond mania burst onto the pop culture stage, James Bond disappeared from the newspapers. But all was not lost for 007.

Wishing to cash in on the release of the *Doctor No* movie, the British arm of the Dell publishing company obtained the rights to produce an adaptation. This was produced by Norman J. Nodel, a former-military field artist and map maker better known as a children's book illustrator. Judging from the art, his adaptation was primarily based on photographs taken during the film's production; a theory seemingly supported by the inclusion of an alternative version of the scene where Bond kills Professor Dent. In the comic Dent and Bond fire simultaneously indicating that Dent still had a round in his gun, unlike the movie. This version of events was filmed but not used in the movie. Some sources suggest that Dell may have in fact only optioned the screenplay rather than the actual movie.

The story first appeared in the British *Classic Illustrated* line (#158A) with translated versions reprinted in Holland, Germany, Denmark, Sweden, and Norway under the

Left: French 39 x 98 inch movie poster from *You Only Live Twice*. Opposite page: Mike Grell original artwork of James Bond.

14 the history of the illustrated 007

Detective Series label with a Dell copyright. However, when the US publishers of *Classic Illustrated* declined to produce a US version, the idea was floated that EON Productions could publish their own comic book for the American market. With no comic book experience they approached the largest comics distributor, Independent News, which at that time shared a parent company with DC Comics. So it was that the US publication rights ended up at the home of Batman and Superman, where the Nodel adaptation was published in #43 (April, 1963) of their *Showcase* title, a book usually reserved for testing out new superheroes and concepts. One unusual aspect of the DC version when compared with the European was that several racial references were omitted and skin tones changed so that non-Caucasian characters, including the Asian Doctor No, became white.

The contract between Eon and DC Comics included an option for the rights to an on-going James Bond series. However, the *Showcase* issue proved to be a one-off appearance. DC did little to promote the book which had basically been forced upon them, and the flat artwork with typeset word balloons looked unlike any other DC comic. It looked positively amateurish compared to their dynamic super-hero titles. Two other strikes against it include the fact that DC published the book too soon and it had disappeared from the newsstands long before the movie had opened in the US.

THE FIRST ADVENTURE OF JAMES BOND takes him to CASINO ROYALE

In addition, it didn't help that the issue's cover sends a somewhat mixed message with a small hand lettered box on the lower left of the cover stating that it is "Based on the novel and now a United Artists film thriller." Perhaps if it had been released a few months later with a Sean Connery photo cover it might have been a different story. As it turned out, Bond wouldn't officially reappear on the American newsstands for another eighteen years.

In 1964 the Japanese comics studio Saito-Production Co. Ltd. produced a series nominally adapting four of the Fleming novels which would appear on a regular basis through 1967. In truth the adaptations had little to do with their source material. All four featured photographs of Sean Connery on the covers, and while the names of the major characters, location and basic plot are Fleming's, the surrounding material is nearly all original story. The manga Bond first appeared in serialized form in an anthology titled *Boys Life* from Shogakukan Inc, and were later collected as "Shinu no ha yatsura da" (It Is Them To Die—based on *Live And Let Die*), "Thunderball Sakusen" (Operation Thunderball—based on *Thunderball*), "Joou heika no 007" (Her Majesty's 007—based on *On Her Majesty's Secret Service*), and "Oogon-

Above: opening "title" newspaper strip from "Casino Royale," 1958, art by John McLusky.

16   the history of the illustrated 007

ju wo motsu otoko" (The Man With The Golden Gun), all published in 1966 under the Golden Comics imprint. While the manga Bond stories were critically acclaimed, the holders of the Bond literary license withdrew permission, most likely because they diverted so far from the source material.

Back in the UK it appears that Ian Fleming apologized to Lord Beaverbrook as in the novels Bond suddenly changed his reading habits to the *Daily Express*. The way was clear for Bond to return, however the decision was made to deviate from Fleming's publication order by skipping the anomalous, *The Spy Who Loved Me*, a literary experiment by Fleming in which the hero hardly appears. On 29th June, 1964 "On Her Majesty's Secret Service" kicked off the second series of Bond comic strips with Henry Gammidge and Jim McLusky once more in creative control. But as it turned out the writer and artist who had adapted Bond's adventures for nearly eight years would only be around for one more story, "You Only Live Twice," before being replaced by the duo considered by many to be the quintessential Bond creative team.

By the time he was asked to take on the James Bond comic strip, American writer Jim Lawrence was a veteran of high concept adventure story telling, including credits such as *The Green Hornet* radio scripts and serial

IAN FLEMING

007 JAMES BOND
M. R.

ZIG ZAG

novels featuring Tom Swift, the Hardy Boys and Nancy Drew among others.

Lawrence gave the audience a new tougher James Bond, a man not afraid of violence. His scripts featured more complex characterization and involved plots. In many ways he got closer to Fleming's Bond than Gammidge had with his almost word for word adaptations. Gammidge sometimes stated that he saw his job as to translate Fleming's work for the comics medium, Lawrence on the other hand was inspired by Fleming. Lawrence also faced the challenge that when he came on board the series was up to Fleming's last novel, *The Man With The Golden Gun*, and it was obvious that Fleming was growing tired of James Bond.

To overcome some of the shortfalls in the novel, Lawrence took the unprecedented step of adding to the original by introducing a whole new subplot at the start of the story that gave substance and a compelling reason for Bond's motivations and actions later on, something that had been missing from Fleming's novel.

"The Man With The Golden Gun" also saw the debut of Chinese born, Australian artist Yaroslav Horak on the strip. Horak, creator of the Australian strips, *The Mask* and *Mark Steel*, had a crisp, detailed cinematic style and was fond of using unusual angles and tight close-ups that would draw the reader into the heart of the action. His use of solid blacks was unusual at the time and at times his art could look scratchy and unfinished, but his skill at depicting both the human face and brutal action made him perfect for the frantic world of James Bond.

Lawrence and Horak would remain on the Bond comic strip for the next seventeen years, making them the longest tenured Bond creators in any media, surpassing even Ian Fleming by four years.

Opposite: cover from ZigZag's comic book adaptation of *Casino Royale*. Right: portrait of James Bond commissioned by his creator, Ian Fleming.

Just as the comic strip was about to enter a new era, Bond also made a return to the pages of a comic book, this time in Scandinavia.

The multi-national publishing company Semic acquired the license to produce a Bond comic book in 1965. Rather than produce original material they decided to use the existing newspaper strips. In order to make the strips fit the different format they were often cropped, stretched and otherwise butchered. In some cases panels were deleted altogether, while at other times new crudely drawn bridging panels were added. The translated text was hand lettered giving the books a very amateurish feel. Perhaps it says something of the popularity of the subject that despite the quality of the product, the James Bond comic books became big sellers with Swedish, Norwegian, and Danish editions being published for many years to come.

In 1965 Spanish publisher Ferma launched *Agente 007, James Bond*. Although the comic featured Bond on the cover only a few of its 52 pages each issue featured Bond. These were heavily edited and translated reprints of the *Daily Express* strips often with "extended" artwork added by local artists. Only short excerpts were printed each issue so that a single story ran over many issues.

The same year Portugese versions of the *Daily Express* strips were published in Brazil under the title *Uma Aventura de James Bond* by Rio Gráfica Editora. The strips were heavily edited and most of the comics featured Sean Connery and movie style images on the covers.

In 1966 following the release of *Thunderball*, Argentinian publisher Editora Columba started to produce an unauthorized periodic series of original, Spanish-language movie adaptations. These adaptations were usually fairly short (around 14-16 pages), and were published in the various *D'artagnan* comic magazines usually when the films premiered, either in the regular issues of the magazine or in the specials ("Extraordinario," the full color magazine "Todo Color,"). All the Bond films between *Thunderball* and *Moonraker* have most likely been adapted, and possibly also some earlier and later Bond films. The non-EON produced *Never Say Never Again* was also adapted in 1984. Besides the original film adaptations, heavily edited versions of some of the newspaper strip Bond stories have also been printed in the *D'artagnan* comics.

The source of the various foreign reprints, the *Daily Express* newspaper strips continued to go from strength to strength under Lawrence and Horak. Their second story was a straight adaptation of the story that caused the split with the *Daily Express* a few years earlier, *The Living Daylights*. But it wasn't long before Lawrence began to add significantly to Fleming's work. With "Octopussy" he turned Fleming's forty-three page morality tale into a gripping spy drama that ran for twenty-seven weeks. By the time he got to the previously skipped and troublesome, *The Spy Who Loved Me*, Lawrence knew he would be continuing on with new original stories. Most of the comic

Above: opening newspaper strip from "Octopussy," art by Yaroslav Horak. **Opposite page:** cover from ZigZag's *James Bond* #39, "On Her Majesty's Secret Service," published in Chile.

IAN FLEMING
007
JAMES BOND

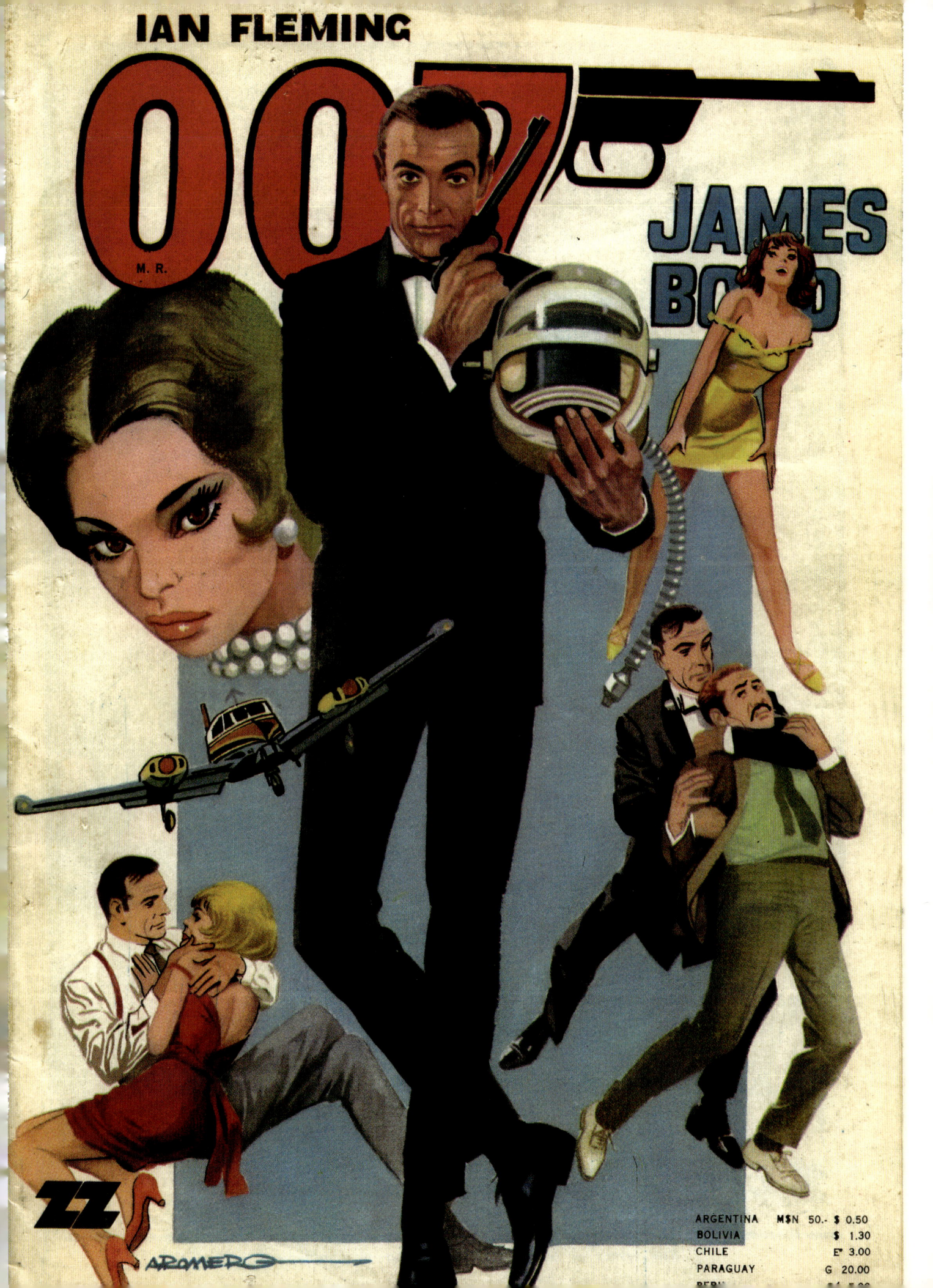

ARGENTINA M$N 50.- $ 0.50
BOLIVIA $ 1.30
CHILE E° 3.00
PARAGUAY G 20.00

strip version of "The Spy Who Loved Me" is a new original plot conceived by Lawrence based on a single throwaway line in Fleming's original novel.

While Bond himself was absent from American comics during this period his spirit lived on when Marvel Comics took the more fantastic elements of the Bond movies and *The Man From U.N.C.L.E.* TV show and built on them with their own super-spy character Nick Fury Agent of S.H.I.E.L.D. who appeared in *Strange Tales* magazine. The stories would occasionally give Bond a name check, for instance in *Strange Tales* #162 published in 1967, the S.H.I.E.L.D. equivalent of Q issues Fury with an invisible car (a full 35 years before Pierce Brosnan would get one in *Die Another Day*) with the quip "Wait till that guy Bond gets a load of that baby." The implied idea that Fury and Bond knew each other, and maybe occasionally worked together, was reinforced a few issues later, in *Strange Tales* # 164, when a familiar figure in a tuxedo turns up at the door to the barber shop that serves as the secret entrance to S.H.I.E.L.D.'s headquarters, only to get the door firmly shut in his face.

The year after Bond's attempt to enter S.H.I.E.L.D., another attempt would be made to launch Bond into the world of comic books. In 1968 Chilean publisher, ZigZag, obtained a license to produce a series of James Bond adventures. The books were mainly produced by Germán Gabler, who got the job because he was fluent enough in English to be able to work from Fleming's original novels. Although the ZigZag license was with the holders of the Bond literary library rather than the movie company, Gabler's Bond looked a lot like Sean Connery, plus he also adapted the movie technique of the "pre-title" sequence for most of his stories. The ZigZag books were a mix of ad-hoc adaptations and original tales. Despite some fairly crude artwork and poor production values, the book was a strong and steady seller. But a change in the political climate in Chile following the 1970 election of a Marxist government meant the book was cancelled almost overnight. It had run for two years and a total of 59 issues.

With the exhaustion of the Fleming canon[1], the Fleming estate gave its first official permission for the creation of new Bond stories to the *Daily Express* team who debuted the first Bond continuation story "The Harpies" on 4th October 1968, just a few weeks before the first continuation novel *Colonel Sun*, by Kingsley Amis, under the pen-name Robert Markham, was published.

Given the amount of changes Lawrence had made to the later Fleming stories, *The Harpies* read like a logical continuation of Fleming's work and started a run of thirty-three original Bond tales written by Jim Lawrence. (By way of comparison Ian Fleming wrote twenty Bond stories, and the most prolific Bond movie screen writer Richard Marbaum has written thirteen.)

With Lawrence at the helm James Bond entered a world where the fantastic rubbed shoulders with reality. He used plot devices ranging from real science to almost science-fiction. His stories ranged from the straight forward espionage thriller to the more esoteric, yet Lawrence always maintained the Fleming tenant that while his surroundings may appear fantastic, Bond was always a serious character. He also had no problem adding to Bond's world while at the same time adapting and extrapolating on Fleming's creations. From new 00 agents to additional Secret Service stations around the world, from a variety of aliases to new villains and resurrected old ones, Lawrence almost single handedly kept the Bond literary franchise alive throughout the 1970s.

Opposite page: U.S. 81 x 81 inch movie poster from *The Spy Who Loved Me*, 1978, art by Bob Peak. Right: cover to the Swedish comic book adaptation of *A View to a Kill*.

While the movie Bond was continuing to pull in audiences, interest in the literary and comic strip Bond was waning throughout the 1970s with no new Bond novels published and a shrinking readership for the newspaper strip. In an attempt to boost readership in late 1977 the strip moved from the *Daily Express* to the *Sunday Express*, but the experiment only lasted for one story before James Bond quietly disappeared from the British papers.

But Lawrence and Horak continued to work, and produced four stories between 1977 and 1981 which appeared in various newspapers around Europe and in the Scandinavian Semic comic books. Semic was also experiencing circulation problems and had placed the Norwegian title on an eight year hiatus with no issues published between 1971 and 1979. Their other editions were reduced in frequency dropping as low as releasing just two issues a year filled with reprints of already adapted strips.

While Semic was struggling, Bond comics were flourishing in Italy where translated high quality reprints of the *Express* strips were appearing in *Albi dell'Avventura – serie James Bond*, an anthology title that included a variety of newspaper strips which ran for over 170 issues, until the mid 1980s.

By the end of the 1970s it looked as if James Bond would only survive on the movie screen.

All that changed in 1981 following the death of Ian Fleming's widow, who had traditionally been averse to anyone else working with her husband's creation, the movies and the *Daily Express* comic strip being the notable exceptions. Her departure cleared the way for the holders of the literary license to work with the Fleming estate to launch a new series of Bond novels. Thriller writer John Gardner was commissioned to reboot the Bond franchise with a new contemporary look and a more modern James Bond. Bond returned to the book stores in *License Renewed*, the first of fourteen original novels from Gardner.

With the new Bond selling well it was decided to try and resurrect the comic strip. This time it would be published in the popular tabloid member of the *Express* family, the *Daily Star*. Jim Lawrence was still at the helm and, for the first story only, "Doomcrack," the art was provided by *MAD* magazine. Harry North altered the characters appearance drastically to the point where Bond was almost unrecognizable. He was soon replaced by original Bond artist John McLusky. Lawrence

Left: Marvel comic book adaptation of *For Your Eyes Only* #1, artwork by Howard Chaykin. Opposite page: panel from Eclipse Comic's movie adaptation of *Licence to Kill*.

made a few minor changes in order to fit into the new Gardner continuity without ever doing any direct adaptations of Gardner stories. In retrospect the *Daily Star* audience was probably not the right audience for the sophisticated Bond of Jim Lawrence and it could be suggested that the strip would have been better served by returning to its spiritual home at the more conservative *Daily Express*. Whatever the reason the strip faded and was quietly pulled from the paper halfway through a story without explanation, bringing to an end twenty-five years of the comic strip Bond. The future now seemed to lie with comic books.

After the demise of the newspaper strip three translated, and unlicensed, versions of the *Daily Express* newspaper adaptations appeared in Germany.

Over in Sweden Semic used the Gardner reboot as an excuse to renegotiate its license and received permission to also create their own original stories. Unfortunately, the resulting stories varied in quality ranging from those that were clearly based on Fleming's creation to some that were so over the top, such as Bond aiding a group of stranded aliens, that they were verging close to super-spy movie parody territory. The Danish version of the Semic book ceased publication in 1984, while the Norwegian version struggled on to 1994 after changing into an anthology title. In Sweden the ailing Bond book merged with the equally struggling title featuring another British hero, The Saint. Together the two managed to limp along to 1996, ending an erratic thirty-one year run.

In 1985 Semic produced an adaptation of the Roger Moore movie *A View To A Kill*, the first official movie adaptation by a non-English language publisher. It was also published in France and Germany. Eight of the original Semic stories saw publication in Spain in 1985, and in Holland between 1984 and 1985.

But what of the United States? Also in the pivotal year of 1981, Marvel would make an attempt to capture the movie audience with an adaptation of the fifth Roger Moore movie, *For Your Eyes Only*. Written by Larry Hamma with art by Howard Chaykin, it was published as both a regular sized two-part mini-series and as the tabloid sized *Marvel Super Special* #19.

A paperback version was also published that broke the panels apart to fit the smaller format which ended up with a very disjointed story flow. Chaykin's artwork is lacking in his usual level of detail and gives the impression of being rushed, perhaps due to tight deadlines and changes made during the movie production. The slower pace of the comic format also exposes several plot holes that were easy to overlook in the fast paced movie. This adaptation was also published in the UK as a hardcover *James Bond Annual*, and in Spain as a special color album.

Marvel tried again two years later with an adaptation of the next Moore movie, *Octopussy*. This time it appears that writer Steve Moore and artist Paul Neary had more time to work on the project as the result rates among the better Bond movie adaptations. Most of the cinematic establishing shots are full of excellent background detail missing from the previous adaptation, all the principal players are recognizable and the plot is followed closely without any obvious logic jumps. "Octopussy" was only published as a 48 page *Marvel Super Special* #26, yet close reading hints that perhaps it had been originally scheduled to be two 24 page issues.

The late eighties saw a new Bond in Timothy Dalton, and a new publisher in Eclipse. The 1989 Eclipse adaptation of Dalton's debut *Licence To Kill* suffered from two major problems, both unfortunately common to media tie-ins. Firstly the production was rushed to meet the movie release date so that writer Richard Ashford's tale ended up being handled by four different artists. Mike Grell did the breakdowns while final art chores were divided between Chuck Austen, Tom Yates and Stan Woch. The deadline rush probably also accounts for the fact that the last three pages of the story are rushed and the final scene from the movie is missing altogether. The second problem facing this particular adaptation was that they didn't have permission to use Timothy Dalton's likeness. As a result Bond's appearance is inconsistent, his facial features changing slightly depending on which artist is drawing any given page. Despite its flaws this adaptation was translated and reprinted in several countries including Holland, Germany and France.

Right: U.S. 27 x 40 inch movie poster from *Licence to Kill*, 1981. Opposite page: cover from the Dark Horse comic book *A Silent Armageddon* #1, art by John Byrns.

26   the history of the illustrated 007

"Licence To Kill" was followed by the first original Bond story to appear in US comics. "Permission To Die," also published by Eclipse in 1989, was a solo effort from writer/artist Mike Grell. The three issue mini-series was hampered by scheduling delays with a two year delay between issues two and three. The plot revolves around a US based scientist offering a new cheap method of launching payloads into space to the British Secret Service in exchange for them rescuing his niece from behind the Iron Curtain. The simple premise ends up as a fairly complex and multi-layered plot that is peppered with references to the Bond movies and the, then-current, John Gardner Bond novels.

In 1989 the Indian publisher Diamond Comics produced a James Bond title that ran for approximately ninety issues. Published in Hindi, Bengali as well as English, it appears to have consisted mainly of reprints of the *Daily Express* strips.

When the Bond license switched to Dark Horse Comics in 1992 they continued with the concept of telling original stories rather than movie adaptations. "Serpent's Tooth," a three issue mini-series by the team of Dough Moench and Paul Gulacy, is regarded by some Bond scholars and fans as approaching the level of parody. Moench seems to have thrown in every Bond cliché and it's easy to spot several scenes lifted almost straight from various movies. The sense of the ridiculous is not helped by a plot featuring flying saucers and a bad guy who looks like a human lizard. However Gulacy's distinctive art and his stylized take on the world of Bond make this an interesting interpretation. Despite its flaws for the Bond purist, it is a fun read and perhaps the slickest looking Bond adventure. Maybe it's for this reason that it is perhaps the most well known, and most widely reprinted, of the various US Bond series. It was translated and published by Feest Comics in Germany in 1993, and by Dark Horse France in 1995. The following year Dark Horse published the first two issues of "A Silent Armageddon," a planned four issue mini-series by writer Simon Jowett and artist John Burns. The basic plot concerned a "super network" called Omega and included several cyberpunk ideas and concepts. Artist Burns was well known for illustrating newspaper strips such as *Modesty Blaise*, and others that often featured curvaceous women losing various articles of clothing. He had also produced several beautifully rendered TV tie-in strips for various British comics magazines such as *TV-21*, *Look-In* and *Countdown*. His

THE OFFICIAL COMICS ADAPTATION OF THE HIT FILM!
topps COMICS
JAMES BOND 007™
GOLDENEYE™
1
OF 3
$2.95 US
$4.15 CANADA
FIRST COLLECTORS ITEM ISSUE
DON MCGREGOR
CLAUDE ST. AUBIN
RICK MAGYAR
BRIAN STELFREEZE

style seemed ideally suited to the smooth, sophisticated world of Bond. Unfortunately the series was cancelled after the first two issues with Dark Horse citing a six month delay in art for issue 3 from Burns as the cause. Perhaps the switch from producing a few pages a week for the British style comics to the twenty-plus pages a month demanded by American comics was too much. Looking at the first two issues you can see the reason for the delay in Burn's artwork as each page is a fully painted delight combining Burns excellent panel layouts, deceptively simple inking, and trademark color washes. For fans of Burns' art style these two issues are worth looking out for. While black and white images of the planned covers for the missing issues 3 and 4 have emerged online so far its not clear if any work was ever done on the second half of the story[2].

The next Bond story from Dark Horse, also published in 1993, is unusual for several reasons. First, it includes the return of a character from the Fleming novels in Tatiana Romanova was who featured in *From Russia With Love*. Secondly this is the only serialized original Bond tale published in the traditional US comic book format. All the other Dark Horse series had been published in the high-gloss squarebound "prestige" format. "Light Of My Death" appeared in *Dark Horse Comics* #8 to #11. Written by Das Petrou with art by John Watkiss, the story was divided into 4 eight page chapters and suffers slightly from trying to fit in a globe-trotting adventure with action, romance and a plot twist into such a confined space. Having said that, Petrou manages to weave a compelling if slightly rushed tale with plenty of subtle Bond references to keep the observant fans happy. This story is notable for being the only Bond "period piece" in that it is firmly set in 1961 as opposed to the ubiquitous "now" of all other Bond stories, be they movies, novels, or comics. This unique Bond story has yet to be collected in a stand alone format, which is a shame as it deserves a wider audience.

Nineteen ninety-four saw a return to the world of Bond for writer Simon Jowett, this time teamed with artists David Lloyd, and David Jackson on "Shattered Helix." The two issues of "Shattered Helix" were intended as a direct sequel to the incomplete "Silent Armageddon" but, beyond a few off hand references to events from the unpublished concluding issues, manages to stand alone as a tightly plotted self contained story. The basic plot revolves around Bond working alongside the US marines in trying to protect a bio-dome in the middle of Arizona from an attack that eventually leads to him taking on a criminal organization known

Opposite page: Topps Comic's movie adaptation of *GoldenEye*, artwork by Brian Stelfreeze. Above: interior page from *Dark Horse Comics* #9, for "Light of My Death," art by John Watkiss.

James Bond — A Comics History

as Cerebus. The story follows the model of the early Bond novels and movies by making good use of interesting locations to help drive the plot. The fast paced narrative and cinematic art style propel the story forward in an entertaining manner that helps you overlook some basic plot holes – such as why would Bond be working with the US marines in the first place?

James Bond returned to the pages of Dark Horse Comics with the series' 25th and final issue. Instead of the usual anthology format the whole issue was in "flip book" format with the James Bond story, "Minute Of Midnight," occupying the back half. The story, written by Doug Monech with art on this occasion supplied by Russ Heath, concerned Bond taping secret meetings in Washington D.C. and concluding with a plot to kidnap M. It is presented in three parts, although on reading it becomes fairly obvious that it was designed to run over several more installments across future issues of Dark Horse Comics, but it was brought to a rapid conclusion with the title's cancellation.

Nineteen hundred and ninety-four also saw Bond comics briefly appear in Russia, the one market where just a few years earlier they would have been banned. Two issues of a Bond comic were published, both containing reprints of original stories first published by Semic in Sweden.

Back in the USA, the last Dark Horse Bond story was published in 1995. Written by Don McGregor, with art from Gary Caldwell, "The Quasimodo Gambit," a three issue mini-series, returns Bond to Jamaica where he ends up taking on mercenary gun runners. The story is told in a very text heavy style with a lot of information crammed into each panel. The fact that some pages run to 24 panels per page adds to the feeling that perhaps this story would have worked better as a novel than a comic book. "The Quasimodo Gambit" was also released in trade paperback format.

Above: Mike Grell pastel portrait of James Bond. Opposite page: James Bond logo used for Eclipse Comics.

The following year McGregor was back scripting a James Bond comic, this time for new license holder Topps, who had decided to return to the adaptation format. Pierce Brosnan's debut as Bond in *GoldenEye* turned out to be 007's swansong in US comic book form as only the first issue of the planned three was published. No clear reason for the withdrawal of issues 2 and 3 has ever been published, although some speculate that a disagreement between Topps and the license holders over the intended audience for the book may have been an issue. There were some concerns about the overt sexual nature of the planned cover for issue 2 and art that shows the female villain, Xenia Onatopp, clearly getting sexually aroused when killing. From the evidence of the first issue, this could have been the best Bond movie adaptation yet as the artist, Claude St.

Aubin, moved away from the convention of trying to recreate the exact movie scenes in favor of retelling the story using comic book techniques. The result was a dynamic looking book with strong action sequences that played to the strength of the four color medium. Some copies of issues #2 and #3 are in circulation as writer Don McGregor had an extremely limited run printed up at his own cost. There is also a 00 issue of "GoldenEye" produced as a special for the 1995 James Bond convention in New York.

It is now over a decade since James Bond appeared in an original story in either comic strip or comic book format, but he hasn't totally disappeared from the comic book stores.

Between 1987 and 1990 UK publisher Titan Books released four collections of the *Daily Express* newspaper strips. The strips included in these volumes were chosen for their availability rather than with any consideration given to order or continuity. In 2004 Titan relaunched and extended the series with new editions complete with additional material placing the strips in context, as well as providing notes on the complete publishing history of the Bond phenomenon. As with the previous editions, the collections are based on the availability of the artwork for any given strip but an attempt is made to keep the individual collections logically in order. The aim is to eventually present every James Bond newspaper strip produced. These collections at this time are up to fourteen volumes, are available in US comics and book stores and are essential reading for anyone interested in this classic character.

While, as far as the author is aware, there are no current plans for any new original Bond stories in comic book format, it appears that Bond, or at least a version of him, will be returning to stores. Ian Fleming Publications has announced a series of graphic novels, with art by Kev Walker, adapting the "Young Bond" novels, with "Silverfin" scheduled to be in stores at some point during the Fleming centenary year of 2008.

Notes

[1] To be strictly accurate three Ian Fleming Bond stories remain that have yet to be adapted into comics, *Quantum of Solace*, *The Property of a Lady*, and *007 in New York*.

[2] In fact the art for Issue #3 was completed and reportedly delivered six months late. Art for Issue #4 was never started.

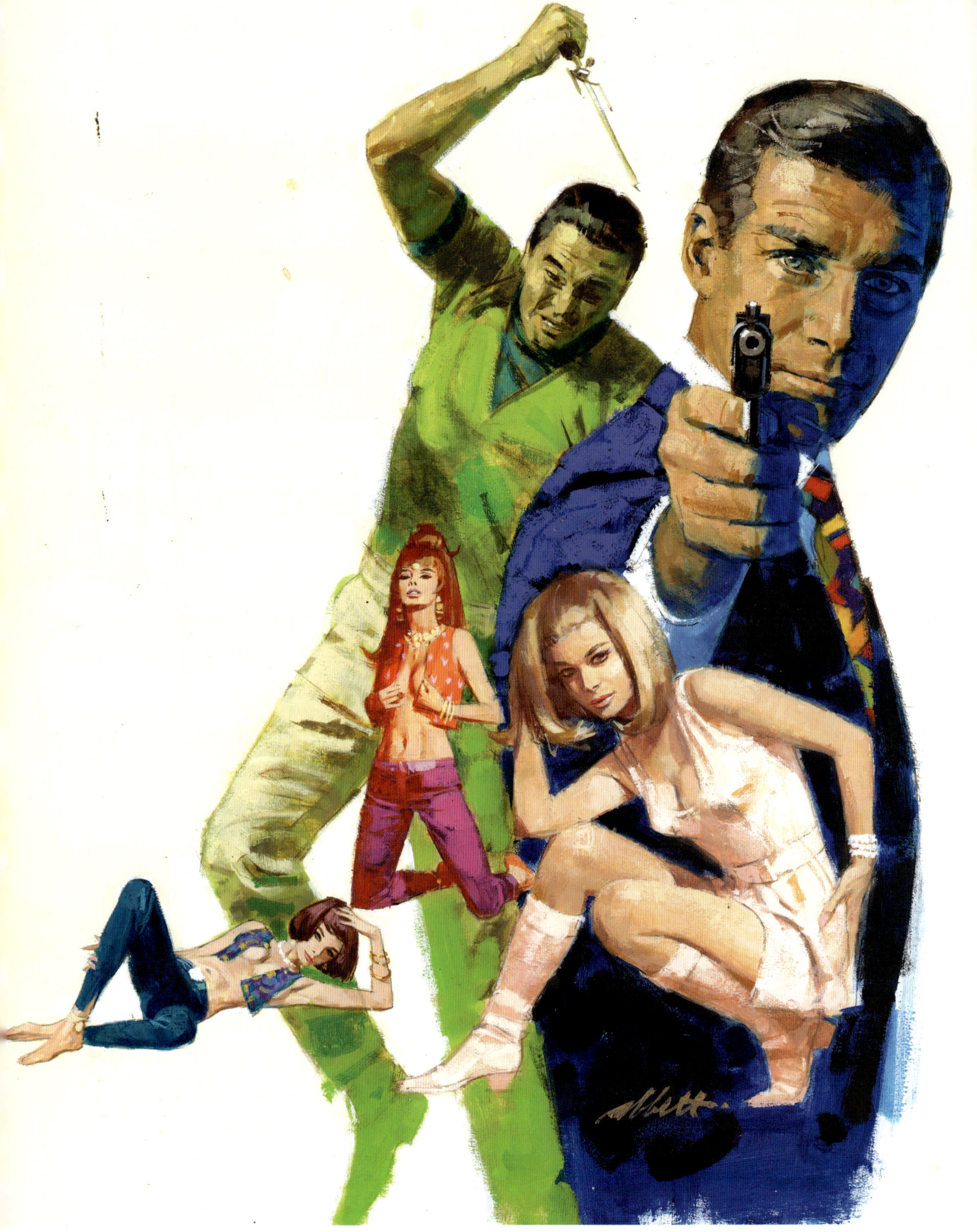

chapter 2
The Series

During the research for this book I came across references to James Bond comics of one sort or another being published in twenty-three different countries. Most used translated versions of existing material such as the *Daily Express* newspaper strips, the original comic book stories from Swedish publisher Semic, or some of the US produced original stories.

The following is an attempt to list all the series by country and publisher. While in most cases this information is well documented, in other cases, China for instance, little is known beyond the fact that at some point a James Bond comic was published.

Argentina

Editorial Columba

- D'artagnan and D'artagnan Extraordinario (1965-1984) - occasional unauthorized movie adaptations

Original artwork by Robert Abbett for the magazine novelization of *Colonel Sun*.

Extra

- Extra newspaper (1964-1983) at least two unauthorized movie adaptations

Brazil

Rio Grafica Editora (GRE)

- Uma Aventura de James Bond #1-18 (1964-1965) - reprinted newspaper strips

Sabar

- 007 James Bond #1-6 (1971-1972) - reprinted newspaper strips

Editoria Brasil-America (EBA)

- 007 James Bond #1-4 (1978) - reprinted newspaper strips

Opera Graphica

- James Bond 007 (2003) - reprinted newspaper strip

China

Unknown publisher

- Unknown titles (date?) - unlicensed reprints of Japanese adaptations

Chile

ZigZag

- 007 James Bond #1-59 (1968-1971) - mix of novel adaptations and original stories

Denmark

International Productions

- Detektiv Serien (1963) - reprints *Doctor No* movie adaptation

A/S Interpresse

- James Bond, Agent 007 #1-66 (1965-1983) - reprints newspaper strips plus one Semic story.

- 007 Samle Album (1978) - reprints newspaper strips

- 007 James Bond Special: Moonraker (1979) - reprints newspaper strips

- 007 James Bond: Strengt Fortoligt (1982) - reprints Marvel movie adaptation of *For Your Eye's Only*

- 007 James Bond: Octopussy (1983) - reprints Semic movie adaptation of *Octopussy*

- James Bond #1-7 (1983-1984) - reprints Semic stories

- Agent X-9 (1988-1990) - occasional reprints of Semic stories

- James Bond: Slangens Liga #1-3 (1995) - reprints Dark Horse series *Serpent's Tooth*

Finland

Kustannus Oy Semic

- James Bond, Agent 007 #1-3 (1975) - reprinted newspaper strips

- James Bond, Agent 007 #1-6 (1976) - reprinted newspaper strips

- James Bond, Agent 007 #1-6 (1977) - reprinted newspaper strips

- James Bond, Agent 007 #1-4 (1978) - reprinted newspaper strips

- James Bond, Agent 007 #1-4 (1979) - reprinted newspaper strips

- James Bond, Agent 007 #1-4 (1980) - reprinted newspaper strips

Above: cover for the Titan reprint of the "Casino Royale" strip. Opposite page: Opposite page: Danish comic book adaptation of *For Your Eyes Only*.

34   the history of the illustrated 007

JAMES BOND AGENT 007

Nr. 8 — Pris Kr. 2,00

FRA EN DRÆBENDE SYNSVINKEL

- James Bond, Agent 007 #1-4 (1981) - reprinted newspaper strips
- James Bond, Agent 007 #1-4 (1982) - reprinted newspaper strips
- James Bond, Agent 007 #1-4 (1983) - reprinted newspaper strips
- Octopussy (1983) - reprint of Semic movie adaptation of *Octopussy*
- James Bond, Agent 007 #1-6 (1984) - reprinted newspaper strips
- James Bond: Tappave Juoni (1984) - reprint of Semic story *Deadly Duplicity*
- James Bond, Agent 007 #1-6 (1985) - reprinted newspaper strips
- 007 ja kuoleman katse (1985) - reprint of Semic movie adaptation of *View To A Kill*
- James Bond, Agent 007 #1-4 (1986) - reprinted newspaper strips
- James Bond, Agent 007 #1-4 (1987) - reprinted newspaper strips
- James Bond, Agent 007 #1-3 (1988) - reprinted newspaper strips
- 007 ja lupa tappaa (1989) - reprint of Eclipse movie adaptation of *Licence To Kill*

Semic

- Agentti X-9 (1991-1992) - occasional reprinted newspaper strips and reprinted Semic stories

France

Glenat Editions

- James Bond 007 #1 (1966) - reprinted newspaper strips

Unknown publisher

- James Bond 007 Rien que pour vos Yeaux (1981) - reprints Marvel movie adaptation of *For Your Eye's Only*

Himalaya

- James Bond Permis De Tuer (1989) - reprints Eclipse movie adaptation of *License To Kill*

Dark Horse France

- James Bond 007 La Dent du Serpent #1-3 (1995) - reprints Dark Horse series *Serpent's Tooth*

the history of the illustrated 007

Germany

Bildschriften Verlag

- Bildschirm Detektiv #706 (1964) - reprints *Doctor No* movie adaptation

Pollischansky Verlag

- Comic Gallery Piccolo #1 and 3 (1980) - unauthorized reprints of newspaper strips

Semic

- Octopussy (1983) - reprints Semic movie adaptation

Ehapa

- Im Angesicht des Todes (1985) - reprints Semic movie adaptation of *View To A Kill*

Alpha Comic

- Lizenz zum Töten (1989) - reprints Eclipse movie adaptation of *License To Kill*

Feest Comics

- Ian Fleming's James Bond 007 #1-3 (1993-1994) - reprints Dark Horse series *Serpent's Tooth*

Greece

Unknown publisher

- unknown title (1965?) - reprints *Doctor No* movie adaptation

Holland

Unknown publisher

- Beled Scherm Detective (1964) - reprints *Doctor No* movie adaptation

Semic

- James Bond #1-8 (1984-1985) - reprints Semic stories

Loempea

- James Bond: Licence To Kill (1989) - reprint of Eclipse movie adaptation of *Licence To Kill*

Hungary

Semic Interprint Nyomdai es Kiadoi Kft

- James Bond #1-6 (1989-1990) - reprints Semic stories

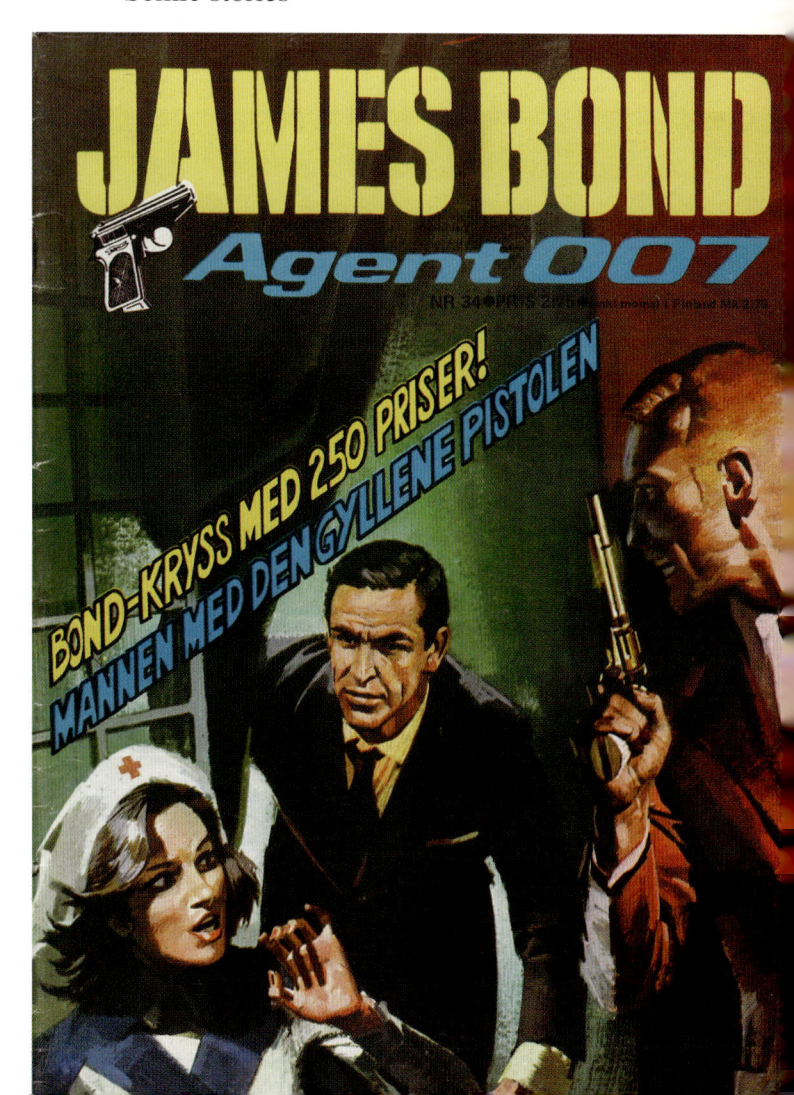

Right: Swedish comic book adaptation for *The Man with the Golden Gun* recasting Sean Connery instead of Roger Moore as Bond. Opposite page: Danish comic book adaptation of *Live and Let Die* using photo reference from *The Spy Who Loved Me*.

India

Diamond Comics

- James Bond #1-90 (1989-?) - reprints newspaper strips

Italy

Camillo Conti

- Albi dell'Avventura - serie James Bond (1974-1982) - occasional reprints of newspaper strips

Unknown Publisher

- L'avventoroso Anno #1 (1973) - reprinted newspaper strip

Corno

- Super Fummetti #16 (1979) - reprinted newspaper strip

Unknown Publisher

- Eureka (1979-1983) - reprinted newspaper strip plus reprint of Marvel movie adaptation of *Octopussy*

Star Comics

- Hyperion - Oddisea Nel Fantastico (1992) - reprints various Dark Horse stories

Japan

Shogakukan Inc

- Boys Life (1964-1967) - serialized novel adaptations

Golden Comics

- Shinu no ha yatsura da (1966) - collected version of serialized adaptation of *Live and Let Die*
- Thunderball Sakusen (1966) - collected version of serialized adaptation of *Thunderball*
- Joou heika no 007 (1967) - collected version of serialized adaptation of *On Her Majesty's Secret Service*
- Oogaon-ju wo motsu otoko (1967) - collected version of serialized adaptation of *The Man With The Golden Gun*

Shogakukan Bunko

- Shinu no ha yatsura da (1980) - collected version of serialized adaptation of *Live and Let Die*
- Thunderball Sakusen (1980) - collected version of serialized adaptation of *Thunderball*

Right: U.S. 27 x 41 inch movie poster for *From Russia With Love*. Opposite page: interior page from the Semic adaptation of *View to a Kill*, Frederico Maidagan artwork.

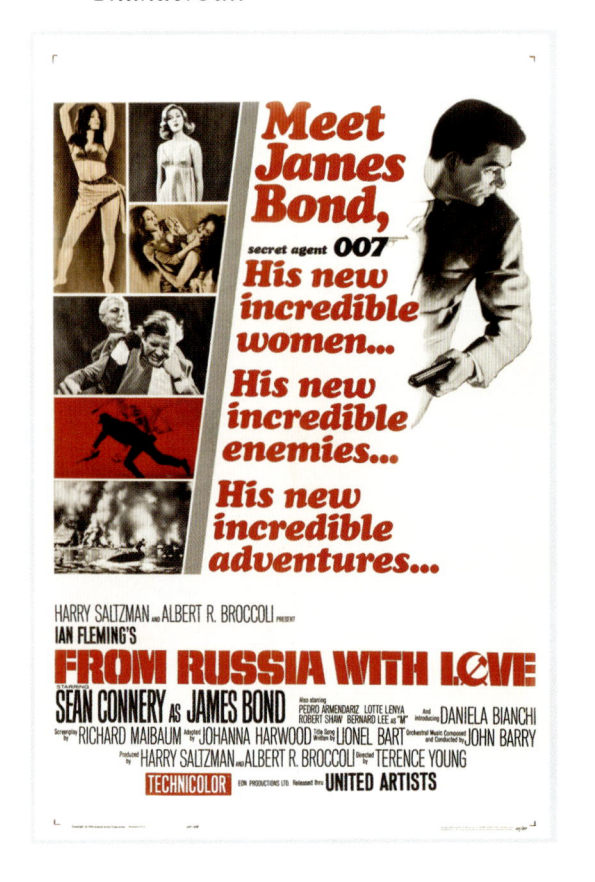

38 the history of the illustrated 007

The Series

IAN FLEMING
007
JAMES BOND

ZIG-ZAG

M.R.

- Joou heika no 007 (1980) - collected version of serialized adaptation of *On Her Majesty's Secret Service*
- Oogaon-ju wo motsu otoko (1980) - collected version of serialized adaptation of *The Man With The Golden Gun*

Norway

International Productions

- Detektiv Serien #6 (1963) - reprints *Doctor No* movie adaptation

Semic Press

- James Bond - Agent 007 #1-4 (1965) - reprinted newspaper strips
- James Bond - Agent 007 #1-4 (1966) - reprinted newspaper strips
- James Bond - Agent 007 #1-13 (1967-1970) - reprinted newspaper strips
- Agent X-9 #6-8 (1977) - reprinted newspaper strips
- Agent 007 - James Bond #1-2 (1979) - reprinted newspaper strips
- Agent 007 - James Bond #1-6 (1980) - reprinted newspaper strips
- Agent 007 - James Bond #1-6 (1981) - reprinted newspaper strips
- James Bond: Kun for dine oyne (1981) - reprints Marvel movie adaptation of *For Your Eye's Only*
- Agent 007 - James Bond #1-7 (1982) - reprinted newspaper strips
- Agent 007 - James Bond #1-8 (1983) - reprinted newspaper strips and reprinted Semic stories
- James Bond: Octopussy (1983) - reprint of Semic movie adaptation of *Octopussy*
- Agent 007 - James Bond #1-7 (1984) - reprinted newspaper strips and reprinted Semic stories
- James Bond #8 (1984) - reprinted newspaper strip
- James Bond #1-8 (1985) - reprinted newspaper strips and reprinted Semic stories
- James Bond Arsalbum (1985) - reprint of Semic story
- James Bond: Med Doden I Sikte (1985) - reprint of Semic movie adaptation of *View To A Kill*
- James Bond #1-8 (1986) - reprinted newspaper strips and reprinted Semic stories

Above: French 47 x 63 inch movie poster for *From Russia with Love*, art by Boris Grinsson. Opposite page: ZigZag comic book cover from "Child's Play," 1969.

41 **The Series**

- James Bond #1-8 (1987) - reprinted newspaper strips and reprinted Semic stories

- James Bond: I Skuddlinjen (1987) - reprint of Semic movie adaptation of *The Living Daylights*

- James Bond #1-8 (1988) - reprinted newspaper strips and reprinted Semic stories

- James Bond #1-8 (1989) - reprinted newspaper strips and reprinted Semic stories

- James Bond: Med rett til a drepe (1989) - reprint of Eclipse movie adaptation of *Licence To Kill*

- James Bond #1-12 (1990) - reprinted newspaper strips and reprinted Semic stories

- James Bond #1-8 (1991) - reprinted newspaper strips and reprinted Semic stories

- James Bond #1-8 (1992) - reprinted newspaper strips and reprinted Semic stories

- James Bond #1-8 (1993) - reprinted newspaper strips, reprinted Semic stories and reprint of Dark Horse Comics series *Serpent's Tooth*

- James Bond #1-8 (1994) - reprinted newspaper strips and reprinted Semic stories

- X-9 Spesial #7-9 (1995) - reprints various Dark Horse Comics series

- James Bond #1-5 (2000-2001) - reprints newspaper strips

Left: U.S. 14 x 36 inch movie poster for *Diamonds Are Forever*, art by Bob McGinnis.

42   the history of the illustrated 007

Russia

Unknown Publisher

- James Bond #1-2 (1994) - reprints Semic stories

Serbia

Unknown publisher

- Unknown title (date?) - reprints of newspaper strips

Spain

Ferma

- Agente 007, James Bond #1-34 (1965-1966) - reprinted newspaper strips

Burulan

- James Bond - Fasciculo semanal #1-30 (1973-1974) - reprinted newspaper strips
- James Bond - Episodios completos #1-5 (1973-1974) - reprinted newspaper strips
- Zeppelin #2 (1973) - reprinted newspaper strip

Ediciones Recreativas

- James Bond 007: Solo para sus ojos (1981) - reprints Marvel movie adaptation of For Your Eye's Only

Bruguera

- James Bond #1-3 (1985) - reprinted Semic stories

Forum

- James Bond 007: Panorama para matar (1985) - reprints Semic movie adaptation of View To A Kill

Planeta de Agostini

- James Bond #1-7 (1988-1989) - reprinted newspaper strips
- Biblioteca Grandes del Comic: James Bond #1-8 (2006-2007) - reprinted newspaper strips

Sweden

International Productions

- Detektiväventyr Serien #6 (1963) - reprints Doctor No movie adaptation

Semic Press AB

- James Bond, Agent 007 #1-73 (1965-1981) - reprinted newspaper strips

Atlantics Forlags

- Ur Dodlig Synvinkel (1981) - reprints Marvel movie adaptation of For Your Eye's Only

Semic Press AB

- James Bond, Agent 007 #1-8 (1982) - reprinted newspaper strips and original stories
- James Bond, Agent 007 #1-8 (1983) - reprinted newspaper strips and original stories
- Semic Album #1 (1983) - movie adaptation of Octopussy
- James Bond, Agent 007 #1-8 (1984) - reprinted newspaper strips and original stories
- Semic Album #2 (1984) - original story
- James Bond, Agent 007 #1-8 (1985) - reprinted newspaper strips and original stories

- Semic Album #3 (1985) - movie adaptation of *View To A Kill*
- James Bond, Agent 007 #1-12 (1986) - reprinted newspaper strips and original stories
- Semic Album #4 (1986) - original story
- James Bond, Agent 007 #1-12 (1987) - reprinted newspaper strips and original stories
- Semic Album #5 (1987) - movie adaptation of *The Living Daylights*
- James Bond, Agent 007 #1-12 (1988) - reprinted newspaper strips and original stories
- Semic Album #6 (1989) - reprints Eclipse film adaptation of *Licence To Kill*

Alvglans Forlags AB

- James Bond Agent 007 (1988) - hardcover album reprinting newspaper strips

Semic Press AB

- James Bond, Agent 007 #1-12 (1989) - reprinted newspaper strips and original stories
- James Bond, Agent 007 #1-12 (1990) - reprinted newspaper strips and original stories
- James Bond, Agent 007 #1-6 (1991) - reprinted newspaper strips and original stories
- James Bond, Agent 007 #1-6 (1992) - reprinted strips and original stories
- James Bond, Agent 007 #1-6 (1993) - reprinted newspaper strips and original stories
- James Bond, Agent 007 #1-4 (1994) - reprinted newspaper strips and original stories
- James Bond, Agent 007 #1-4 (1995) - reprinted newspaper strips and original stories
- James Bond, Agent 007 #1-4 (1996) - reprinted newspaper strips and original stories

Thailand

Unknown publisher
- Unknown title (1981?) - reprints Marvel movie adaptation of *For Your Eyes Only*

Turkey

Unknown Publisher
- unknown title (date) - reprinted newspaper strips

ALFA
- James Bond #1-12 (date?) - reprinted newspaper strips

UK

Express Newspapers
- Daily Express, Series 1 Strips #1-1128 (1958-1962) - adaptations of Ian Fleming stories
- Daily Express, Series 2 Strips #1-475 (1964-1966) - adaptations of Ian Fleming stories

- Daily Express, Series 3 Strips #1-815 (1966-1968) - adaptations of Ian Fleming stories
- Daily Express, Series 3 Strips # 816-3437 (1968-1977) - original stories
- Sunday Express, Series 4 Strips #1-636 (1977-1981) - original stories (only one story of the five in this series was published in UK).
- Daily Star, Series 5 Strips #1-965 (1981-1983) - original stories (UK publication stopped suddenly at strip #673)

Dell

- Classics Illustrated #158a (1963) - *Doctor No* movie adaptation

World Distributors

- James Bond Annual (1968) - reprinted newspaper strip

Marvel Comics UK

- For Your Eyes Only #1-2 (1981) Hardcover Annual – reprints Marvel (US) movie adaptation
- Octopussy (1983) Hardcover Annual – reprints Marvel (US) movie adaptation

Titan Books

- James Bond Albums #1-4 (1987-1988) - reprinted newspaper strips
- James Bond Albums #1-17 (2004-2009) - reprinted newspaper strips

U.S.A

DC Comics

- Showcase #43 (1963) - reprints *Doctor No* movie adaptation

James Bond Fan Club

- The Illustrated James Bond, 007 (1981) - reprinted newspaper strips

Marvel Comics

- *For Your Eyes Only* (1981) movie adaptation
- *Octopussy* (1983) movie adaptation
- James Bond Jr, #1-12 (1992)

Eclipse Comics

- *Licence To Kill* (1989) - movie adaptation
- Permission To Die #1-3 (1991) - original story

Dark Horse Comics

- Serpent's Tooth #1-3 (1993) - original story
- A Silent Armageddon #1-2 (1993) - original story
- Dark Horse Comics #8-11, 25 (1993) - original stories
- Shattered Helix #1-2 (1994) - original story
- Quasimodo Gambit #1-2 (1995) - original story

Topps Comics

- *GoldenEye* #1 (1996) - movie adaptation

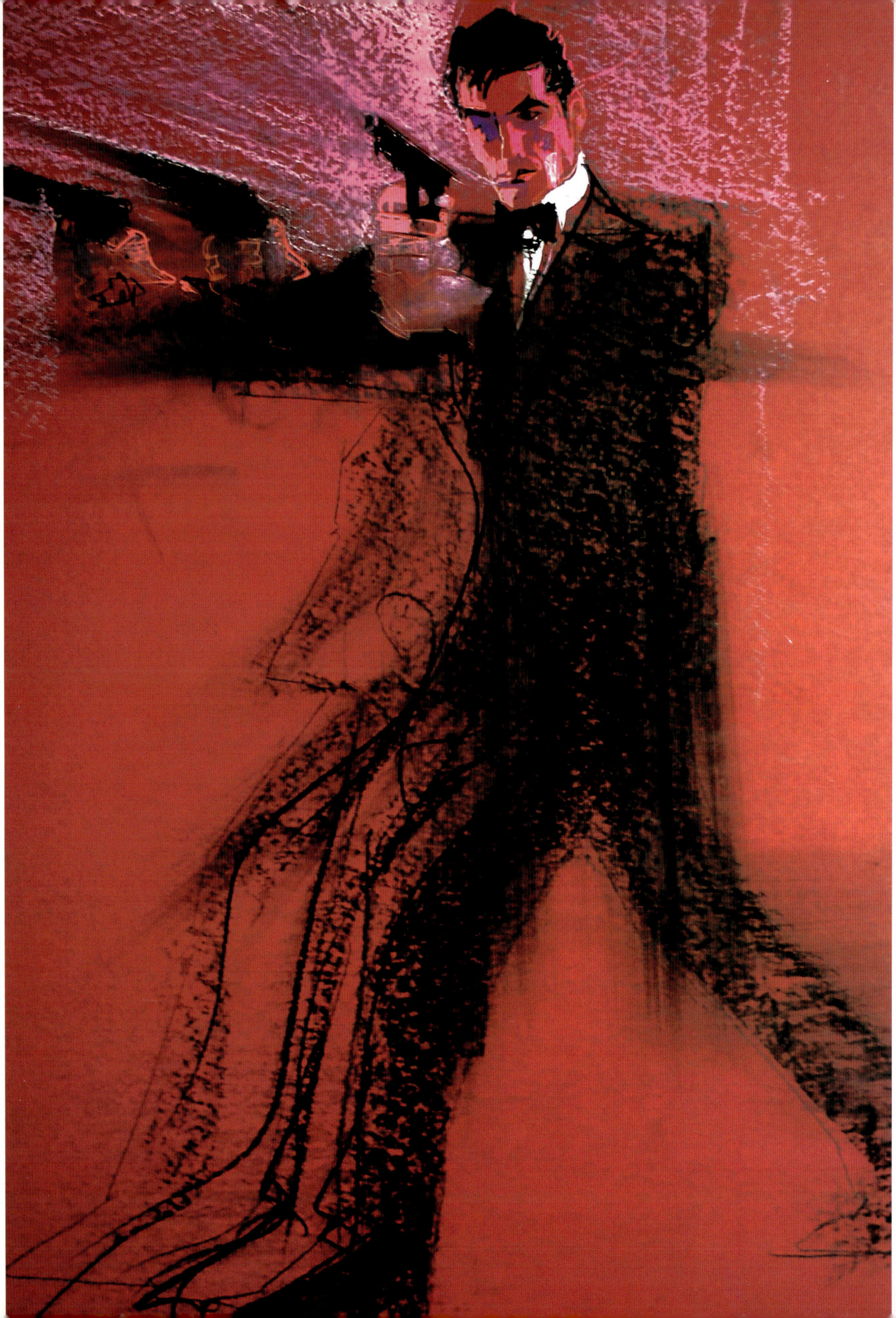

chapter 3
The Missions

Most people are familiar with various James Bond adventures from the twenty-one movies and the fourteen original novels. The more informed Bond fans may also be familiar with the twenty-six continuation novels. Even if you add all these together the total still falls well short of the number of Bond stories published as comics. More Bond stories have been told in comics than in any other medium.

Between the 1957 *Daily Express* adaptation of Casino Royale and the aborted 1996 TOPPS comics adaptation of *GoldenEye*, James Bond has appeared in one hundred and forty-five different stories in either newspaper strips or comic books.

The following section provides a detailed summary of each of those stories. Wherever possible I have included a plot summary, publication details, information on the writers and artists (if known) and notes on items of interest.

The stories are listed chronologically based on the date they were first published.

Proposal for unused movie poster artwork for *Licence to Kill*, artwork by Bob Peak.

Where possible reprints and translations have also been noted. If a story has been adapted multiple times, (For instance *On Her Majesty's Secret Service* which has been published as a newspaper strip, a comic book and a movie adaptation), it is listed based on the publication date of the first occurrence.

CASINO ROYALE

NEWSPAPER STRIP

Type: *Daily Express* comic strip

Writer: Anthony Hearn

Artist: John McLusky

Originally Published: 7 July, 1958 to 13 December, 1958 (Series #1, 1- 138)

Source: Based on the first Bond novel *Casino Royale* by Ian Fleming, published in 1953

Plot Summary: Monsieur Le Chiffre, "the cipher", is an agent for the Soviet assassination bureau SMERSH, running a baccarat game at a French casino to raise needed operational funds, namely, to recover SMERSH's money that he lost in a failed attempt to establish a chain of brothels. Expert baccarat player James Bond is assigned the job of beating Le Chiffre in the hope that the his gambling debts will provoke SMERSH into killing him. After hours of intensive play, Bond manages to beat Le Chiffre, but only with extra money provided by Felix Leiter of the CIA, who is in attendance as a covert observer. Bond has been provided with an assistant, the beautiful but emotionally turbulent Vesper Lynd, who becomes his lover. But she is holding a terrible secret, she is actually a Russian double agent, under orders to see that Bond does not escape Le Chiffre.

Notes: The James Bond strip debuted in the 7th July, 1958 edition of the *Daily Express* with a somewhat subdued opening title panel and on reflection, when compared with what was to come later, is a bit of an oddity. With the benefit of hindsight it can be seen to bear many of the hallmarks of a debut piece. The characterization is a little inconsistent and not yet on target. There are also frequent breaks in the pacing where writer Hearn's almost literal translation of the Fleming novel leads to an over reliance on captions as opposed to keeping the story moving through action and dialog. Given that the paper's editors were also aware that the potential readership for the strip was wider than that of the novels, i.e. anyone in the family could pick it up and read it, including children, several of the book's more graphic scenes were toned down or rewritten.

One of the most prominent examples of these changes is the notorious torture scene. While in the strip you see Bond being tied to a chair by Le Chiffre, you don't see any of the subsequent actions that Fleming described in excruciating detail. Also the players in that particular drama are drawn in positions which would be physically impossible for them to have carried out those particular actions.

In the novel Bond treats the betrayal and suicide of Vesper Lynd coldly and brutally, closing the book with a terse "the bitch is dead now." The comic strip has Bond expressing disbelief that his love could have been a double agent. The strip ends with a new bridging piece that ties up the end of "Casino Royale" and leads into Bond being sent on assignment to New York for the start of "Live and Let Die."

English Reprints:

"Casino Royale" was reprinted in the 1990 and 2005 Titan Book collections *Casino Royale*.

Above: U.S. 27 x 40 inch movie poster for the 2007 version of *Casino Royale*. **Below:** Italian 55 x 79 inch movie poster for the 1967 version of *Casino Royale*. **Opposite page:** daily newspaper strip "Casino Royale."

Translations:

Brazil

- Uma Aventura de James Bond #5 (1965?)—"Casino Royale"
- 007 James Bond # 2 (1971)—"James Bond em: Cassino Royale"
- 007 James Bond #1(1978)—"Cassino Royale"

Denmark

- James Bond, Agent 007 #1 (1965)—"Højt spil i Monte Carlo"
- James Bond, Agent 007 #56 (1980)—"Casino Royale"

Finland

- James Bond, Agent 007 #2— Series 14 (1988)—"Casino Royale"
- Agentti X-9 #5 (1992)—"Kovaa peliä Monte Carlossa"

Italy

- Albi dell'Avventura—serie James Bond #12 (1974 ?)—"Casino Royale"

Norway

- James Bond, Agent 007 #3 (1965)—"Høyt spill i Monte Carlo"
- James Bond #4 (1988)—"Casino Royale"
- James Bond #1 (2000)—"Casino Royale"

Spain

- Agente 007, James Bond #19-33 (1966?)–"Casino Royale"

Sweden

- James Bond, Agent 007 #3 (1965)—"Högt spel i Monte Carlo"
- James Bond, Agent 007 #18 (1972?)—"Högt spel i Monte Carlo"
- James Bond, Agent 007 #68 (date?)—"Casino Royale"
- James Bond, Agent 007 #2—Series 12 (1992)—"Casino Royale"

COMIC BOOKS

Chile

Type: Adaptation of Ian Fleming novel

Writer: German Gabler

Artist: German Gabler

Originally Published: 007 James Bond #8 (1969) published by Zig Zag

LIVE AND LET DIE

NEWSPAPER STRIP

Type: *Daily Express* comic strip
Writer: Henry Gammidge
Artist: John McLusky

Originally Published: *Daily Express* from 15th December 1958 to 28th March 1959 (Series 1, strip #139-225)

Source: Based on the second Bond novel *Live and Let Die* by Ian Fleming, published in 1954

Plot Summary: James Bond 007 is sent to New York City to investigate "Mr. Bigs," an underworld voodoo leader who is suspected by M of selling 17th century gold coins to finance Soviet spy operations in America. These gold coins have been turning up in Harlem and Florida. Although Bond was reluctant to take on the mission when he was briefed, Bond's attitude quickly changes upon learning that Mr. Big is an agent of SMERSH and that this mission offers him a chance of retaliation for previously being tortured by SMERSH operative Le Chiffre and branded on his hand by Le Chiffre's SMERSH assassin in *Casino Royale*. In Harlem, Bond meets up with his counterpart in the CIA, Felix Leiter, and the two are captured by Mr. Big where Bond is subsequently quizzed by Mr. Big's fortune-telling girlfriend, Solitaire. After escaping with Solitaire, they all go to St. Petersburg, Florida where they confirm in a warehouse that Mr. Big is indeed smuggling 17th century coins underneath sand in fish tanks. While at the warehouse, Solitaire is recaptured by Mr. Big's minions and Leiter loses an arm and a leg after being fed to a shark. Bond continues his mission in Jamaica where he meets Quarrel and John Strangways, the head of station in Jamaica. Later Bond swims through shark and barracuda infested waters to Mr. Big's island and manages to plant a limpet mine on the hull of his boat before being captured. Mr. Big ties both Solitaire and Bond up to his boat and attempts to drag them over the shallow coral reef, however, they are saved once Bond's limpet mine explodes.

Notes: Writer Henry Gammidge came on board for the second Bond adventure with the approach that he was employed to "translate" Fleming into a comic strip format. However as this strip was scheduled for a 15 week run as opposed to the 20 weeks that had been allotted for "Casino Royale" he had to truncate the story and left out much of the detail and background information from the novel. Thus, despite Gammidge's intentions, the result is a less faithful adaptation than its predecessor.

Gammidge also adopted the device of having Bond narrate the adventure. While this worked in some cases it lead to occasions when Bond became either omniscient or questioned his own actions.

For the modern Bond fan, perhaps the most startling thing about this strip is a sense of sudden familiarity in two key scenes. The Bond movie writers and producers often lifted sequences from Fleming's novels and used them out of their original context in other stories. This happened twice with *Live and Let Die*, but reading this strip it also looks like the directors used the comic art as storyboards for those sequences. The maiming of Felix Lieter and the follow up fight in the fish farm was used in the Timothy Dalton movie, *Licence To Kill,* while the keel-hauling of Bond and his female lead was transferred into the Roger Moore movie *For Your Eyes Only*.

English Reprints

Eight years after the strip completed its run in the *Daily Express* it was reshot from the original art and reformatted to appear in the 1967/68 hardback *James Bond Annual*, the only newspaper strip ever included in the UK Annuals.

"Live And Let Die" was reprinted in the 1990 and 2005 Titan Books collections *Casino Royale*.

Below: newspaper strip "Live and Let Die." Opposite page: U.S. 27 x 41 inch move poster from *Live and Let Die*.

Translations

Brazil
- Uma Aventura de James Bond #6 (1964)—"Os outros que se danem"
- 007 James Bond #3 (1971)—"Viver e deixar de morrer"
- 007 James Bond #1 (1978)—"Viver e deixar de morrer"

Denmark
- James Bond, Agent 007 #3 (1965)— "Leve... og lad dø"
- James Bond, Agent 007 #50 (Dec 1979)— "Leve... og lad dø"

Finland
- James Bond #2 (1986)—"Elä ja anna toisten kuolla"

Italy
- Albi dell'Avventura—serie James Bond # ? (1975?)—"Vivi e lascia morire"

Norway
- James Bond, Agent 007 #2 (1965)—"Leve og la dø"
- James Bond #7 (1986)—"Leve og la dø"
- James Bond #1 (2000)—"Live And Let Die"

Spain
- Agente 007, James Bond #11-18 (1965)—"Vive y deja vivir"

Sweden
- James Bond, Agent 007 #2 (1965)—"Leva och låta dö"
- James Bond, Agent 007 #16 (date ?)—"Leva och låta dö"
- James Bond #2 (1986)—"Leva och låta dö"

COMIC BOOKS

Japan

Type: Manga Serial / Collections
Writer/Artist: Takao Saito

Originally Published: December 1964 to August 1965 in nine parts serialized in *Boys Life*

Notes: In 1966 "Live and Let Die" was collected into a single album format (19 cm x 14 cm B&W) under the title of *Shinu no ha yatsura da* (literal translation – "It is Them To Die"), the first of four Bond manga albums published under the Golden Comics label. They were again reprinted in 1980 with new covers this time under the Shogakukan Bunko imprint. At some point the manga Bond was translated into Chinese and reprinted in Hong Kong in both serialized and collected formats.

MOVIE ADAPTATION

Argentina

Type: Unofficial Movie Adaptation - Color
Writer: Percival W. Lytton
Artist: Enio

Originally Published:. D'artagnan Extraordinario #310 (August 1973)

Notes: "Live and Let Die" was a 15 page adaptation under the title "*Vivir Y Dejar Morir* " and appeared in the D'artagnan "Special" dated August 1973.

MOONRAKER

NEWSPAPER STRIP

Type: *Daily Express* comic strip
Writer: Henry Gammidge
Artist: John McLusky

Originally Published: *Daily Express* from 30th March, 1959 to 8th August, 1959 (Series 1, strip #226-339)

Source: Based on the third James Bond novel, *Moonraker*, by Ian Fleming, first published in 1955

Plot Summary: Bond is asked by M to observe Sir Hugo Drax, who is winning money playing bridge at M's club, *Blades*, and whom M suspects of cheating. Although M claims to not really care, he is concerned why a multimillionaire and national hero such as Drax would resort to cheating at a card game. Bond later confirms Drax's deception, and manages to 'cheat the cheater' (with a little help from Benzedrine and champagne), winning £15,000 and infuriating Drax. As it turns out, Drax is the backer of the 'Moonraker' missile project being built to defend the UK against its Cold War enemies. The Moonraker rocket is essentially an upgraded V-2 rocket that uses liquid hydrogen and fluorine as propellants; it can withstand the ultra-high combustion temperatures in its engine thanks to the use of columbite, on which Drax has a monopoly. Because the engine can withstand more heat the Moonraker therefore can use more powerful fuels which results in the rocket having a vast improvement in range. Partly due to the cheating episode, M asks Bond to infiltrate Drax's missile-building organization on the coast of England. Bond uncovers a dreadful and fiendish plot to destroy London, which he foils with the assistance of a female (and, of course, attractive) Special Branch agent, Gala Brand.

Notes: Writer Gammidge continues with his "Bond as narrator" technique and takes it a step further in this strip by having Bond break the fourth wall and address the readers directly. Artist McLusky seemed to struggle with transferring what is one of the most staid of Bond stories into interesting visuals. He resorts to several panels that show newspaper headlines (under a *Daily Express* masthead of course) and even several panels explaining how to play bridge.

However once the story moves to Drax's headquarters, McLusky's style gets looser and the action starts to come fast and furious. The strip is notable for the first appearance of Bond's Bentley in action during a car chase in which McLusky's use of speed lines and shadows give a real sense of movement. Overall the strip is a pretty faithful adaptation of Fleming's book with the only real departure being the omission of a scene where Bond uses stimulants to get himself through the crucial card game.

English Reprints

"Moonraker" was reprinted in the 2000 Titan Books collection *Casino Royale*.

TRANSLATIONS

In the Titan volume it states "This strip hasn't been reprinted in any form since it first appeared." Perhaps they should have said reprinted in the UK, as several foreign language versions have been produced, as well as an English language reprint published in India.

Brazil
- Uma Aventura de James Bond #7 (1965)—O Foguete da Morte
- 007 James Bond (1978)—O Foguete da Morte

Denmark
- James Bond, Agent 007 #7 (1966)—Den Dodbringende Raket"
- James Bond, Agent 007 #31 (date?)—Den Dodbringende Raket"

Finland
- James Bond, Agent 007 #2 (1979)—"Moonraker"

Italy
- Albi dell'Avventura—serie James Bond #22 (1976?)—"La sonda lunare"

Norway
- James Bond, Agent 007 #3 (1966)—den dødbringende raketten"
- James Bond #1 and #2 (1990)—"den dødbringende raketten"
- James Bond #2 (2000)—"Moonraker"

Sweden

Opposite page: two sequential daily newspaper strips from "Moonraker." Above: Swedish comic book adaptation of *Diamonds Are Forever*.

- James Bond, Agent 007 #3 (1966)—"Moonraker"
- James Bond, Agent 007 #30 (date?)—"Moonraker"
- James Bond, Agent 007 #50 (date?)—"Moonraker"
- James Bond, Agent 007 #4 (1991)—"Moonraker"

COMIC BOOKS

Chile

Type: Adaptation of Ian Fleming novel

Writer: German Gabler

Artist: German Gabler

Originally Published: 007 James Bond #18 (1969) as "Sabotaje" published by ZigZag

53   The Missions

MOVIE ADAPTATION

Argentina

Type: Unofficial Movie Adaptation - Color
Writer: unknown
Artist: unknown

Originally Published: *D'artagnan Todo Color #1* (1979)

Notes: This Argentinean title has a *Moonraker* strip listed in its contents and as it was published the same year (1979) that the Roger Moore movie was released, there's a strong possibility this was an unofficial movie adaptation.

DIAMONDS ARE FOREVER

NEWSPAPER STRIP

Type: *Daily Express* comic strip
Writer: Henry Gammidge
Artist: John McLusky

Originally Published: *Daily Express* from 8 October 1959 to 30 January 1960 (Series 1, strip #340-487)

Source: Based on the fourth James Bond novel, *Diamonds Are Forever*, by Ian Fleming, first published in 1956

Plot Summary: M instructs Bond to infiltrate a smuggling ring, which is running diamonds from African mines to the United States. Bond's job is to travel down the "pipeline" as far as he can and find out who is behind it all. Under the name of Peter Franks, a petty crook already known as a diamond smuggler, he meets a mysterious "go-between" named Tiffany Case, with whom he falls in love. Bond discovers that the smuggling ring is operated by a ruthless American gang called "The Spangled Mob," which is run by the brothers Jack Spang and Seraffimo Spang. Bond learns that the

Below: introduction "title" of the "Diamonds are Forever" newspaper strip.

pipeline ends in Las Vegas where Seraffimo Spang owns the Tiara hotel and a ghost town named "Spectreville" that acts as the headquarters for the Spangled Mob.

Notes: Like the previous two strips, Henry Gammidge continued to use the Bond as narrator technique, and although not as blatant as it had been in *Moonraker* it still lead to moments of Bond sharing information about things that he should have had no knowledge of. Overall, script wise, it is a fairly faithful adaptation of Fleming's story. One notable feature of this strip is that for the first time another name appeared alongside Ian Fleming's in the credit box each day. The strip was now credited as "by Ian Fleming, Drawing by John McLusky."

Diamonds Are Forever was the first strip where McLusky started to experiment with ways to break away from the strict three-panel layout with the use of montages, or by using some of the art elements to imply a panel border.

English Reprints

UK—*Diamonds Are Forever* was reprinted in the 2005 Titan Books *Doctor No*.

USA—In 1981 *Diamonds Are Forever* was one of the three strips reprinted in *The Illustrated James Bond, 007* issued by the US branch of the James Bond Fan Club.

TRANSLATIONS

Brazil
- Uma Aventura de James Bond #8 (1965)—"Os Diamantes são eternos"

Denmark
- James Bond, Agent 007 #9 (March 1967)—"Død og Diamanter"
- James Bond, Agent 007 #54 (August 1980)—"Diamanter varer evigt"

Finland
- James Bond, Agent 007 #4 (1981)—"Timantit ovat ikuisia"

Italy
- Albi dell'Avventura—serie James Bond #29 (1974?)—"I diamanti sono eterni"

Norway
- James Bond, Agent 007 #1 (1967)—"Død og Diamanter"
- James Bond, Agent 007 #4 and #5 (1990) — "Diamanter varer evig"
- James Bond #2 (2000)—"Diamonds Are Forever"

Sweden
- James Bond, Agent 007 #1 (1967)—"Död och diamanter"
- James Bond, Agent 007 #20 (Date?)—"Diamantfeber"
- James Bond, Agent 007 #71 (Date?)—"Diamantfeber"
- James Bond #5 and #6 (1988)—"Diamantfeber"
- James Bond, Agent 007 Album (1988)—"Död och diamanter"
- James Bond #2 (1996)—"Diamantfeber"

COMIC BOOKS

Chile

Type: Novel adaptation—Color
Writer: German Gabler
Artist: Lincoln Fuentes

Originally Published: James Bond, Agent 007 #23 as "Diamantes Eternos"

MOVIE ADAPTATION

Argentina

Type: Unofficial Movie Adaptation - Color
Writer: unknown
Artist: unknown

Originally Published:. D'artagnan Extraordinario #? (1971)

Notes: This Argentinean title has a "Diamonds Are Forever" strip listed in its contents and as it was published the same year (1971) that the Sean Connery movie was released, there's a strong possibility this was an unofficial movie adaptation.

FROM RUSSIA WITH LOVE

NEWSPAPER STRIP

Type: *Daily Express* comic strip
Writer: Henry Gammidge
Artist: John McLusky

Published: *Daily Express* from 3rd February 1960 to 21st May 1960 (Series 1, strip #488-583)

Source: Based on the fifth James Bond novel, *From Russia With Love,* by Ian Fleming, first published in 1957

Plot Summary: *From Russia with Love* is perhaps the most complex of Fleming's novels and revolves around a series of elaborate plots and counterplots between the British and the Russian intelligence agencies. It begins with SMERSH, seeking to redeem itself from a series of failures that have made some within the Soviet government begin to criticize the organization. SMERSH plans to commit a grand act of terrorism in the intelligence field and has targeted James Bond. Mainly through the agency of Kronsteen, the chess-playing master planner, and Colonel Rosa Klebb, SMERSH lays a trap for Bond by setting pretty young cipher clerk, Corporal Tatiana Romanova, to pretend to defect from her post in Istanbul, claiming to have fallen in love with Bond after a glimpse from his file photograph. As an added incentive, Tatiana will provide the British agent with a Spektor decoder. The ultimate goal is to set up James Bond for assassination and cause a scandal, but SMERSH doesn't count on Tatiana actually falling in love with 007. As events unfold in Istanbul the reader (and Bond himself) get the satisfying feeling that Bond is taking the initiative but this is a complete illusion. After all the fighting, Bond unwittingly plays the precise role predicted and defined in the SMERSH plan and boards the Orient Express on the journey from Istanbul to Paris — and heads directly into the hands of SMERSH killer Grant. Amazingly Bond readily accepts Grant as a fellow MI6 agent and goes to sleep under Grant's watchful eye, after having obligingly handed Grant his gun. Instead of killing Bond without further ado as Kronsteen's plan called for, Grant cannot resist the temptation to crow at the top British agent, humiliate him and engage in a long boastful conversation. Growing careless and overconfident, Grant gives Bond the chance to improvise a desperate ploy which works against all odds — with the result that Grant loses his life and the entire careful Soviet scheme falls into ruin. Later, after successfully delivering Tatiana to his superiors, Bond has a final encounter with Rosa Klebb — which leaves her captured but 007 poisoned and nearly dead from the final kick of her poisoned toe.

Notes: The biggest problem with adapting Fleming's novel into a newspaper strip was that the first third of the novel is told from the SMERSH point of view as their intricate plans are laid. In fact Bond doesn't appear in the narrative until he arrives in Istanbul. Most of this background material was omitted from the strip, including several key scenes between Tatania and Klebb. It also made writer Gammidge's "Bond as narrator" technique useless as, for the story to work, Bond had to be totally ignorant of the trap laid for him. As a result the first three weeks of the strip use an odd dispassionate objective third person narration in caption boxes to explain the settings and action prior to Istanbul. It would be the last time that this narration technique would be used on a Bond strip.

McLusky's art continued the development begun in "Diamonds Are Forever" with greater use of montages, speed lines and shadows to help build atmosphere and action. The famed gypsy camp fight scene is a fairly frenetic example of this technique. While the novel ends with uncertainty about Bond's fate, the strip expands its time frame by showing Bond being treated and starting on the road to recovery following his poisoning. The dialog in the last panel even segues directly into the opening for *Doctor No*.

English Reprints

UK—"From Russia With Love" was reprinted in the 2005 Titan Books collection "Doctor No."

USA—"From Russia With Love" is one of the only three newspaper strips to be reprinted in the US when it was included in the US James Bond Fan Club book *The Illustrated James Bond 007* published in 1981.

TRANSLATIONS.

Brazil
- Uma Aventura de James Bond #2 (1964)—"Moscou Contra 007"
- 007 James Bond #2 (1980)—"Moscou Contra 007"

Denmark
- James Bond, Agent 007 #5 (1966)—Agent 007 Jages
- James Bond, Agent 007 #59 (1981)—Agent 007 Jages

Finland
- James Bond, Agent 007 #2 (1980—"007 Istanbulissa"
- James Bond, Agent 007 #1 (1988)—"Salainen agentti 007 Istanbulissa"

Germany
- Comic Gallery Piccolo #3 (1980)—"Liebesgrüsse aus Moskau"

Italy
- Albi dell'Avventura—serie James Bond #34 (date?)—"Dalla Russia con amore"
- Super Fummetti #16 (1979)—"Dalla Russia con amore"

Norway
- James Bond, Agent 007 #1 (1966)—"Agent 007 ser rødt"
- James Bond, Agent 007 #7 (1987)—"From Russia – With Love"
- James Bond Album #3 (2000)—"From Russia With Love".

Sweden
- James Bond, Agent 007 #1 (1966)—"Agent 007 ser rött"
- James Bond, Agent 007 #24 (1975)—"Agent 007 ser rött"
- James Bond, Agent 007 #62 (1977)—"Agent 007 ser rött"
- James Bond #12 (1981)—"Agent 007 ser rött."
- James Bond Collection #4 (1995) —"Agent 007 ser rött"

COMIC BOOKS

Chile

Type: Novel adapataion

Writer: German Gabler

Artist: German Gabler

Originally Published: 007 James Bond #22 (1969) as "De Rusia con Amor" published by ZigZag

Above: U.S. 81 x 81 inch movie poster for *From Russia With Love*.

DOCTOR NO

NEWSPAPER STRIPS

Type: *Daily Express* comic strip

Writer: Peter O'Donnell

Artist: John McLusky

Published: *Daily Express* from 23rd May, 1960 to 1st October, 1960 (Series 1, strip #584-697)

Source: Based on the sixth James Bond novel, *Doctor No*, by Ian Fleming, first published in 1958

Plot Summary: *Doctor No* starts with Bond's recovery from the poison administered by Rosa Kleb at the end of *From Russia With Love*. Once healthy, Bond is sent by M on a "rest cure" to Jamaica to investigate the disappearance of Strangways, the head of a station in Kingston, who had previously appeared in *Live and Let Die*. He learns that Strangways had been investigating the activities of Dr. Julius No, a Chinese-German who lives on an island called "Crab Key" that is said to be the home of a vicious dragon. With the help of, Quarrel (who also appeared in *Live and Let Die*), as well as the beautiful Honeychile Rider, who visits the island to collect valuable shells, Bond discovers that Dr. No, who ostensibly operates a business harvesting and exporting guano, is in fact working with the Russians. They have supplied him with several million dollars worth of equipment to sabotage nearby American missile tests. Bond and Honeychile are captured by Dr. No, but Quarrel is burned to death by the (mechanical) dragon. Doctor No's specialty is torture and he tortures Bond to discover and record his powers of endurance. But Bond survives, kills Doctor No, and rescues Honey.

Notes: This adaptation marked a one-off assignment on 007 for writer Peter O'Donnell, who two years later would create his own super spy, *Modesty Blaise*. In *Doctor No*, O'Donnell adapted his style to closely mirror that of regular writer Henry Gammidge, adopting some of Gammidge's objective narration technique. The strip was faithful to the novel including several scenes that were later left out by the movie producers, such as a frankly ludicrous battle between Bond and a giant squid. As with *From Russia With Love*, the fact that the movie producers stayed relatively faithful to the novel means that from today's perspective it looks like this newspaper strip could have been used for storyboarding the first Bond movie which went into production two years after the strip was published.

During one of the extended torture sequences (also excised from the movie) O'Donnell and artist John McLusky added in a couple of guards casually watching the scene, with the effect that in some ways it emphasized Dr No's brutality in a way that wasn't explored in Fleming's novel. Doctor No also marked a departure from McLusky's use of opening title bars on the strip's first day. McLusky also started to use more zip-a-tone for several of his backgrounds and shading on this strip in place of his usual cross-hatching, with mixed results.

English Reprints

UK—"Doctor No" was reprinted in the 2005 Titan Books collection *Doctor No*.

USA—"Doctor No" is one of the only three newspaper strips to be reprinted in the US when it was included in the US James Bond Fan Club book *The Illustrated James Bond 007* published in 1981.

TRANSLATIONS.

Brazil

- Uma Aventura de James Bond #3 (1964)—"O satanico Dr. No"
- 007 James Bond #6 (1971)—"O satanico Dr. No"
- 007 James Bond #2 (1978)—"O satanico Dr. No"

Denmark

- James Bond, Agent 007 #4 (1965)—"Doktor No"

Finland

- James Bond, Agent 007 #2 (1987)—"Tohtori E*i*"

Italy

- Albi dell'Avventura—serie James Bond #40—#46 (date?)—"Dr. No"

Spain

- Agente 007, James Bond #1-10 (1965)—"Agente 007 contra Dr. No"

Sweden

- James Bond, Agent 007 #4 (1965)—"Doktor No"
- James Bond, Agent 007 #22 (date?)—"Döden på Jamaica"
- James Bond, Agent 007 #60 (date?)—"Döden på Jamaica"
- James Bond, Agent 007 #3 (1988)—"Döden på Jamaica"
- James Bond, Agent 007 #1 (1996)—"Döden på Jamaica"

Norway

- James Bond, Agent 007 #4 (1965)—"Doktor No"
- James Bond #6 (1988)—"Doktor No"
- James Bond Collection #3 (2000)—"Doktor No"

COMIC BOOKS

Chile

Type: Novel adaptation—Color

Writer: German Gabler

Artist: German Gabler

Originally Published: in 007 James Bond #20 (1970) by ZigZag

MOVIE ADAPTATION

UK

Type: Movie Adaptation - Color

Writer: Norman J. Nodel

Artist: Norman J. Nodel

Originally Published: *Classics Illustrated* 158a (1962)

Notes: Wishing to cash in on the release of the *Doctor No* movie, the British arm of the Dell publishing company obtained the rights to produce an adaptation. This was produced by Norman J. Nodel, a former-military field artist and map maker better known as a children's book illustrator. Judging from the art, his adaptation was primarily based on photographs taken during the film's production; a theory seemingly supported by the inclusion of an alternative version of the scene where Bond kills Professor Dent. In the comic Dent and Bond fire simultaneously indicating that Dent still had a round in his gun, unlike the movie. This version of events was filmed but not used in the movie. Some sources suggest that Dell may have in fact only optioned the screenplay rather than the actual movie. This version of the story first appeared in the British *Classics Illustrated* line #158a in late 1962.

English Reprints

USA – When, for some as yet unknown reason, the US publishers of *Classics Illustrated* declined to produce a US version, the idea was floated that Eon Productions could publish their own comic book for the American market. With no comic book experience they approached the largest comics distributor, Independent News, which at that time shared a parent company with DC Comics. So it was that the US publication rights ended up at the home of *Batman* and *Superman*, where the Nodel adaptation was published in *Showcase* #43 (April, 1963). One unusual aspect of the DC version when compared with the European was that several racial references have been omitted and skin tones changed so that non-Caucasian characters, including the Asian Doctor No, became white. The contract between Eon and DC Comics included an option for the rights to an on-going *James Bond* series. However, the *Showcase* issue proved to be a one-off appearance. DC did little to promote the book which had basically been forced upon them. Two other strikes against it include the fact that DC published the book too soon and it had disappeared from the newsstands long before the movie had opened in the US. In addition, it didn't help that the issue's cover failed to mention that it was a movie adaptation. In fact it sends a somewhat mixed message with a small hand lettered box on the lower left of the cover stating that it is "Based on the novel and now a United Artists film thriller." The story has not been reprinted in the US since.

TRANSLATIONS:

NOTE: The translated reprints of the Dell/Classic Illustrated adaptation was the first appearance of Bond in the comics format in the countries listed below. All the translated reprints used the same cover art as the UK Classic Illustrated original. DC Comics was the only publisher to create their own *Doctor No* movie comic cover art.

Denmark

- Detektiv serien #6 (1963)—"Doktor No"

Germany

- Bildschirm Detektiv # 706 (1964)—"James Bond: WXN antwortet nicht"

Norway

- Detektiv serien #6 (1963)—"Doktor No"

Sweden

- Detektiväventyr serien # 6 (1963)—"Doktor No"

GOLDFINGER

NEWSPAPER STRIP

Type: *Daily Express* comic strip
Writer: Henry Gammidge
Artist: John McLusky

Originally Published: *Daily Express* between 10 March 1960 and 1st April 1961 (Series 1, strip #698-849)

Source: Based on the seventh James Bond novel, *Goldfinger,* by Ian Fleming, published in 1959

Plot Summary: Bond is at the Miami airport musing over the killing of a drug dealer in Mexico when he is recognized by Junius DuPont (one of the card players from *Casino Royale*). DuPont asks Bond to observe a two-handed Canasta game between him and one, Auric Goldfinger. Du Pont suspects Goldfinger of cheating and offers to pay Bond to confirm his suspicions. Bond discovers that Goldfinger is using his "companion" Jill Masterson to watch duPont's cards through binoculars from his hotel suite. Bond stops the charade and forces Goldfinger to admit his guilt and pay back Du Pont due compensation. Bond also takes Masterson as a "hostage" until the debt is paid. Back in England Bond coincidently starts to research Goldfinger at the same time that his name comes up associated with a possible gold smuggling operation. With M's permission Bond once again places himself in Goldfinger's path and the two engage in a high stakes golf game, during which Bond spots Goldfinger cheating. By reversing the cheat, Bond forces Goldfinger to concede the game. Bond follows Goldfinger through Europe to his factory in Switzerland where he uncovers how Goldfinger is smuggling the gold to India. En-route he encounters Tilly Masterson, Jill's sister, who informs Bond how Goldfinger suffocated Jill with gold paint. Tilly is out for revenge. Bond and Tilly are captured and Bond is tortured for information by being placed on a buzz saw table. After blacking out Bond awakes to incredulously discover that Goldfinger has decided that Bond and Tilly Masterson should work for him as secretaries. Goldfinger includes the pair in his briefing of "Operation Grand Slam" a plan to break in to Fort Knox. At the briefing are the heads of several American crime syndicates, including Pussy Galore, head of the all female "cement mixers." Bond manages to sneak a message out to his friend Felix Leiter that outlines Goldfinger's plan, and with the cooperation of Pussy Galore they manage to thwart the robbery, but not before Tilly Masterson is killed by Goldfinger's man servant Oddjob.

Opposite page: newspaper strip from "Dr. No."
Right: 31 x 16 inch French movie poster from *Dr. No* with artwork by Boris Grinsson.

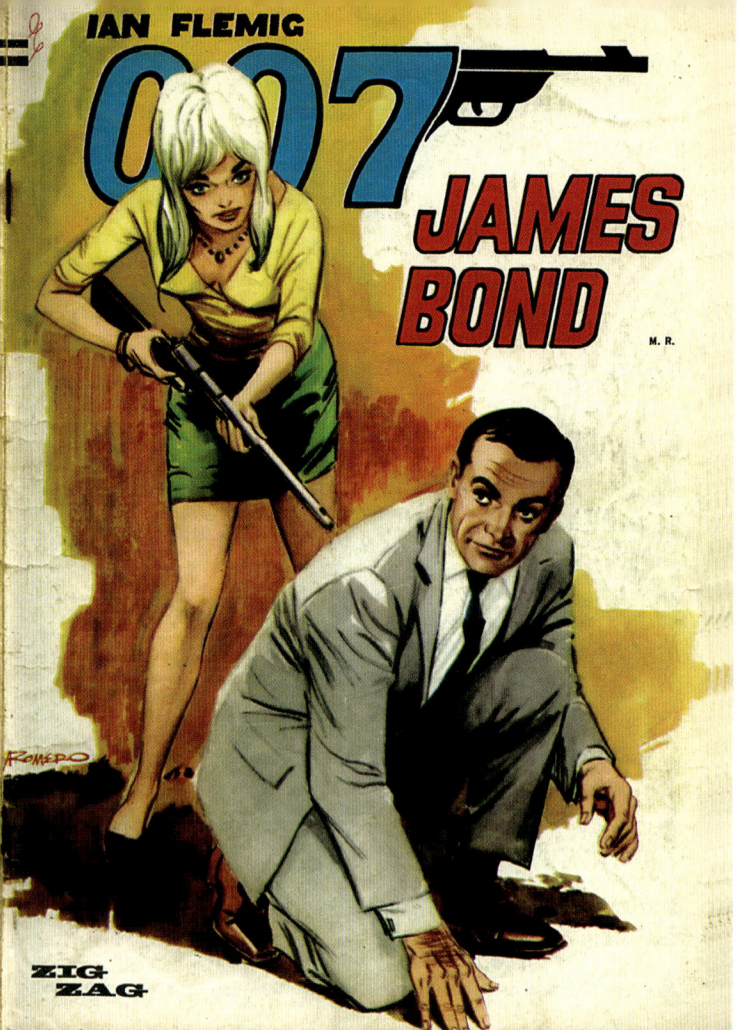

Notes: One of the most faithful adaptations of a Fleming novel to the comics format, the *Daily Express* strip follows the novel's story beat for story beat. However the editors did make two noticeable changes. The iconic murder of Jill Masterson by being covered in gold paint, which was described in detail in the novel and even recreated in the movie version, is omitted. The strip just includes a line of dialog that says that she was killed. In the UK version of the strip Bond's climatic fight with Oddjob is toned down with the knife play removed, however an unlicensed translated version of the strip published in Germany included the original art showing Oddjob using a knife against Bond. This strip is also the first time we see Bond driving an Aston Martin.

English reprints—Titan Books 2004 *Goldfinger*

Translations

Brazil
- Uma Aventura de James Bond #1 (1964)—"007 contra Goldfinger"

Denmark
- James Bond, Agent 007 #2 (1965)—"Contra Goldfinger"
- James Bond, Agent 007 #57 (1987)—"Contra Goldfinger"

Finland
- James Bond, Agent 007 #1 (1987)—"Kultasormi!"

Germany
- Comic Gallery Piccol #1(1980)—"Goldfinger" This was an unlicensed reprint of the "Goldfinger" strip with unedited original art.

India
- James Bond #74 (1989)—"Goldfinger"

Italy
- Albi dell'Avventura—serie James Bond #45 (1975) "Goldfinger"

Norway
- James Bond, Agent 007 #1 (1965)—"Operasjon Storeslem"
- James Bond #2 (1988) —"Operasjon Storeslem"
- James Bond #4 (2001)—"Operasjon Storeslem"

Spain
- Agente 007, James Bond #34 (1966)—"Goldfinger" First 10 strips only, the title was cancelled and story never completed.
- Biblioteca Grandes del Comic: James Bond #3 (2006)—"Goldfinger"

Sweden
- James Bond, Agent 007 #1 (1965)—"Operation Storslam"
- James Bond, Agent 007 #14 (1971)—"Goldfinger"
- James Bond, Agent 007 #64 (date?)—"Goldfinger"
- James Bond, Agent 007 #7 and #8 (1989)—"Goldfinger"
- James Bond Collection (1988)—"Goldfinger"

COMIC BOOKS

Chile

Type: Novel adaptation—Color
Writer: German Gabler?
Artist: Hernan Jiron

Originally Published: 007 James Bond #10, #13 and #14

Notes: This adaptation of the Ian Fleming novel was spread across three issues. Issue 10 contained "Mision en Mexico" (Mission in Mexico) a self contained tale loosely based on the first chapter of the novel, with the rest of the story told in "Encrucijada Fatal" (Fatal Crossroad) in issue #13 and "El Oro de Fort Knox" (The Gold of Fort Knox) in issue #14.

Opposite page: covers from ZigZag's *James Bond* #13 and #14, 1969, adaptations of *Goldfinger*. Below: a daily from the "Goldfinger" strip.

RISICO

NEWSPAPER STRIP

Type: *Daily Express* comic strip
Writer: Henry Gammidge
Artist: John McLusky

Originally Published: *Daily Express* between 3rd April 1961 and 24th June, 1961 (Series 1, strip #850 - #921)

Source: Based on the James Bond short story Risico by Ian Fleming, published as part of the *For Your Eyes Only* collection, published in 1960

Plot Summary: James Bond is sent by M to investigate a drug smuggling operation based out of Italy that is pumping narcotics into England. M instructs Bond to get in touch with a CIA informant, Kristatos, who in turn tells Bond that a man named Enrico Colombo is behind the racket. When Bond sets out to find more information on Colombo, he is captured by him and brought aboard Colombo's ship, the *Colombina*. While in captivity Colombo informs Bond that Kristatos is actually the one in charge of the drug smuggling operation and that he is being backed by the Russians. The next day, the *Colombina* arrives at Santa Maria, where men are loading another shipment. Bond, Colombo, and the crew of the *Colombina* attack the warehouse and discover Kristatos inside. While trying to escape, Kristatos is killed by Bond.

Notes: A fairly faithful adaptation of the Fleming short story. Risico provided the major part of the plot line for the Roger Moore movie *For Your Eyes Only* and in places the strip reads almost like a storyboard for the relevant movie sequences, especially the raid on Kristatos' warehouse.

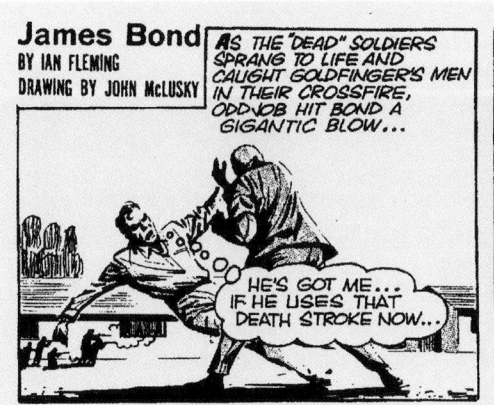

English Reprints

"Risico" was reprinted in the 2004 Titan Books collection *Goldfinger*.

Translations

Brazil
- Uma Adventure de James Bond #15 (date?)—"O falso agente"

Denmark
- James Bond, Agent 007 #10 (1967)—"Risicoligaen"
- James Bond, Agent 007 #37 (1976)—"Risicoligaen"

Italy
- Albi dell'Avventura—serie James Bond #48 (date?) – "Rischio"

Norway
- James Bond, Agent 007 #2 (1967)—"Risico—de hensynsløse opiumssmuglerne"
- James Bond #3 (1987)—"Risiko-ligaen"
- James Bond #4 (2001)—"Risico"

Spain
- Biblioteca Grandes del Comic: James Bond #3 (2006) —"Risico"

Sweden
- James Bond, Agent 007 #2 (1967)—"Risico"
- James Bond, Agent 007 #6 (1986)—"Risico"

Above: opening title for the "For Your Eyes Only" newspaper strip, 1961. **Opposite page:** British 30 x 40 inch movie poster from *For Your Eyes Only*.

COMIC BOOKS

Chile

Type: Novel adaptation—Color
Writer: German Gabler?
Artist: Hernan Jiron

Originally Published: 007 James Bond #1 (1968) as "Operacion Riesgo" (Operation Risk)

Notes: The little known Risico was the surprising choice as the first adaptation to appear in the Chilean publisher ZigZag's James Bond series.

FROM A VIEW TO A KILL

NEWSPAPER STRIP

Type: *Daily Express* comic strip
Writer: Henry Gammidge
Artist: John McLusky
Published: *Daily Express* between 25th June 1961 and 9th September, 1961 (strip #922-987)

Source: Based on the James Bond short story "From A View To A Kill" by Ian Fleming, published as part of the *For Your Eyes Only* collection, published in 1960

Plot Summary: While taking a break in Paris Bond is sent to investigate the murder of an army dispatch-rider who was carrying intelligence documents. To unravel the mystery Bond disguises himself as a dispatch-rider and follows the same journey as the previous ride. The assassin attempts to kill Bond, however, Bond is ready and ends up killing the assassin, and uncovering his base of operations hidden in an old gypsy encampment.

Notes: The strip reverts back to starting with a full width title graphic with no action or narrative on the first day. This is then followed by a two panel strip on the second day before settling into the more traditional three panels per strip layout. At various points artist John McLusky switches back to two panels as if to stretch out the action and make this short story fit the days allocated.

English Reprints
From A View To A Kill was reprinted in the 2004 Titan Books *Goldfinger*.

Translations

Brazil
- Uma Aventura de James Bond #16 (1965)—"Fator Invisíve"
- 007 James Bond #5 (1972)—"De uma visão a um assassinato"

Denmark
- James Bond, Agent 007 #13 (1968)—"Livsfarlig opgave"
- James Bond, Agent 007 #43 (1978)—"Dødelig opgave"

Germany
- Comic Gallery Piccolo #3 (1980) – "Mörder ohne skrupel"—an unlicensed translated reprint

Italy
- Albi dell'Avventura—serie James Bond #51 (date?) — "Appuntamento con il killer"

Norway
- James Bond, Agent 007 #5 (1968)—"Med døden til følge"
- James Bond, Agent 007 #8 (1990)—"Med døden til følge"
- James Bond Collection #5 (2001)—"From A View To A Kill"

Spain
- Biblioteca Grandes del Comic: James Bond #3 (2006) —"From A View To A Kill"

Sweden
- James Bond, Agent 007 #5 (1968)—"Dödligt uppdrag"
- James Bond, Agent 007 #43 (date?)—"Dödligt uppdrag"
- James Bond, Agent 007 #2 (1990)—"Dödligt uppdrag"

COMIC BOOKS

Chile

Type: Short Story adapataion

Writer: German Gabler

Artist: Artist Unknown

Above left: interior page from the Indian version of "For Your Eyes Only," 1981, using rearranged panels from the daily newspaper strip with John McLusky art. Right: cover from 007 James Bond #28, 1969, published in Chile by ZigZag featuring "Thunderball." Opposite page: cover to the Swedish film adaptation of "Thunderball."

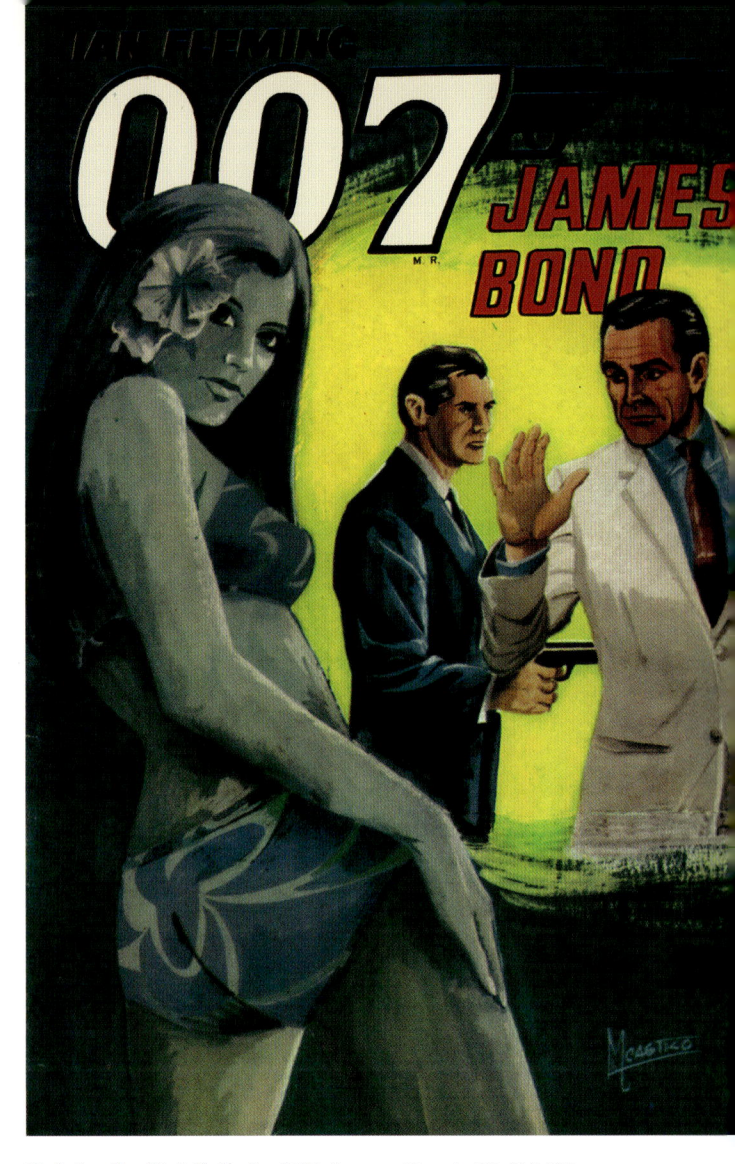

Originally Published: 007 James Bond #9 (1969) as "Cacería" published by ZigZag

MOVIE ADAPTATION

Sweden

Type: Movie Adaptation—Color
Writer: Jack Sutter
Artist: Frederico Maidagan

Originally Published: Semic Album #3 (1985)

Notes: The movie title drops the "From A" from the original and is correctly referred to as "*View To A Kill.*" This adaptation appears to suffer from most of the problems common to movie adaptations, rushed art and static storytelling. This particular adaptation is not helped by its garish coloring and corny dialog which gives it a somewhat amateurish look.

Translations:

Finland
- Published under the title "007 ja kuoleman katse" by Semic

Germany
- Published under the title "Im Angesicht des Todes" by Ehapa publications

Norway
- Published as "Med Døden I Sikte." By Semic

Spain
- Published as "James Bond 007: Panorama para matar" by Forum

FOR YOUR EYES ONLY

NEWSPAPER STRIP

Type: *Daily Express* comic strip
Writer: Henry Gammidge
Artist: John McLusky

Published: *Daily Express* between 11th September, 1961 and 9th December, 1961 (Series 1, strip #988-1065)

Source: Based on the James Bond short story *For Your Eyes Only* by Ian Fleming, published as part of the *For Your Eyes Only* collection in 1960

Plot Summary: Close friends of M are murdered by Cuban hitman Major Gonzales after they refuse to sell their Jamacian homestead to his boss, Herr von Hammerstein. A few weeks later M, after finding out that Von Hammerstein is in Vermont, gives Bond a voluntary assignment, "off-book" from sanctioned Secret Service duties, to prevent any harm to the Havelocks's only daughter, Judy, by any means necessary. When Bond arrives on the scene, however, he finds Judy Havelock has arrived there first and intends to carry out her own mission of revenge. With only a bow and arrow, Judy kills von Hammerstein from 100 yards by shooting him in the neck at the exact moment he dives into a lake. A shootout later occurs with the rest of von Hammerstein's men, all of whom, including Major Gonzales, are killed by Bond.

Notes: Instead of being a direct adaptation, "For Your Eyes Only" hints that writer Henry Gammidge may have wanted to add his own interpretation to Fleming's work and characters. While the story remains faithful to the source material, Gammidge's take on M is less forceful than Fleming's. He also introduces the idea of the by play between Bond and Moneypenny that would become a staple of the movie series, which was still two years in the future.

English Reprints

"For Your Eyes Only" was reprinted as part of the 2004 Titan Books *Goldfinger*.

Translations

Brazil
- Uma Aventura De James Bond #12 (1964)—"Para Você Sòmente"
- 007 James Bond #6 (1971)—"Olho Por Olho"

Denmark
- James Bond, Agent 007 #8 (1966) "Fra dødelig vinkel"
- James Bond, Agent 007 #29 (1974)—"Fra en dræbende synsvinkel"

Finland
- James Bond, Agent 007 #3 (1975) —"Erään tapon tarin a"

India
- James Bond #? (date?)—title unknown

Italy
- Albi Dell'avventura—Serie James Bond #60 (date?) —"Solo per i tuoi occhi"

Norway
- James Bond, Agent 007 #4 (1966)— "Fra en drep ende synsvinkel"
- James Bond, Agent 007 #1 (1987)—"Kun for dine øyne"
- James Bond #5 (2001)—"For Your Eyes Only"

Spain
- Biblioteca Grandes Del Comic: James Bond #4 (2006) —"For Your Eyes Only"

Sweden
- James Bond, Agent 007 #4 (1966)—"Ur dödlig synvinkel"
- James Bond, Agent 007 #28 (1970)—"Ur dödlig synvinkel"
- James Bond, Agent 007 #4 (1986)—"Ur dödligsynvinkel"

COMIC BOOKS

Chile

Type: Novel adaptation—Color
Writer: German Gabler ?
Artist: Herman Jiron
Originally Published: 007 James Bond #3 (1968) as "Solo para tus Ojos"

MOVIE ADAPTATION

USA

Type: Movie Adaptation—Color
Writer: Larry Hamma
Artist: Howard Chaykin

Originally Published: *Marvel Super Special* #19 (1981), simultaneously published as a two-part regular comic sized mini-series and as a mass market paperback

Notes: Howard Chaykin's artwork is lacking in his usual level of detail and gives the impression of being rushed, perhaps due to tight deadlines and changes made during the movie production. The slower pace of the comic format also exposes several plot holes that were easy to overlook in the fast paced movie. The comics adaptation diverts from the movie in a couple of different areas which suggest that it was based on an early draft of the screen play. The comic includes an appearance by M, who was in the early screen play drafts but was written out following the death of M actor Bernard Lee in early 1981. The dialogue between Bond and the young skater Bibi is also more suggestive in the comic than appeared on film, where it may have been toned down due to the apparent age differences.

The mass market paperback version broke the panels apart to fit the smaller format which ended up with a very disjointed story flow.

English Language Reprints

Reprinted in the 1981 Marvel Comics UK hardback *James Bond Annual*.

Translations:

Denmark
- 007 James Bond: Strengt Fortroligt (1982)

France
- James Bond 007 Rien que pour vos yeux (1981)
- Les 3 grands films de l'annee en bande dessinée. (date?)

Norway
- Kun for dine øyne (1981)

Spain
- James Bond 007: Solo para sus ojos (1981)

Sweden
- Ur Dödlig Synvinkel (1981)

THUNDERBALL

NEWSPAPER STRIP

Type: *Daily Express* comic strip
Writer: Henry Gammidge
Artist: John McLusky

Published: *Daily Express* between November 12th 1961 and 10th February 1962 (strip Series 1 # 1066-1128)

Source: Based on the James Bond novel *Thunderball* by Ian Fleming, published in 1961

Plot Summary: After a poor medical assessment Bond is sent by M to the Shrubland health clinic. At the clinic Bond encounters SPECTRE agent Count Lippe and the two engage in a torturous game. Shortly after Bond's return to active duty SPECTRE issues a ransom demand to the governments of the world informing them that it has acquired two NATO nuclear devices. On a hunch M assigns Bond to the Bahamas as part of the plan, codenamed Operation Thunderball, to recover the bombs. Bond once again teams up with Felix Leiter of the CIA. In the Bahamas Bond meets Domino Vitalli, the mistress of local "treasure hunter" Emil Lago, who is in reality the SPECTRE agent in charge of the operation. Bond and Lieter locate the hijacked NATO aircraft from which the bombs had been stolen. With Domino's help Bond connects Largo to SPECTRE and the story climaxes in a graphic underwater battle between Largo's men and US divers, during which Domino kills Largo with a spear gun.

Opposite page: The hasty conclusion tacked onto the end of the suddenly cancelled "Thunderball" newspaper strip, art by John McLusky, 1962. **Above:** U.S. 27 x 41 inch movie poster from *Thunderball*, 1965.

69 The Missions

Notes: Just as *Thunderball* started to appear in the *Daily Express*, rival newspaper the *Sunday Times* approached Ian Fleming asking for his assistance with the launch of a new color magazine. As Fleming often cited *The Times* as Bond's favorite reading material in the novels, he agreed and gave them permission to print "*The Living Daylights*." Lord Beaverbrook, the publisher of the Express group of papers, who believed he had a first refusal agreement with Fleming on any new Bond stories was furious and ordered that the Bond comic strip be withdrawn, immediately. Writer Henry Gammidge and illustrator John McLusky were given only a few days' notice and were forced to conclude the story in only two daily strips. The story had only reached the hijacking of the bomber. The new ending simply stated that SPECTRE communicated its demands to the governments and that all intelligence agents, including James Bond, were sent to search for the missing bombs. The last line reads: "Bond finds them and the world is safe". Six more panels for the *Daily Express* version were originally completed by John McLusky detailing the hijacking of the bomber; however, they were never published. A further six panels also were created to expand and conclude the story; these were used in the various translated versions of the comic strip. Even this expanded "conclusion" doesn't follow the plot of the book as it basically involves an underwater fight between Bond and a SPECTRE agent during which Bond's mask gets ripped off, he faints, blacks out and wakes up in hospital where Leiter tells him that the bombs have been recovered.

English Reprints—Titan Books, as part of the 2004 *Goldfinger* (includes the missing "Thunderball" strips)

Translations

Brazil
- Aventura DE JAMES BOND #4 (date?)—"007 contra a Chantagem Atômica"
- 007 James Bond #3 (1971)—"Thunderball Operação Atômica"

Denmark
- James Bond, Agent 007 #6 (1966)—"Thunderball"
- James Bond, Agent 007 #52 (1980)—"Thunderball"

Finland
- James Bond, Agent 007 #4 (1987)—"Pallosalama"

Italy
- Albi Dell'avventura—Serie James Bond #65 (date?)—"Thunderball"

Norway
- James Bond, Agent 007 #2 (1966)—"Thunderball"
- James Bond, Agent 007 #6 (1990)—"Operasjon Tordensky"
- James Bond Collection (2001)—"Thunderball"

Spain
- Biblioteca Grandes Del Comic: James Bond #4 (2006)—"Thunderball"

Sweden
- James Bond, Agent 007 #3 (1966)—"Åskbollen" James Bond, Agent -007 #26 (date)— "Åskbollen"
- James Bond, Agent 007 #65 (date)—"Åskbollen"
- James Bond, Agent 007 #3 (1990)—"Åskbollen"

COMIC BOOKS

Chile
Type: Novel adaptation—Color
Writer: German Gabler
Artist: Lincoln Fuentes

Originally Published: *007 James Bond* #28 and #33 by ZigZag

Notes: *Thunderball* was adapted in two parts, the first part, "SPECTRE," was published in issue #28 with the concluding part "Operacion Trueno" in issue #33.

Japan

Type: Manga Serial / Collections
Writer: Takao Saito
Artist: Takao Saito

Originally Published: September 1965 to March 1966 in seven parts serialized in "Boys Life"

Notes: In 1966 *Thunderball* was collected into a single album format (19 cm x 14com B&W) under the title of *"Thunderball Sakusen"*, the second of four Bond manga albums published under the "Golden Comics" label. They were again reprinted in 1980 with new covers this time under the Shogakukan Bunko imprint. At some point the manga Bond was translated into Chinese and reprinted in Hong Kong in both serialized and collected formats.

MOVIE ADAPTATION

Argentina

Type: Unofficial Movie Adaptation
Writer: unknown
Artist: Daniel Haupt
Originally Published: D'artagnan #122 (1966) as "Operacion Trueno"

Above: opening title for the "On Her Majesty's Secret Service" newspaper strip, art by John McLusky, 1964. Opposite page: French 39 x 98 inch movie poster from *On Her Majesty's Secret Service*, 1969.

71   **The Missions**

ON HER MAJESTY'S SECRET SERVICE

NEWSPAPER STRIP

Type: *Daily Express* comic strip
Writer: Henry Gammidge
Artist: John McLusky

Published: *Daily Express* between 29th June 1964 and 17th May 1965 (Series 2, strip # 1-274)

Source: Based on the James Bond novel *On Her Majesty's Secret Service* by Ian Fleming, published in 1963

Plot Summary: The story opens with Bond quietly observing a woman on a beach who he then rescues from an attempted suicide by drowning. Shortly afterwards the pair are captured by a pair of thugs and brought before Marc-Ange Draco, the head of the Union Corse. Draco turns out to be the father of the woman, the Contessa Teresa di Vincnzo ("Tracy"). Draco sees in Bond the sort of man who can tame and look after his daughter and offers Bond a million dollars to marry her. Bond refuses, but agrees to keep romancing her. Bond also asks Draco to use his contacts to locate Blofeld, the head of SPECTRE, who he has spent that last year hunting. Draco finds out that Blofeld is in Switzerland, but doesn't have a precise location. Back in London Bond receives another clue when the Royal College of Arms receives a request from Blofeld to confirm his right to the title of Comte de Bleuville. Disguised as "Sir Hilary Bray" from the College of Arms, Bond travels to Switzerland and is escorted to Blofeld's clinic in the Alps by his assistant Irma Blunt. At the clinic Bond finds that Blofeld is brainwashing a selection of British girls to unconsciously launch a biological weapons attack on British food and wildlife stocks on their return to the UK. After another agent is caught near the facility, Bond believes his cover is blown and makes a daring ski escape down the mountain. At the climax of the chase in the village below, Bond is rescued by Tracy who had been told by her father that Bond may be in the area. The two escape several SPECTRE traps and at the end of the chase, Bond amazes himself by proposing to Tracy before he returns to London. With tacit approval from M, Bond and Draco plan an assault on Blofeld's headquarters. Blofeld escapes down a bob sled run with Bond in close pursuit. Despite Bond's best efforts Blofeld escapes, but his clinic is destroyed and his biological warfare plans thwarted. A short while later Bond and Tracy marry, but as they drive away from their wedding they are attacked in a drive by shooting by Blofeld and Irma Blunt and Tracy is killed.

Notes: Taking almost a full year to run, this is one of the longest comic strip adaptations and one of the most faithful being close to a scene by scene adaptation. A few minor changes were made to cover small plot holes, but otherwise it is almost verbatim Fleming's story. Considering that the 1969 movie version of this story also adhered closely to Fleming's story the strip reads almost like a storyboard for the movie.

English Reprints

"On Her Majesty's Secret Service" is reprinted in the 2004 Titan Books *On Her Majesty's Secret Service*.

Translations

Brazil
- Aventura DE JAMES BOND #9 (date?)— "A Servico de sua Majestade"

Denmark
- James Bond, Agent 007 #11 (1967)—"I hendes Majestæts hemmelige tjeneste

- James Bond, Agent 007 #33 (1975)—" I hendes Majestæts hemmelige tjeneste"

Finland
- James Bond, Agent 007 #1 (1986)—"as Hänen Majesteettinsa Salaisessa Palvelussa"

Italy
- Albi Dell'avventura—Serie James Bond #76 (date?)—"Al servizio segreto di sua maesta" (Part 1)
- Albi Dell'avventura—Serie James Bond #77 (date?)—"Operazione corona" (Part 2)
- Albi Dell'avventura—Serie James Bond #78 (date?)—"La vendetta di Blofeld" (Part 3)

Norway
- James Bond, Agent 007 #3 (1967)—"I hennes majestets hemmelige tjeneste"
- James Bond, Agent 007 #4 (1989)—"I hemmelig tjeneste"

Spain
- Biblioteca Grandes Del Comic: James Bond #4 (2006)—"Al servicio secreto de su majestad"

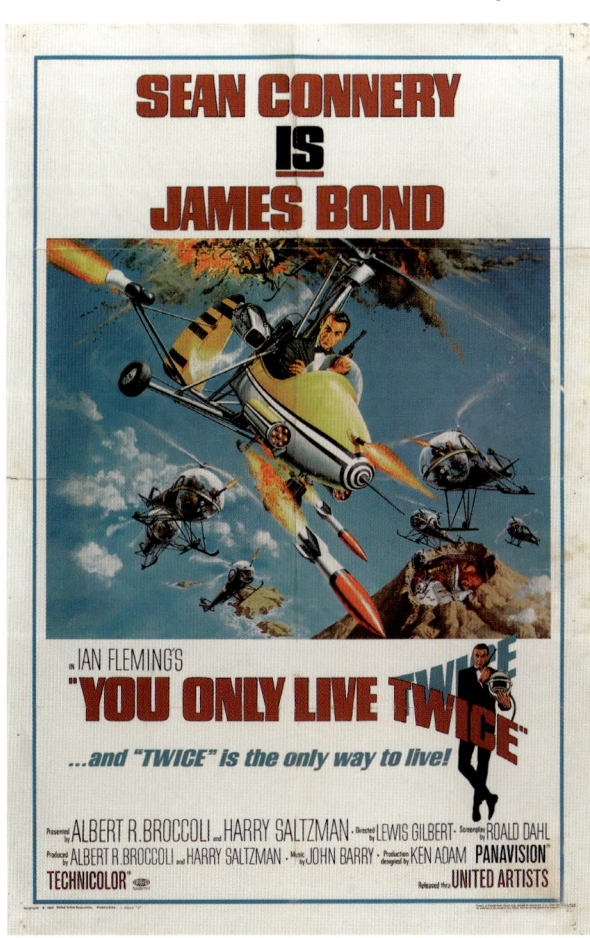

Sweden
- James Bond, Agent 007 #3 (1967)—"I hennes majestäts hemliga tjänst"
- James Bond, Agent 007 #32 (1970)—"I hennes majestäts hemliga tjänst"
- James Bond, Agent 007 #69 (date?)—"I hennes majestäts hemliga tjänst" (Part 1)
- James Bond, Agent 007 #70 (date?)—"I hennes majestäts hemliga tjänst" (Part 2)
- James Bond, Agent 007 #9 (1989)—"I hennes majestäts hemliga tjänst" (Part 1)
- James Bond, Agent 007 #10 (1989)—"I hennes majestäts hemliga tjänst" (Part 2)

COMIC BOOKS

Chile

Type: Novel adaptation—Color
Writer: German Gabler
Artist: Lincoln Fuentes

Originally Published: 007 James Bond #38 and #39 by ZigZag

Notes: "On Her Majesty's Secret Service" was adapted in two parts, the first part, "El Archicriminal" was published in issue #38 with the concluding part "Al Servicio Secreto de su Majestad" in issue #39.

Japan

Type: Manga Serial / Collections
Writer: Takao Saito
Artist: Takao Saito

Originally Published: April to December 1966 in nine parts serialized in "Boys Life"

Notes: In 1967 "On Her Majesty's Secret Service" was collected into a single album format (19 cm x 14com B&W) under the title of *"Joou heika no 007,"* the third of four Bond manga albums published under the Golden Comics label. They were again reprinted in 1980 with new covers this time under the Shogakukan Bunko imprint. At some point the manga Bond was translated into Chinese and reprinted in Hong Kong in both serialized and collected formats.

Opposite page: first edition dustjacket from *On Her Majesty's Secret Service*. Left: U.S. 27 x 41 inch, style A, movie poster from *You Only Live Twice*, 1967.

MOVIE ADAPTATION

Argentina

Type: Unofficial movie adaptation
Writer: unknown
Artist: unkown

Originally Published: D'artagnan Extraordinario #? (1969) as "On Her Majesty's Secret Service"

YOU ONLY LIVE TWICE

NEWSPAPER STRIP

Type: *Daily Express* comic strip
Writer: Henry Gammidge
Artist: John McLusky

Published: *Daily Express* between 18th May 1965 and 8th January 1966 (Series 2, strip #275-475)

Source: Based on the James Bond novel *You Only Live Twice* by Ian Fleming, published in 1964

Plot Summary: Disconsolate after the murder of his wife Tracy, James Bond has started to botch missions and loose interest in the secret service. In a last ditch effort to save Bond's career M "promotes" him and sends him on an impossible mission to Japan to try and convince the head of the Japanese secret service, Tiger Tanaka, to share information he has about the Soviet Union. Tiger and Bond form a deep friendship and Tiger agrees to Bond's request, if Bond will carry out one task. Kill a Dr. Shatterhand, who is operating a politically embarrassing 'Garden of Death' where people go to commit suicide. Bond is amazed to discover that Shatterhand is in fact Blofeld and is happy to set out on his own revenge. With the help of Tanka and Kissy Suzuki, a former Japanese movie star who returned to her roots as a pearl diver, Bond infiltrates Blofeld's castle. Eventually facing Blofeld in a sword duel Bond kills his nemesis, but as he escapes he suffers a head injury that leaves him with no memories. Kissy Suzuki hides the amnesiac Bond and lives with him as lovers. Eventually Bond comes across a mention of Vladivostok in a paper and it starts to spark memories of his past life. A life he sets off to rediscover.

Notes: In his last Bond story writer Gammidge moves away from doing strict "translations" of Fleming and instead focuses on the central plot. While the book spends a fair amount of time describing Japanese culture, the comic strip skips them and instead adds fresh elements to drive the plot forward. In the strip Blofeld's motives for opening his "Garden of Death" seem more in keeping with the villain of the previous two stories. Gammidge also adds Kissy Suzuki to the final fight scene and makes Blofeld's final fate a little more dramatic. The aftermath of the destruction of Blofeld's headquarters and the investigation into Bond's disappearance are also fleshed out, while a few seeds are sown that lead directly into the next story, *The Man With The Golden Gun*.

English Reprints
"You Only Live Twice" was reprinted in the 2004 Titan Books *On Her Majesty's Secret Service*.

Translations

Brazil
- Uma Aventura De James Bond #10 (date?)—"Só se vives duas vêzes"

Denmark
- James Bond, Agent 007 #12 (1967)—"Djævlens urtegård"

Finland
- James Bond, Agent 007 #1 (1981)—"as Elät vain kahdesti"

Italy
- Albi Dell'avventura—Serie James Bond #91 (date?)—"Si vive solo due volte" (Part 1)
- Albi Dell'avvent—Serie James Bond #92 (date?)—"Si vive solo due volte" (Part 2)

Norway
- James Bond, Agent 007 #4 (1967)—"Djevelens urtegård - man lever bare to ganger"
- Agnet 007 – James Bond #1 (1981)—"Djevelens urtegård—man lever bare to ganger"

Spain
- Biblioteca Grandes Del Comic: James Bond #5 (2007)—"You Only Live Twice"

Sweden
- James Bond, Agnet 007 #4 (1967)—"Djävulens trädgård"
- James Bond, Agent 007 #38 (date?)—"Man lever bara två ganger"

- James Bond, Agent 007 #66 (date?)—"Man lever bara två ganger"

COMIC BOOKS

Chile

Type: Novel adaptation—Color
Writer: German Gabler
Artist: German Gabler

Originally Published: 007 James Bond #40 as "Solo se vive dos vecesin" by ZigZag

THE MAN WITH THE GOLDEN GUN

NEWSPAPER STRIP

Type: *Daily Express* comic strip
Writer: Jim Lawrence
Artist: Yaroslav Horak

Published: *Daily Express* between 10th January 1966 and 10th September 1966 (Series 3, strip #1-209)

Source: Based on the James Bond novel *The Man With The Golden Gun* by Ian Fleming, published in 1965

Plot Summary: A year after his disappearance, a man claiming to be James Bond reappears in London. After passing several MI6 checks Bond eventually meets up with M and tries to assassinate his boss. The assassination plot is foiled and it is revealed that Bond was brain washed by the KGB after he traveled to Vladivostok to recover his memory. Once deprogrammed M sends Bond on an apparent suicide mission to take out the renowned Cuban—backed gunman Francisco Scramanga, also known as The Man With The Golden Gun. Bond locates Scaramanga in Jamaica and using the cover name Mark Hazard manages to get himself hired as a minder/personal assistant. Unknown to Bond, Felix Leiter is also working the case and the two eventually cross paths and meet up. Eventually Bond's cover is blown and Sacramanga tries to kill him. After a gun battle on a train, the two face off in a swamp. Bond eventually kills Scaramanga but, once again, is severely wounded.

Notes: New Bond writer Jim Lawrence takes what is arguably one of Fleming's thinner Bond stories and expands on it to create a gripping tale that gives a hint of the things to come once he would start writing original Bond tales. Here he adds a complete subplot at the start of the tale which adds depth to the villain Scaramanga and gives Bond a more personal motivation for going after him. Lawrence also introduces a new Bond girl—the femme fatale Taj Mahal. The third day's strip references back to the events of *You Only Live Twice* with a brief cameo by Kissy Suzuki grieving for her "lost" Bondo-San.

English Reprints
"The Man With The Golden Gun" is reprinted in the 2004 Titan Books album *The Man With The Golden Gun*.

Translations

Brazil
- Uma Aventura De James Bond #11 (date)—"O homem do revolver de ouro"
- James Bond 007 #1 (2003)—"O homem da Pistola de Ouro"

Denmark
- James Bond, Agent 007 #15 (1968)—"Manden med den gyldne pistol"
- James Bond, Agent 007 #35 (1976)—"Manden med den gyldne pistol" (part 2)
- James Bond, Agent 007 #40 (1977)—"Manden med den gyldne pistol" (part 1)

Finland
- James Bond, Agent 007 #5 (1976)—"Aivopesty" (part 1 only)
- James Bond, Agent 007 #3 (1986) – "007 James Bond ja kultainen ase"

France
- James Bond 007 #1 (1988)—"L'homme au pistolet d'or"

India
- James Bond #44 (date?)—"Scaramanga"

Italy
- Albi Dell'avventura - Serie James Bond #104 (date?)—"L'homme au pistolet d'or" (part 1)
- Albi Dell'avventura—Serie James Bond #105 (date?)—"L'homme au pistolet d'or" (part 2)

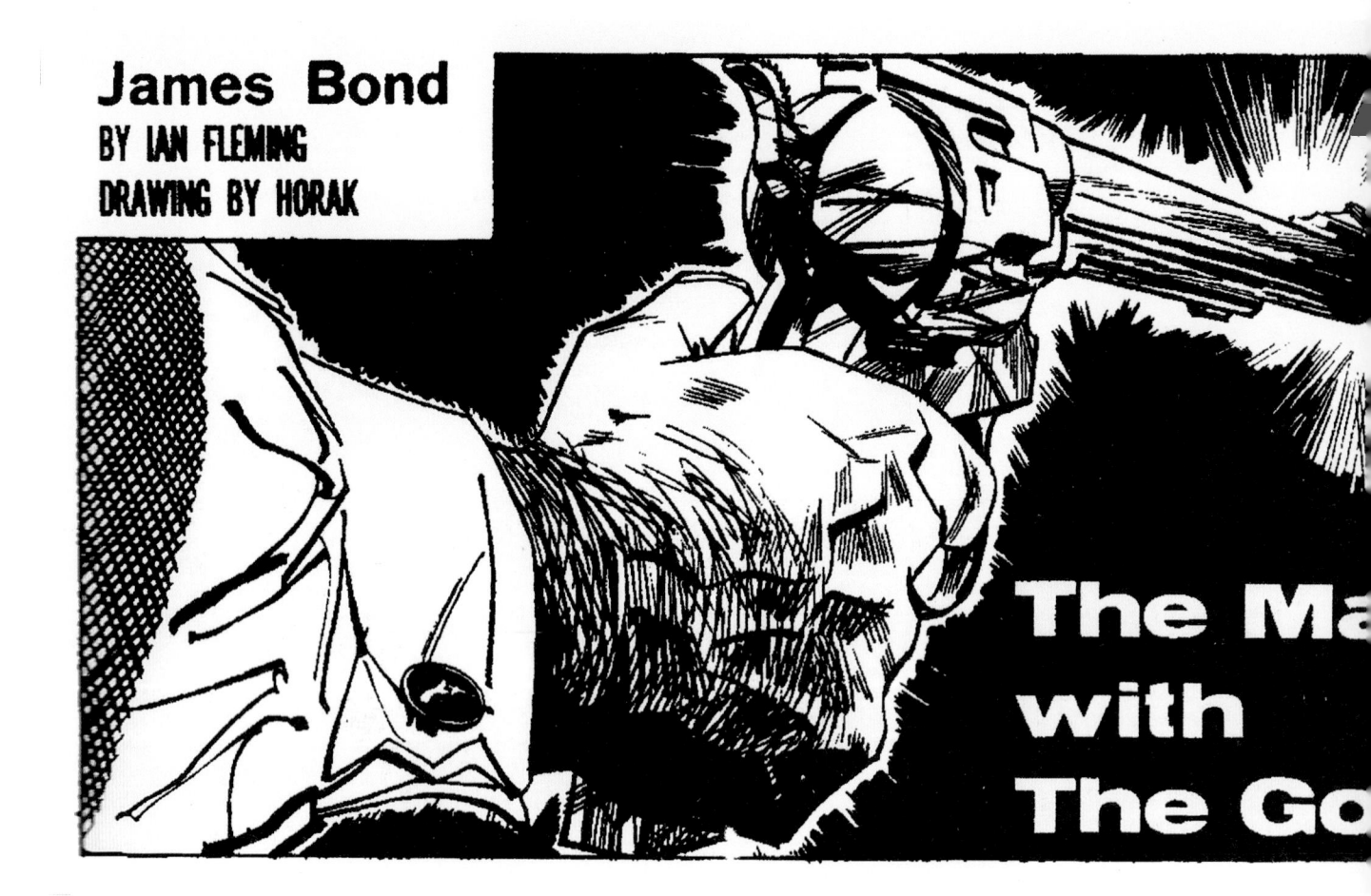

Norway
- James Bond, Agent 007 #7 (1968)—"Mannen med gullpistolen"
- James Bond, Agent 007 #2 (1982)—"Hjernevasket" (part 1)
- James Bond, Agent 007 #3 (1982)—"Hjernevasket" (part 2)
- James Bond, Agent 007 #7 (1992)—"Drep M!" (part 1)
- James Bond, Agent 007 #8 (1992)—"Mannen med den gylne pistol" (part 2)

Spain
- James Bond #1 (1988)—"El hombre de las pistolas de Oro" (part 1)
- James Bond #2 (1988)—"El hombre de las pistolas de Oro" (part 2)
- Biblioteca Grandes Del Comic: James Bond #5 (2006)—"Man With The Golden Gun"

Sweden
- James Bond, Agent 007 #7 (1968)—"Manden med den gyllene pistolen"
- James Bond, Agent 007 #34 (date?)—"Manden med den gyllene pistolen"
- James Bond, Agent 007 #7 (1987)—"Manden med den gyllene pistolen" (part 1)
- James Bond, Agent 007 #34 (1987)—"Manden med den gyllene pistolen" (part 2)

COMIC BOOKS

Chile

Type: Novel adaptation—Color
Writer: German Gabler
Artist: Lincoln Fuentes

Originally Published: 007 James Bond #41 as "El Hombre del revolver de Oro" by ZigZag

Above: opening title for "The Man With The Golden Gun" newspaper strip, art by Yaroslav Horak, 1968.

Japan

Type: Manga Serial / Collections
Writer: Takao Saito
Artist: Takao Saito

Originally Published: January to August 1967 in eight parts serialized in *Boys Life*

Notes: In 1967 "The Man With The Golden Gun" was collected into a single album format (19 cm x 14 cm B&W) under the title of *"Oogon-ju wo motsu otoko"*, the last of four Bond manga albums published under the Golden Comics label. They were again reprinted in 1980 with new covers in 1985 under the Shogakukan Bunko imprint. At some point the manga Bond was translated into Chinese and printed in Hong Kong in both serialized and collected formats.

MOVIE ADAPTATION

Argentina

Type: Unofficial Movie Adaptation
Writer: Fred W. Seymour
Artist: Fernandez

Originally Published: D'artagnan Extraordinario #350 (1975) as "El Hombre del Revolver de Oro"

THE LIVING DAYLIGHTS

NEWSPAPER STRIP

Type: *Daily Express* comic strip
Writer: Jim Lawrence
Artist: Yaroslav Horak

Published: *Daily Express* between 12th September 1966 and 12th November 1966 (Series 3, strip #210 - 263)

Source: Based on the James Bond short story "The Living Daylights" originally published in The Sunday Times in February 1962 by Ian Fleming and included in the 1966 collection *Octopussy*.

Plot Summary: Set just after the events of *Thunderball*, Bond is assigned as a sniper to cover the escape of a Russian defector known only as "272." MI6 has reports that a KGB assassin known as "Trigger" has been ordered to kill "272." Bond is surprised to discover that "Trigger" is a beautiful woman. Instead of killing her Bond shoots the butt of her rifle to stop her firing. While "272" escapes unharmed the mission is deemed a failure.

Notes: Given the time of its original publication in 1962 this story's most logical placement is just after *Thunderball*, the tone and mood of Bond does not fit with the rest of the comic strip continuity by placing it straight after *The Man With The Golden Gun*. Once again Jim Lawrence fleshes out Fleming's throw away characters by adding back story to Agent 272's decision to defect. The female "Trigger" is made into an almost "anti-Bond" figure and, unlike the novel and movie, pays the ultimate price for her failure.

English Reprints
"The Living Daylights" was reprinted in the 2004 Titan Books album "*The Man With The Golden Gun*"

Translations

Brazil
- Uma Aventura De James Bond #13 (date?) — "Encontro em Berlim"
- 007 James Bond #5 (date)—"Encontro em Berlim"

Denmark
- James Bond, Agent 007 #14 (1968)—"Spionen fra øst"
- James Bond, Agent 007 #40 (1977)—"Spionen fra øst"

France
- James Bond 007 #1 (1988)—"Tuer n'est pas jouer"

Finland
- James Bond, Agent 007 #5 (1976)—"Vakooja idasta"
- James Bond, Agent 007 #2 (1986)—"Vakooja idasta"

Italy
- Albi Dell'avventura—Serie James Bond #111 (date)—"Accompagnamento per un delitto"

Norway
- James Bond, Agent 007 #6 (1968)—"Spionen fra øst"
- James Bond, Agent 007 #2 (1986)—"Spionen fra øst"

Spain
- James Bond #1-6 (1973)—"A traves del muro"
- James Bond #1 (1973)—"A traves del muro"
- James Bond #2 (1988)—"Alta Tensión" (part 1)
- James Bond #3 (1988)—"Alta Tensión" (part 2)
- Biblioteca Grandes Del Comic: James Bond #5 (2006)—"The Living Daylights"

Sweden
- James Bond, Agent 007 #6 (1968)—"Spionen från öst"
- James Bond, Agent 007 #39 (date)—"Spionen från öst"
- James Bond, Agent 007 #5 (1985)—"Spionen från öst"
- James Bond, Agnet 007 #2 (1993)—"Spionen från öst"

Left: detail from the cover from *Agent James Bond 007* #11, a 1986 Swedish "Octopussy" comic book.

78   the history of the illustrated 007

MOVIE ADAPTATION
Sweden

Type: Movie Adaptation
Writer: Jack Sutter
Artist: Juan Sampros

Originally Published: as "Iskallt Uppdrag," by Semic in 1987

Notes: This 45 page color adaptation of the first Timothy Dalton movie was a slight improvement on the other Semic movie adaptations. However it is very unevenly paced—going from six or seven panels per page to an incredibly cramped fifteen panels per page at the end. It was as if the page count caught the creators off guard with story to tell and not many pages left. The result is that the climax of the story is reduced to little more than expository dialog with no room for the visual action.

Translations

Norway
- James Bond: I Skuddlinjen (1987)

OCTOPUSSY

NEWSPAPER STRIP

Type: *Daily Express* comic strip
Writer: Jim Lawrence
Artist: Yaroslav Horak

Published: *Daily Express* between 14th November 1966 and 27th May 1965 (Series #3, strip 264-428)

Source: Based on the James Bond short story "Octopussy" by Ian Fleming and included in the 1966 collection *Octopussy*

Plot Summary: Bond is assigned to apprehend Major Dexter Smythe, a World War II hero who has been implicated in a murder that links back to a horde of missing Nazi gold. Bond only appears for a brief time in this story, which is told mostly in flashback from Smythe's point of view.

Notes: Once more writer Jim Lawrence rather than doing a straight adaptation of the Fleming story used it more as a springboard to tell his own tale. Here he adds a lot more action to the mix and switches the focus of the story more on Bond (which is what the *Daily Express* readers would expect) Lawrence's Bond in this story is also more akin to the screen action hero than Fleming's "civil servant." The result is that Lawrence turns Fleming's forty-three page morality tale into high adventure.

"Octopussy" also features a slightly different take by Horak on the opening strip as it combines the title in with the action, drawing the reader's eye along the strip, rather than just having the traditional static label on the first panel.

English Reprints

"Octopussy" was reprinted in the 1988 and 2004 Titan Books albums *Octopussy*.

Translations

Brazil
- Uma Aventura De James Bond #14 (date?) — "James Bond Acusa"

Denmark
- James Bond, Agent 007 #16 (1969)—"Undervandsdøden"
- James Bond, Agent 007 #42 (1977)—"Undervandsdøden"

Italy
- Albi Dell'avventura—Serie James Bond #112 and #113 (date?)—"Octo Pussy and Scorpaena plumierei"

Norway
- James Bond, Agent 007 #8 (1968)—"Octopussy – undervannsdøden"
- James Bond, Agent 007 #6 (1980)—"Octopussy —undervannsdøden"

Spain
- James Bond #19-24 (1974)—"El Octopodo asesino"
- James Bond Episodios completos #4 (1974) — "El Octopodo asesino"
- James Bond #3 and #4 (1988)—"Octopussy"
- Biblioteca Grandes Del Comic: James Bond #6 (2006)—"Octopussy"

Sweden
- James Bond, Agent 007 #8 (1968)—"Octopussy—undervattensdöden"
- James Bond, Agent 007 #41 (date?)—"Octopussy—undervattensdöden"
- James Bond, Agent 007 #11 and #12 (1986) — "Octopussy—undervattensdöden"

MOVIE ADAPTATIONS

Octopussy is the only James Bond movie to have two different official movie adaptations produced.

Sweden

Type: Movie Adaptation
Writer: Jack Sutter ?
Artist: Frederico Maidagan

Originally Published: as "Octopussy" in Semic Album #1 (1983)

Notes: In comparison to the Marvel USA adaptation (see below) this version comes across as flat and dull due to the somewhat sketchy artwork and flat color palette.

Translations

Denmark
- James Bond 007: Octopussy—color album (1983)

Finland
- Octopussy—color album (1983)

Germany
- Octopussy—color album (1983)

Norway
- Octopussy—color album (1983)
- James Bond - Agent 007 #1 (1994) - title

USA

Type: Movie Adaptation
Writer: Steve Moore
Artist: Paul Neary

Originally Published: as *Marvel Super Special* #26

Notes: On this occasion it appears that the creative team had more time to work on the project as the result rates among the better Bond movie adaptations. Most of the cinematic establishing shots are full of excellent background detail missing from the previous adaptation, all the principal players are recognizable and the plot is followed closely without any obvious logic jumps. *Octopussy* was only published as a 48 page Marvel Super Special #26, yet close reading hints that perhaps it had been originally scheduled to be two 24 page issues.

Opposite page: cover to the Danish edition of "Octopussy," 1969.

English reprints

Reprinted in 1983 Marvel UK hardback *James Bond Annual*

Translations

Italy
- EUREKA! #? (1983)—"Octopussy"

Sweden
- James Bond, Agent 007 #5 (1991)—"Octopussy"

THE HILDEBRAND RARITY

NEWSPAPER STRIP

Type: *Daily Express* comic strip
Writer: Jim Lawrence
Artist: Yaroslav Horak

Published: *Daily Express* between 29th May 1967 and 16th December 1967 (Series #3, strip 429-602)

Source: Based on the James Bond short story *The Hildebrand Rarity* by Ian Fleming and included in the 1960 collection *For Your Eyes Only*

Plot Summary: While vacationing in the Seychelles Islands with his friend, Fidele Barbey, James Bond is introduced to objectionable and sadistic millionaire Milton Krest, who is in search of a rare fish in order to keep his "Krest Foundation" legitimate and preserve it as a tax write-off. Krest invites Bond and Barbey to join him and his young wife Elizabeth aboard his boat, Wavekrest, in the hunt for the fish. Once on board Bond discovers that Krest is in the habit of whipping his wife with a stingray's tail. During an onboard party to celebrate the discovery, a drunken Krest threatens Elizabeth and insults Bond. During the night Bond hears Krest choking and later finds him dead with the fish lodged in his throat. Bond throws the body in to the sea and cleans up the crime scene. When the Wavekrest reaches port everyone assumes the drunken Krest fell overboard. Bond keeps his suspicion that Elizabeth Krest took her revenge on her abusive husband to himself.

Notes: For some reason there was a six year gap between the adaptation of the other short stories from *For Your*

JAMES BOND
AGENT 007

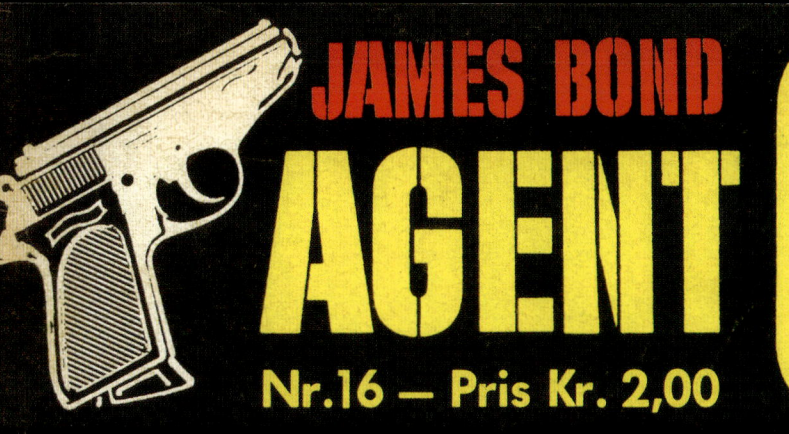

Nr. 16 — Pris Kr. 2,00

OCTOPUSSY-UNDERVANDSDØDEN

Eyes Only and *The Hildebrandt Rarity*. Once again writer Jim Lawrence takes the basic concept, themes and characters of Fleming's story and expands on them to tell his own story. Added to the search for the elusive titular fish is a mission to rescue a secret project from the seabed (as later used in the movie *For Your Eyes Only*), in fact it's 36 days into the strip before the first sequence from the Fleming story even appears. Lawrence dropped the character of Fidele Barbey from the story while at the same time developing the character of Milton Krest, making him appear much closer to the version portrayed on screen in 1989's *License To Kill* than the one dimensional villain of the original story.

English Reprints

"The Hildebrandt Rarity" was reprinted in the 1988 and 2004 Titan Books album *Octopussy*.

Translations

Brazil
- Uma Aventura De James Bond #17 (date?)—"A raridade de Hildebrand"

Denmark
- James Bond, Agent 007 #17 (1969)—"U-båd savnes"
- James Bond - Agent 007 #4 (1981)—"Ubåt savnet"

Finland
- James Bond, Agent 007 #4 (1986)—"Sukellusvene kateissa"

Italy
- Albi Dell'avventura - Serie James Bond #125 (1974)— "Missione "Sea Slave" (part 1)
- Albi Dell'avventura—Serie James Bond #126 (1974) - "La Rarità Hildebrand" (part 2)

Norway
- James Bond, Agent 007 #9 (1968)—"Ubåt savnet"

Spain
- James Bond Fasciculo semanal #1-6 (1973)—"Un extraño ejemplar"
- James Bond Episodios completos #1 (1973)—"Un extraño ejemplar
- James Bond #4-6 (1988)—"La Rareza de Hildebrand"
- Biblioteca Grandes Del Comic: James Bond #6 (2006)—"The Hildebrand Rarity"

Sweden
- James Bond, Agent 007 #9 (1968)—Ubåt saknas
- James Bond, Agent 007 #45 (date?)—Ubåt saknas

- James Bond, Agent 007 #8-9 (1986)—Ubåt saknas
- James Bond, Agent 007 #2 (1994)—Ubåt saknas

COMIC BOOKS

Chile

Type: Short story adaptation
Writer: German Gabler
Artist: Hernan Jiron

Originally Published: 007 James Bond #2 (1968) as *La Rareza de Hildebrand* by ZigZag

THE SPY WHO LOVED ME

NEWSPAPER STRIP

Type: *Daily Express* comic strip
Writer: Jim Lawrence
Artist: Yaroslav Horak

Published: *Daily Express* between 18th December 1967 and 3rd October 1968 (Series #3, strip 603-815)

Source: Based on the James Bond novel *The Spy Who Loved Me* by Ian Fleming first published in 1962

Opposite page top: opening title for "The Spy Who Loved Me" newspaper strip leading into the original story that was added as a prequel to the events of the novel, art by Yarsolav Horak, 1967. Below: halfway through the newspaper adaptation of "The Spy Who Loved Me" catches up with the events of Fleming's novel, art by Yaroslav Horak. Below this page: opening title for "The Harpies" newspaper strip, art by Yaroslav Horak, 1968.

Plot Summary: "The Spy Who Loved Me" is told entirely from the point of view of Vivienne Michel, a young Canadian woman trapped in an isolated American motel. The first part deals with Vivienne's background, the second part introduces a couple of thugs who have been sent to burn down the hotel in an insurance fraud, and trap Vivienne on the premises. The third part of the book tells of the arrival of James Bond at the motel and his subsequent protection and rescue of Vivienne during which he kills the two thugs.

Notes: Ian Fleming had refused to allow *The Spy Who Loved Me* to be adapted during his lifetime so it had been skipped over in the strip chronology. It should have fit between *Thunderball* and *On Her Majesty's Secret Service*. This jump in sequence created some story telling problems for Lawrence in adapting the story, as did its unusual nature. Rather than do a straight adaptation of the tale, in which Bond hardly appears and then only from the viewpoint of the female narrator, Lawrence took a throw away line that Fleming included in the story and expanded it into a totally new back story with Bond investigating espionage within the Canadian Royal Airforce which turns out to be connected to SPECTRE Lawrence also introduces his first original villain, the mysterious masked Madame Spectra. The actual adaptation of Fleming's story doesn't start until strip #708, about half way through the story. The split between Lawrence's original story and the adaptation was exploited in several foreign language reprints where they were treated as two separate stories. In some cases the two parts were even published in reverse order.

English Reprints

"The Spy Who Loved Me" was reprinted in the 1989 and 2005 Titan Books album *The Spy Who Loved Me*.

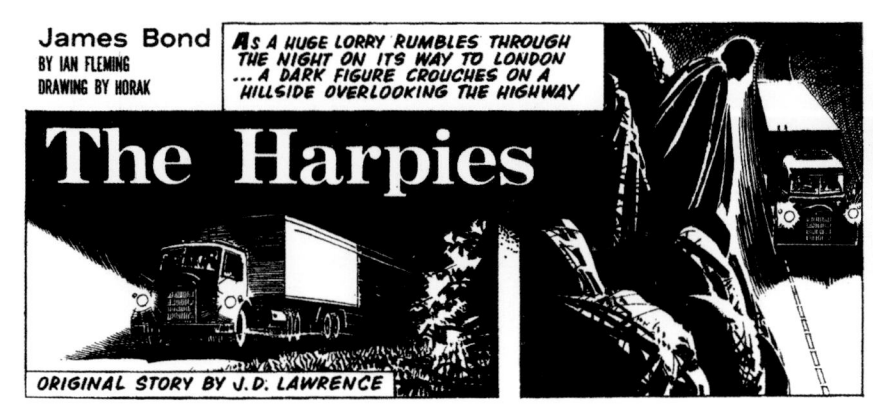

Translations

Brazil
- Uma Aventura De James Bond #18 (date?) — "Espiáo e amante"
- 007 James Bond #4 (date?)—"O Plano Sinistro"

Denmark
- James Bond, Agent 007 #18 (1969)—"Operation Spøgelsesfly"
- James Bond, Agent 007 #20 (1970)—"Rædslernes nat"

Finland
- James Bond - Agent 007 #6 (1977)—"Operaatio aavelento"
- James Bond - Agent 007 #2 (1978)—"Kauhun yö"

Italy
- Albi Dell'avventura - Serie James Bond #141 (date?)—"Il ritorno della SPECTRE"
- Albi Dell'avventura—Serie James Bond #142 (date?)— "La spia che mi amava"

Norway
- James Bond, Agent 007 #10 (1969)—"Operasjon Spøkelsesfly"
- James Bond, Agent 007 #11 (1969)—"Redselsnatten"
- Agent 007 - James Bond #3 (1980) – "Skrekkens Nat"
- Agent 007, James Bond #4 (1980)—"Spionflyet"
- Agent 007, James Bond #6 (1992) —"Skrekkens Nat"
- Agent 007, James Bond #3 (1993)—"Spionflyet"

Spain
- James Bond #6-7 (1989)—"La Espia que Me Amo"
- Biblioteca Grandes Del Comic: James Bond #7 (2007)—"La Espía que me amó"

Sweden
- James Bond, Agent 007 #10 (1969)—"Operation Spökflyg"
- James Bond, Agent 007 #11 (1969)—"Skräcknatten"
- James Bond, Agent 007 #47 (date?) – "Operation Spökflyg"
- James Bond, Agent 007 #49 (date?)—"Skräcknatten"
- James Bond, Agent 007 #10 (1989)—"Operation Spökflyg"
- James Bond, Agent 007 #7 (1990)—"Skräcknatten"

COMIC BOOKS

Chile

Type: Novel adaptation
Writer: German Gabler
Artist: German Gabler

Originally Published: 007 James Bond #37 (1979) as "El Espía que me amo" by ZigZag

THE HARPIES

NEWSPAPER STRIP

Type: *Daily Express* comic strip
Writer: Jim Lawrence
Artist: Yaroslav Horak

Published: *Daily Express* between 4th October 1968 and 23rd June 1969 (Series #3, strip 816-1037)

Source: Original story

Plot Summary: Dr John Phineus, inventor of the Q-Ray is kidnapped by The Harpies, a gang of female villains who use hang gliders and rocket packs. Bond infiltrates the operations of Phineus's chief rival, Simon Nero, by posing as a corrupt police officer Mike Hazard and gaining employment as the new Head of Security. With the help of Nero's daughter he uncovers Nero's connections to The Harpies and rescues Phineus.

Notes: The first original James Bond comics story was published just a few months before the first non-Fleming Bond novel, so it is highly probable that novelist Kingsley Amis and strip writer Jim Lawrence were working in parallel as the first people other than Ian Fleming to write an original Bond story. Lawrence's story read like a natural continuation of the last three strips in which he had been adding in more and more original material. The one area where the change is noticeable is in the dialog, as without Fleming's dialog to fall back on, Lawrence seems to be struggling to find a true voice for Bond.

The first day of the strip acknowledges Lawrence's work with a small "original story by J.D. Lawrence" caption, but for the rest of the story carries just the regular "James Bond by Ian Fleming, Drawing by Horak" credits. The plot is a little tenuous in places with Bond jumping to some surprising conclusions based on little or no evidence. Lawrence also reintroduces Bond's alias Mark Hazard, first used by Fleming in *The Man With The Golden Gun*.

English Reprints

"The Harpies" was reprinted in the 2005 Titan Books album *The Spy Who Loved Me*.

Translations

Denmark
- James Bond, Agent 007 #19 (1970)—"Fuglekvinderne ..."

Italy
- Albi Dell'avventura—Serie James Bond #173 (date?)—"Raggio Q"
- Albi Dell'avventura—Serie James Bond #174 (date?)—"Le arpie"

Norway
- James Bond, Agent 007 #12 (1970)—"Flaggermuskvinnen"
- Agent 007—James Bond #2 (1979)—"Fuglekvinnene"
- Agent 007—James Bond #5 (1994)—"Fuglekvinnene"

Spain
- James Bond Fasciculo semanal #25-30 (1974)—"Tratamiento de Shock"
- James Bond, Episodios completos (1974)—"Tratamiento de Shock"
- Biblioteca Grandes Del Comic: James Bond # 7 (2007)—"The Harpies"

Sweden
- James Bond, Agent 007 #12 (1969)—"Fågelkvinnorna"
- James Bond, Agent 007 #55 (date?)—"Fågelkvinnorna"
- James Bond, Agent 007 #4-5 (1989)—"Fågelkvinnorna"

Opposite page: page from *007 James Bond* #7, art by Hernan Jiron, 1969. Below: title page from ZigZag original story "Chinese Puzzle," art by Luis Avila, 1969.

DEADLY GOLD

COMIC BOOKS

Chile

Type: Original Story
Writer: German Gabler
Artist: German Gabler

Originally Published: 007 James Bond #4 (1968) as "Oro Morta" by ZigZag

Notes: This story features Le Chiffre from *Casino Royale*, the first example of another writer using one of Fleming's villains in an original story.

GOLD FOR LE CHIFFRE

COMIC BOOKS

Chile

Type: Original Story
Writer: German Gabler
Artist: Hernan Jiron

Originally Published: 007 James Bond #5 (1968) as "Oro para Le Chiffre" by ZigZag

Notes: This is probably a sequel to "Deadly Gold" published in the previous issue.

ULTRA SECRET

COMIC BOOKS

Chile

Type: Original Story
Writer: German Gabler
Artist: German Gabler

Originally Published: 007 James Bond #6 (1968) as "Ultrasecreto" by ZigZag

Notes: The third issue in a row to feature Le Chiffre. As these three issues were published prior to the ZigZag adaptation of *Casino Royale* they may have been some sort of prequel story.

CHILD'S PLAY

COMIC BOOKS

Chile

Type: Original Story
Writer: German Gabler
Artist: Hernan Jiron

Originally Published: 007 James Bond #7 (1968) as "Juego de Niños" by ZigZag

GOLD AND DEATH

COMIC BOOKS

Chile

Type: Original Story
Writer: German Gabler
Artist: German Gabler

Originally Published: 007 James Bond #11 (1968) as "Oro y Muerte" by ZigZag

RELENTLESS PURSUIT

COMIC BOOKS

Chile

Type: Original Story
Writer: German Gabler
Artist: German Gabler

Originally Published: 007 James Bond #12 (1969) as "Persecucion Implacable" by ZigZag

BERLIN INTRIGUE

COMIC BOOKS

Chile

Type: Original Story
Writer: German Gabler
Artist: German Gabler

Originally Published: 007 James Bond #15 (1969) as "Intriga en Berlin" by ZigZag

Above: Danish edition of "River of Death," 1971. Opposite page: cover from *007 James Bond #27*, from ZigZag, 1969, featuring the the story "Sacrilege."

HOLIDAY FOR A SPY

COMIC BOOKS

Chile

Type: Original Story
Writer: German Gabler
Artist: Abel Romero

Originally Published: 007 James Bond #16 (1969) as "Vacaciones para un Espia" by ZigZag

THE CRIME AT THE DISCOTHEQUE

COMIC BOOKS

Chile

Type: Original Story
Writer: German Gabler
Artist: German Gabler

Originally Published: 007 James Bond #17 (1969) as "El Crimen de la Discotheque" by ZigZag

The Missions

TENEMOS TODO UN CASO ENTRE MANOS. SI NO FUERA POR EL TESTIGO, NO SABRÍAMOS NI SIQUIERA LO QUE OCURRIÓ. NO QUEDA MÁS QUE APELAR A LA BUENA SUERTE.
QUIERE DECIR QUE...
QUE TENDRÉ QUE RECORRER EL MAR BUSCANDO LA ISLA QUE SIRVE DE REFUGIO A ESA EXTRAÑA BANDA DE SECUESTRADORAS, AUNQUE ME TOME TODA MI VIDA ENCONTRARLA.
AL DÍA SIGUIENTE, BOND COMENZÓ LA QUE PROMETÍA SER UNA LARGA BÚSQUEDA...
LA PRIMERA ETAPA DEL VIAJE ES UNA ISLA A QUINCE MILLAS AL OESTE.
NO SE VE NADA EXTRAÑO AQUÍ. ¡VÁMONOS!
QUINCE DÍAS DESPUÉS, LUEGO DE INNUMERABLES FRACASOS, BOND DECIDIÓ LLAMAR A LONDRES...
¿M? HABLA BOND. NO HE CONSEGUIDO NADA. ESTO ES COMO BUSCAR UNA AGUJA EN UN PAJAR.
SERÁ MEJOR QUE DEJE EL CASO. PODEMOS NECESITARLO DE UN MOMENTO A OTRO AQUÍ. DEJAREMOS QUE NUESTRA SECCIÓN DEL CARIBE SE ENCARGUE DEL ASUNTO.
EN TODO CASO, PROBARÉ POR ÚLTIMA VEZ HOY. SI NO OCURRE NADA, ESTARÉ DE VUELTA MAÑANA EN LONDRES.

DEADLY SAFARI

COMIC BOOKS

Chile

Type: Original Story
Writer: German Gabler
Artist: German Gabler

Originally Published: 007 James Bond #19 (1969) as "Safari Mortal" by ZigZag

A BEAUTY IN DISTRESS

COMIC BOOKS

Chile

Type: Original Story
Writer: German Gabler
Artist: Hernan Jiron

Originally Published: 007 James Bond #21 (1969) as "Una Bella en Apuros" by ZigZag

THE C.I.P.E.T. AFFAIR

COMIC BOOKS

Chile

Type: Original Story
Writer: German Gabler
Artist: Luis Avila

Originally Published: 007 James Bond #24 (1969) as "El Asunto C.I.P.E.T." by ZigZag

THE CROWS

COMIC BOOKS

Chile

Type: Original Story
Writer: German Gabler
Artist: German Gabler

Originally Published: 007 James Bond #25 (1969) as "Los Cuervos" by ZigZag

THE MISSING PILOT

COMIC BOOKS

Chile

Type: Original Story
Writer: German Gabler
Artist: German Gabler

Originally Published: 007 James Bond #26 (1969) as "El piloto desaparecido" by ZigZag

SACRILEGE

COMIC BOOKS

Chile

Type: Original Story
Writer: German Gabler
Artist: German Gabler

Originally Published: 007 James Bond #27 (1969) as "Sacrilegio" by ZigZag

THE QUEEN OF THE BEES

COMIC BOOKS

Chile

Type: Original Story
Writer: German Gabler
Artist: Lincoln Fuentes

Originally Published: 007 James Bond #29 (1969) as "La Reina de las Abejas" by ZigZag

Opposite page: interior page from "The Queen of the Bees," art by Lincoln Fuentes, 1969.

INTRIGUE IN THE ARCTIC

COMIC BOOKS

Chile

Type: Original Story
Writer: German Gabler
Artist: German Gabler

Originally Published: 007 James Bond #30 (1969) as "Intriga en el Artico" by ZigZag

RIVER OF DEATH

NEWSPAPER STRIP

Type: *Daily Express* comic strip
Writer: Jim Lawrence
Artist: Yaroslav Horak

Published: *Daily Express* between 24th June 1969 and 29th November 1969 (Series #3, strip 1038-1174)

Source: Original story.

Plot Summary: Bond is assigned to investigate a series of bizarre murders apparently committed by trained animals. Tracing one of the animals, a howler monkey, to its place of origin, Bond ends up in Rio De Janerio where he learns another 00 agent has been killed. All clues point to the sadistic biochemist known as Dr. Cat who has been spotted working deep in the jungle. Bond teams up with native-American CIA agent Kitty Redwing. The two are kidnapped and tortured by Dr. Cat but manage to escape and release the nerve gas that Dr. Cat was working on.

Notes: There's a lot packed into a relatively small amount of space with this original story. However, it is a very solid story and appears to have been much more thoroughly thought out than other strips. There is some speculation that "River of Death" may have been adapted from a proposal for a Bond continuation novel by Jim Lawrence. One small plot mistake does stand out as Kitty Redwing never actually introduces herself to Bond, yet he seems to know her name. She is introduced to the readers via a caption box, as Bond wouldn't be able to see that information we can only assume that she gave him her name off panel. Bond also returns to using a Beretta in this strip, the gun he had been told by M to stop using after the events of *From Russia With Love*.

English Reprints

"River Of Death" was reprinted in the 2005 Titan Books album *Colonel Sun*

Translations

Denmark
- James Bond, Agent 007 #21 (1971)—"Dødens Flod"

Finland
- James Bond, Agent 007 #4 (1979)—"Kuoleman virta"
- Agentti X-9 #3 (1992)—"Kuoleman virta"

Italy
- Albi Dell'avventura - Serie James Bond #174? (date?)—"Il fiume della morte"

Norway
- James Bond, Agent 007 #13 (1970)—"Dødens Flod"
- Agent 007 - James Bond #1 (1980)—"Dødens Flod"

90   the history of the illustrated 007

Spain
- James Bond Fasciculo semanal #13-18 (1973)—"El Rio de la Muerte"
- James Bond Episodios completos #3—(1973) "El Rio de la Muerte"
- Zeppelin #2 (1973)—"El Rio de la Muerte"
- Biblioteca Grandes Del Comic: James Bond #8 (2007)—"River of Death"

Sweden
- James Bond, Agent 007 #13 (1970)—"Dödens Flod"
- James Bond, Agent 007 #59 (date?)—"Dödens Flod"
- James Bond, Agent 007 #1 (1992)—"Dödens Flod"

COLONEL SUN

NEWSPAPER STRIP

Type: *Daily Express* comic strip
Writer: Jim Lawrence
Artist: Yaroslav Horak

Published: Daily Express between 1st December 1969 and 20th August 1970 (Series #3, strip 1175-1393)

Source: Based on the James Bond continuation novel *Colonel Sun* by Kingsley Amis (writing as "Robert Markham") first published in 1968

Plot Summary: After M is kidnapped from his home, Bond sets out to find him. The kidnappers left clues pointing to the Greek islands. Bond uncovers a plot by Chinese agent Colonel Sun to attack a Soviet hosted peace conference and place M's body at the site to implicate the British. Working with Ariadne Alexandrou, a Greek communist Soviet agent, Bond rescues M and thwarts Colonel Sun's plans.

Notes: *Colonel Sun* holds the distinction of being the only non-Fleming Bond novel to be adapted into the comic strip format. The strip is very faithful to the novel with one notable exception being that in the strip "Colonel Sun's" paymasters are not Red China but the recently resurrected SPECTRE As with *Casino Royale*, the novel's brutal and detailed torture scene is omitted from the strip and happens off panel. "Colonel Sun" is generally regarded as one of the best James Bond comic strips.

English Reprints

"Colonel Sun" was reprinted in the 2005 Titan Books album *Colonel Sun*.

Translations

Brazil
- 007 James Bond #1 (1971)—"007 Contra o Coronel Sun"

Denmark
- James Bond, Agent 007 #22 (1971)—"Møde med døden...!"

Norway
- Agent 007, James Bond #6 (1981)—"Dødeligt toppmøte"

Opposite page: opening title for "The River of Death" newspaper strip, art by Yaroslav Horak, 1969. Above: opening title for "Colonel Sun" newspaper strip, art by Yarosalv Horak, 1969.

Spain
- James Bond Fasciculo semanal #25-30 (1974)—"Coronel Sol"
- James Bond Episodios completos #5 (1974)—"Coronel Sol"
- Biblioteca Grandes Del Comic: James Bond #8 (2007) – "Coronel Sol"

Sweden
- James Bond, Agent 007 #15 (1971)—"Dödligt toppmöte"
- James Bond, Agnet 007 #11-12 (1989)—"Dödligt toppmöte"

THE SILK CORD

COMIC BOOKS

Chile

Type: Original Story
Writer: German Gabler
Artist: German Gabler

Originally Published: 007 James Bond #31 (1970) as "El Cordon de Seda" by ZigZag

THE HAND OF FATE

COMIC BOOKS

Chile

Type: Original Story
Writer: German Gabler
Artist: German Gabler

Originally Published: 007 James Bond #32 (1970) as "La Mano del Destino" by ZigZag

DOUBLES

COMIC BOOKS

Chile

Type: Original Story
Writer: German Gabler
Artist: German Gabler

Originally Published: 007 James Bond #35 (1970) as "Sosias" by ZigZag

THE BEACH OF FLOWERS

COMIC BOOKS

Chile

Type: Original Story
Writer: German Gabler
Artist: German Gabler

Originally Published: 007 James Bond #42 (1970) as "La Muerte se divierte" by ZigZag

THE EXECUTIONER

COMIC BOOKS

Chile

Type: Original Story
Writer: German Gabler
Artist: Hernan Jiron

Originally Published: 007 James Bond #43 (1970) as "El Ejecutor" by ZigZag

BAIT

COMIC BOOKS

Chile

Type: Original Story
Writer: German Gabler
Artist: German Gabler

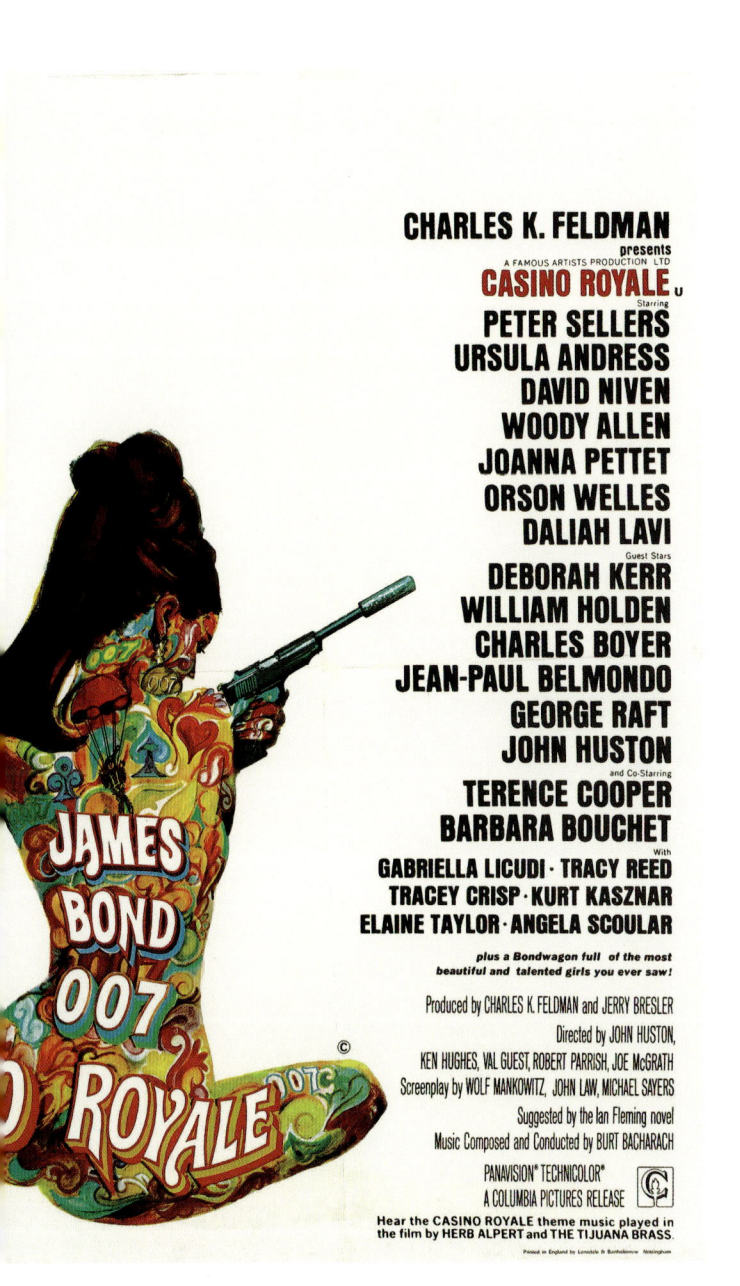

Originally Published: 007 James Bond #44 (1970) as "Señuelo" by ZigZag

CRY OF FREEDOM

COMIC BOOKS

Chile

Type: Original Story
Writer: German Gabler
Artist: German Gabler

Originally Published: 007 James Bond #45 (1970) as "Grito de Libertad" by ZigZag

Originally Published: 007 James Bond #36 (1970) as "La playa de las Flores" by ZigZag

DEATH IS AMUSED

COMIC BOOKS

Chile

Type: Original Story
Writer: German Gabler
Artist: German Gabler

Above: British 30 x 40 inch movie poster from the 1967 version of *Casino Royale*, art by Robert McGinnis.

DANGER AT DOCK 4

COMIC BOOKS

Chile

Type: Original Story
Writer: German Gabler
Artist: German Gabler

Originally Published: 007 James Bond #46 (1970) as "Peligro en el Dique 4" by ZigZag

PRINCE AND THE DRAGON

COMIC BOOKS

Chile

Type: Original Story
Writer: German Gabler
Artist: Lincoln Fuentes

Originally Published: 007 James Bond #47 (1970) as "El Príncipe y El Dragón" by ZigZag

A WARM SUMMER AFTERNOON

COMIC BOOKS

Chile

Type: Original Story
Writer: German Gabler
Artist: German Gabler

Originally Published: 007 James Bond #48 (1970) as "Una Calurosa Tarde de Verano" by ZigZag

BODY GUARD

COMIC BOOKS

Chile

Type: Original Story
Writer: German Gabler
Artist: German Gabler

Originally Published: 007 James Bond #49 (1970) as "Guardaespaldas" by ZigZag

5 DEGREES BELOW ZERO

COMIC BOOKS

Chile

Type: Original Story
Writer: German Gabler
Artist: German Gabler

Originally Published: 007 James Bond #50 (1970) as "5 grados bajo cero" by ZigZag

THE SABOTEURS

COMIC BOOKS

Chile

Type: Original Story
Writer: German Gabler
Artist: German Gabler

Originally Published: 007 James Bond #51 (1970) as "Los Saboteadores" by ZigZag

A PLEASURE TRIP

COMIC BOOKS

Chile

Type: Original Story
Writer: German Gabler
Artist: German Gabler

Originally Published: 007 James Bond #52 (1970) as "Un Viaje de Placer" by ZigZag

Opposite page: U.S. 27 x 41 inch movie poster from *Goldfinger*, 1964.

The Missions

MERCENARIES

COMIC BOOKS

Chile

Type: Original Story
Writer: German Gabler
Artist: German Gabler

Originally Published: 007 James Bond #53 (1970) as "Mercenario" by ZigZag

INFERNO IN SICILY

COMIC BOOKS

Chile

Type: Original Story
Writer: German Gabler
Artist: German Gabler

Originally Published: 007 James Bond #54 (1970) as "Infierno en Sicilia" by ZigZag

YETI

COMIC BOOKS

Chile

Type: Original Story
Writer: German Gabler
Artist: German Gabler

Originally Published: 007 James Bond #55 (1970) as "Yeti" by ZigZag

THE GOLDEN DOLPHIN

COMIC BOOKS

Chile

Type: Original Story
Writer: German Gabler
Artist: German Gabler?

Originally Published: 007 James Bond #56 (1970) as "El Delfín de Oro" by ZigZag

THE RALLY OF DEATH

COMIC BOOKS

Chile

Type: Original Story
Writer: German Gabler
Artist: German Gabler

Originally Published: 007 James Bond #57 (1970) as "La Rallye de la Muerte" by ZigZag

Above: opening title for "The Golden Ghost" newspaper strip, art by Yaroslav Horak, 1970. Opposite page: "The Golden Ghost" newspaper strip. These two sequential strips are reminiscent of the kitchen fight scene from the Timothy Dalton movie *The Living Daylights*.

MYSTERY ON TV

COMIC BOOKS

Chile

Type: Original Story
Writer: German Gabler
Artist: German Gabler

Originally Published: 007 James Bond #58 (1970) as "Misterio en la Television" by ZigZag

THE CONDEMNED

COMIC BOOKS

Chile

Type: Original Story
Writer: German Gabler
Artist: German Gabler

Originally Published: 007 James Bond #59 (1970) as "Los Condenados" by ZigZag

THE GOLDEN GHOST

NEWSPAPER STRIP

Type: *Daily Express* comic strip
Writer: Jim Lawrence
Artist: Yaroslav Horak

Published: *Daily Express* between 21st August 1970 and 16th January 1971 (Series #3, strip 1394-1519)

Source: Original story

Plot Summary: Living up to the "extortion" part of their name, SPECTRE offers the British Secret Service information about a plot against the new nuclear powered airship The Golden Ghost. Their price? One million pounds and James Bond as hostage. Bond agrees and goes to Paris to meet his SPECTRE contact. The SPECTRE agent is killed and tries to leave Bond a clue to the plot. Following various clues Bond eventually gets himself a place on the airship's maiden voyage. All the passengers are drugged and awake to find themselves and the airship held hostage on a deserted island by Felix Bruhl, another SPECTRE agent. Bruhl throws Bond to the sharks as an example, but using a concealed knife Bond escapes. Bond and Bruhl eventually face off in a brutal battle on board the airborne ship from which Bruhl falls to his death.

Notes: While the plot and pacing reads like a typical, if somewhat far fetched, Jim Lawrence tale, the dialog does not. Reading this story it seems as if someone else placed the words in the characters' mouths based on Lawrence's plot and Horak's art. In particular, Bond's British accent which lapses into clichéd pseudo-cockney with the inclusion of numerous 'luvs' and 'mates,' words never used by Bond up until this point. There is also some internal inconsistency with Bond's cover switching between Transworld Consortium to Transworld News.

The keel hauling sequence from *Live and Let Die* also seems to be reprised here. For Bond movie fans, the final showdown between 007 and the villain in a ship's galley is reminiscent of the brutal kitchen fight from *The Living Daylights*.

English Reprints

"The Golden Ghost" was reprinted in the 2006 Titan Books album *The Golden Ghost*

Translations

Denmark
- James Bond, Agent 007 #23 (1972)—"Det gyldne spøgelse"

Italy
- Albi Dell'avventura—Serie James Bond #? (date?)—"Il fantasma D'Oro"

Norway
- Agent 007, James Bond #5 (1982)—"Sporløst forsvunnet"

Spain
- James Bond Fasciculo semanal #7-12 (1973)—"Sombras de Oro"
- James Bond Episodios completos #2 (1973)—"Sombras de Oro"

Sweden
- James Bond, Agent 007 #17 (1971)—"Det gyllene spöket"
- James Bond, Agent 007 #51 (date?)—"Det gyllene spöket"
- James Bond, Agent 007 #3 (1991)—"Det gyllene spöket"

Below: two sequential strips from "Double Jepardy," 1971, art by Yaroslav Horak. A similar sequence was used in the Roger Moore movie *Live and Let Die* two years later. Opposite page: opening title for the "Starfire" newspaper strip, 1971, art by Yaroslav Horak

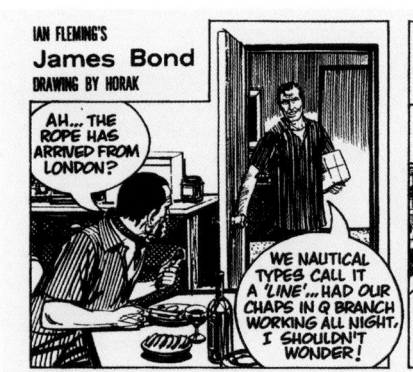

FEAR FACE

NEWSPAPER STRIP

Type: *Daily Express* comic strip
Writer: Jim Lawrence
Artist: Yaroslav Horak

Published: *Daily Express* between 18th January 1971 and 20th April 1971 (Series #3, strip 1520-1596)

Source: Original story.

Plot Summary: Briony Thorne, the former 0013 and Bond's former lover, returns to London where she is suspected of having been turned by the Chinese secret service. Thorne declares her innocence but the only person who believes her is Bond. She claims to have been framed by a man names Kress who has connections to Magnus Mining and someone called Lambert. Their investigations uncover that Lambert has perfected a series of faceless robots and that Magnus means to profit from using Lambert's robots in his mines. However, one of the robots has killed a stripper, and Kress is using that as leverage to sell the plans to whichever foreign power will pay the most.

Notes: Jim Lawrence expands on Ian Flemings Double-0 section with the introduction of female agent Briony Thorne (0013). Lawrence also returns to his SciFi roots with an improbable story featuring remote control robots capable of passing as humans. In many ways the plot reads as if it were inspired by a classic episode of the TV show *The Avengers* featuring faceless "cybernauts" that aired a few years before this story was published.

English Reprints

"Fear Face" was reprinted in the 2006 Titan Books album *The Golden Ghost*

Translations

Brazil
- 007 James Bond #4 (1978)—"A Face do Terror"

Denmark
- James Bond, Agent 007 #25 (1973)—"Stålspionen"
- James Bond, Agent 007 #60 (1981)—"Stålspionen"

Norway
- Agent 007, James Bond #3 (1983)—"Stålspionen"

Spain
- James Bond Fasciculo semanal #19-24 (1974)—"Rostro de Acero"
- James Bond Episodios completos #4 (1974)—"Rostro de Acero"

Sweden
- James Bond, Agent 007 #21 (1972?)—"Stålspionen"
- James Bond, Agent 007 #54 (date?)—"Stålspionen"
- James Bond, Agent 007 #5 (1993)—"Stålspionen"

DOUBLE JEOPARDY

NEWSPAPER STRIP

Type: *Daily Express* comic strip
Writer: Jim Lawrence
Artist: Yaroslav Horak

JAMES BOND
AGENT 007
NR. 27 ● KR. 3,25
Nyt Bond-eventyr, med masser af piger
og spænding. DRÆBENDE BUDSKAB
Johnny Boy som
VILDJUNGLENS KONGE

Published: *Daily Express* between 21st April 1971 to 28th August 1971 (Series #3, strip 1597-1708)

Source: Original story.

Plot Summary: A New York museum art director steals his own paintings, while in Paris a French industrialist steals his own company secrets, then both die in mysterious circumstances. Meanwhile the wife of a top Ministry of Defense official is blackmailed into spying. In order to divert attention from his wife, the MoD official shots himself. Bond is assigned to investigate the shooting and the blackmailer is revealed as an agent of SPECTRE. Bond's investigations lead him to Morocco where he uncovers SPECTRE's plans to replace certain key people with surgically altered body doubles.

Notes: Like the movie *Live and Let Die* one of the set pieces of the strip includes Bond's use of a hang glider to infiltrate an enemy hideout. At the time the strip was printed, hang gliding was a little known sport. Jim Lawrence also introduces another alias for Bond, "Jeremy Blade" of the Ornithological Society, paying homage to Fleming's inspiration for his lead character's name as well as the name of M's club in the novels. At first the story reads like two separate stories, but Lawrence ties the seemingly unrelated subplots together through a somewhat improbable coincidence. Thirty years after this strip was published, continuation novelist Raymond Benson would use the concept of body doubles in his book *Doubleshot* (2000). The concept would also be reworked in a few of the original Swedish produced comics during the 1980s.

English Reprints

"Double Jeopardy" was reprinted in the 2006 Titan Books album *The Golden Ghost*

Translations

Denmark
- James Bond, Agent 007 #24 (1972)—"Mysteriet om dobbeltgængerne"

Norway
- Agent 007 - James Bond #8 (1983)—"Dødens dobbeltgjenger"
- Agent 007 - James Bond #6 (1994)—"Dødens dobbeltgjenger"

Above: cover for the 1974 Danish comic book with the story "Trouble Spot."

Spain
- James Bond, Fasciculo semanal #7-12 (1973)—"Juego Peligroso"
- James Bond Episodios completos #2 (1973)—"Juego Peligroso"

Sweden
- James Bond, Agent 007 #19 (1972)—"Dödens dubbelgångare"
- James Bond, Agent 007 #53 (date?)—"Dödens dubbelgångare"

STARFIRE

NEWSPAPER STRIP

Type: *Daily Express* comic strip
Writer: Jim Lawrence
Artist: Yaroslav Horak

Published: *Daily Express* between 30th August 1971 and 24th December 1971 (Series #3, strip 1709-1809)

Source: Original story.

Plot Summary: Several people who have openly criticized "Lord Astro" the leader of a hippie cult, are mysteriously killed by fireballs that seem to be called down from the skies. One of the people killed is a CIA agent, so Bond is assigned to investigate. The investigations lead him to an electronics expert named Quantrill who seems to have some connection to each victim. It turns out that Quantrill had once sold secrets to the Russians and is now a SPECTRE operative. Bond trails Quantrill to a family party and manages to lure him outside and plant one of Quantrill's own homing devices, used to summon the deadly fireballs, on him.

Notes: One of the most straightforward espionage plots to appear in the Bond newspaper strips. Starfire is full of plot twists, starting a little hesitantly and building pace as the story develops. In many ways it didn't really need Bond in the story. It would have worked just as well with any generic thriller character. Artist Horak also effectively uses the space between the panels to let the reader add to the action with his own imagination. This would be the last time that SPECTRE. is used or mentioned in a Bond strip for close to ten years.

IAN FLEMING'S James Bond
DRAWING BY HORAK

Isle of Condors

Nightfall finds James Bond on a wooded road in Italy...when suddenly...

English Reprints

"Starfire" was reprinted in the 2006 Titan Books album *The Golden Ghost*

Translations

Denmark
- James Bond, Agent 007 #26 (1973)—"Stjernernes herre"

Norway
- Agent 007—James Bond #12 (1990)—"Stjernenes herre"

Spain
- James Bond, Fasciculo semanal #13-18 (1973)—"La Estrella de Fuego"
- James Bond, Episodios completos #3 (1973)—"La Estrella de Fuego"

Sweden
- James Bond, Agent 007 #23 (1973)—"Stjärnornas herre"
- James Bond, Agent 007 #73 (date?)—"Stjärnornas herre"

TROUBLE SPOT

NEWSPAPER STRIP

Type: *Daily Express* comic strip
Writer: Jim Lawrence
Artist: Yaroslav Horak

Published: *Daily Express* between 28th December 1971 and 10th June 1972 (Series #3, strip 1810-1951)

Source: Original story

Plot Summary: Bond has been set on the trail of a mysterious box and imitates an agent called Mike Channing to try and track it down. Channing's girlfriend reveals that she believes Channing's blind wife may have it. They head for California in search of Mrs. Channing, closely persuaded by a Russian commissar who also wants the box. Bond decides to try and convince Folly Channing that he is her husband by imitating his voice. The only positive identification he has for Mrs. Channing is a birthmark on her backside. Luckily for Bond, Folly Channing lives in a nudist colony! After convincing Folly that he is her husband, Bond recovers the box only to be confronted by the Russian. A shoot out occurs and Bond kills the commissar. The box turns out to contain the skull of a Russian double agent.

"WELL, I'LL BE DAMNED!..WHO'S THIS COMING?. LADY GODIVA?"

"HELP! HELP!"

1952

Notes: The central conceit of this story that a blind woman would mistake another man's voice (even a disguised one) for that of her husband strains credulity. Throw in the convenience of the nudist camp identity confirmation and this story approaches farce. However, if you ignore those two features it is in fact close to another straightforward espionage story that doesn't really need 007. Although, the machine gun mounted in the fender of Bond's car adds a nod to the movies. The strip features lots of shots of women without much in the way of clothing. This would become a staple of the Bond strips (and of British newspaper strips in general) during the seventies. This is the first strip not to feature M.

English Reprints

"Trouble Spot" was reprinted in the 2006 Titan Books album *Trouble Spot*.

Above: opening title for "The Isle Of Condors" newspaper strip, art by Yaroslav Horak, 1972. Below: cover of the Swedish "The Isle Of Condors," 1972.

103   **The Missions**

Translations

Denmark
- James Bond, Agent 007 #27 (1974)—"Dræbende budskab"

Italy
- L'avventoroso Anno #1-2 (1973)—"In cerca di guai"

Norway
- Agent X9 #7 (1977)—"Dødelig budskap"
- James Bond #10 (1990)—"Dødelig budskap"

Sweden
- James Bond, Agent 007 #25 (1973)—"Dödligt budskap"
- James Bond, Agent 007 #3 (1989)—"Dödligt budskap"
- James Bond, Agent 007 #4 (1996)—"Dödligt budskap"

ISLE OF CONDORS

NEWSPAPER STRIP

Type: *Daily Express* comic strip
Writer: Jim Lawrence
Artist: Yaroslav Horak

Published: *Daily Express* between 12th June 1972 and 21st October 1972 (Series #3, strip 1952-2065)

Source: Original story

Plot Summary: While in Italy on the trail of a Belgian woman who stole NATO secrets, Bond encounters a nude woman on horseback who claims she is escaping kidnappers. Amazingly Bond returns her to the villa where she claims she was being held prisoner and is then promptly drugged by its owners, the Gallews. Searching Bond's papers, the Gallews find a photo of the Belgian female spy. Panicked, they head for the nearby island of a man called Ucelli who runs a school for female spies. One downside to the school is that after completing a mission the girls are fed alive to Ucelli's pet condors. In the show down confrontation, Bond manages to spray Ucelli with the homing scent he uses to attract the birds, and leaves him to his fate.

Notes: The increasing prominence of unclothed women in the Bond newspaper strips starts right with the second panel of this story. Surprisingly, given the "school for female spies" angle and the focus on the female form, this strip also shows a marked shift in the treatment of female characters from being just window dressing to becoming strong respected protagonists in their own right. This story marks the point where writer Lawrence and artist Horak seemed to settle on how they would handle Bond. The tight story telling structure, the dynamic art and the character of Bond as portrayed here becomes the standard for the newspaper strips going forward.

English Reprints

"Isle of the Condors" was reprinted in the 2006 Titan Books album *Trouble Spot*.

Translations

Denmark
- James Bond, Agent 007 #28 (1974)—"Kondorernes ø"
- James Bond, Agent 007 #62 (1982)—"Kondorernes ø"

Finland
- James Bond, Agent 007 #1 (1982)—"Kondorien saari"

Norway
- Agent 007, James Bond #3 (1982)—"Kondorenes øy"
- James Bond #11 (1990)—"Kondorenes øy"

Sweden
- James Bond, Agent 007 #27 (1974)—"Kondorernas ö"

LEAGUE OF VAMPIRES

NEWSPAPER STRIP

Type: *Daily Express* comic strip
Writer: Jim Lawrence
Artist: Yaroslav Horak

Published: *Daily Express* between 25th October 1972 and 28th February 1973 (Series #3, strip 2066-2172)

Source: Original story

Plot Summary: A vampire cult that is growing across Europe seems to be linked to a series of mysterious deaths, including one of an MI6 agent. MI6 are alerted by shipping magnate Xerxes Xerophanos that his wife may be in the process of being recruited by the vampire cult. Bond infiltrates a cult ceremony where Margo Xerophanos is to be the victim. Bond deciphers that Xerxes is behind the cult and is trying to get her killed so he can inherit her fortune. He also plans to kill off her father using a tactical nuclear missile launched from one of his ships. Bond manages to persuade the crew to mutiny, foiling the plan.

Notes: This is perhaps on of the most far fetched of the Lawrence scripted stories.

English Reprints

"The League of Vampires" was reprinted in the 2006 Titan Books album *Trouble Spot*.

Translations

Denmark
- James Bond, Agent 007 #32 (1975)—"Vampyrligaen"

Finland
- Agnetti X-9 #10 (1991)—"Vampyyrikopla"

Norway
- James Bond, Agent 007 #8 (1977)—"Vampyrligaen"
- Agent 007—James Bond #2 (1981)—"Vampyrligaen"
- Agent 007—James Bond #7 (1993)—"Vampyrligaen"

Sweden
- James Bond, Agent 007 #31 (1974)—"Vampyrligan"
- James Bond, Agent 007 #1 (1982)—"Vampyrligan"
- James Bond, Agent 007 #11 (1990)—"Vampyrligan"

DIE WITH MY BOOTS ON

NEWSPAPER STRIP

Type: *Daily Express* comic strip
Writer: Jim Lawrence
Artist: Yaroslav Horak

Published: *Daily Express* between 1st March 1973 and 18th June 1973 (Series #3, strip 2173-2256)

Source: Original story

Plot Summary: The Mafia are after a new British developed sedative that has been found to have psychedelic properties and is growing in use as a recreational drug. It also leaves the user impervious to pain. Bond is sent to New York to find the niece of the drug's inventor and keep the Mafia from getting hold of her.

Notes: One of the shortest strips in the series, and it seems to suffer from it as, in many ways, it feels rushed. Unlike Lawrence's other strips, it features a simple single layered plot, and some of Bond's dialog is seemingly out of character. There is little actual spy work involved as this seems more like a bodyguard type story than a suitable assignment for the world's best secret agent.

English Reprints

"Die With My Boots On" was reprinted in the 2006 Titan Books album *Trouble Spot*.

Translations

Denmark
- James Bond, Agent 007 #30 (1974—"Narkohandlerne"
- James Bond, Agent 007 #66 (1983)—"Narkohandlerne"

Norway
- James Bond, Agent 007 #4 (1982)—"Narkotikahandlerne"

Sweden
- James Bond, Agent 007 #29 (1974)—"Droghandlarna"
- James Bond, Agent 007 #2 (1982)—"Droghandlarna"
- James Bond, Agent 007 #3 (1992)—"Droghandlarna"

THE GIRL MACHINE

NEWSPAPER STRIP

Type: *Daily Express* comic strip
Writer: Jim Lawrence
Artist: Yaroslav Horak

Published: *Daily Express* between 19th June 1973 and 3rd December 1973 (Series #3, strip 2257-2407)

Source: Original story

Plot Summary: Britain wishes to install the Emir of Hajar on the throne and overthrow his uncle in order to secure oil rights. However the Secret Service must first find out where the Emir is being held. Clues lead Bond to a man called Rashid in Las Palmas, but he is killed before 007 can get information from him. Bond then tries Rashid's sister who turns out to be one of the wives of the regent holding the Emir. Bond is smuggled into Hajar in the titular, girl machine, a large cabinet filled with scents, alcohol and blue movies that was meant to be a bribe for the regent. Bond eventually contacts Rashid's sister, rescues the Emir and the three flee for the border.

Notes: This is a very visual story with the climactic escape to the border sequence bordering on the cinematic, taking over a month's worth of strips just to convey this sequence. Once again some of the dialog is out of character for Bond.

English Reprints

"The Girl Machine" has yet to be reprinted.

Translations

Denmark
- James Bond, Agent 007 #34 (1975)—"Jagten på det Sorte Guld..."

Norway
- Agent X-9 #6 (1977)—"Jakten på det svarte gullet"
- James Bond #2 (1991)—"Jakten på det svarte gullet"

Sweden
- James Bond, Agent 007 #33 (1975)—"Jakten på det svarta guldet"
- James Bond, Agent 007 #9 (1989)—"Jakten på det svarta guldet"
- James Bond, Agent 007 #6 (1993)—"Jakten på det svarta guldet"

BEWARE OF BUTTERFLIES

NEWSPAPER STRIP

Type: *Daily Express* comic strip
Writer: Jim Lawrence
Artist: Yaroslav Horak

Published: *Daily Express* between 4th December 1973 and 11th may 1974 (Series #3, strip 2408-2541)

Source: Original story

Plot Summary: Bond and new 00 agent Suzi Kew are assigned to kill an agent of the Butterfly spy network in Paris, which they do. On leave in Jamaica afterwards, Bond is kidnapped and brain washed. Suzi Kew is assigned to go after Bond and finds him amnesiac in Jamaica. His memory restored by the Secret Service, he infiltrates the Butterfly network and kills Attila, the head of the network.

Above: cover to the Danish edition of "The Nevsky Nude," 1976. **Opposite page:** cover to the Swedish edition of "The Phoenix Project," 1982.

Notes: Female OO agent and ongoing supporting character Suzi Kew, ostensibly the niece of Major Boothroyd (Q), makes her debut in this strip. She will go on to be a semi—regular in the comic strips as Bond's assistant, and occasional lover.

English Reprints

"Beware of Butterflies" has yet to be reprinted.

Translations

Denmark
- James Bond, Agent 007 #36 (1976)—"Operation Sommerfugl"

Norway
- Agent 007—James Bond #7 (1982)—"Operasjon Sommerfugl"
- James Bond #4 (1994)—"Operasjon Sommerfugl"

Sweden
- James Bond, Agent 007 #35 (1975)—"Operation Fjäril"

NEVSKY NUDE

NEWSPAPER STRIP

Type: *Daily Express* comic strip
Writer: Jim Lawrence
Artist: Yaroslav Horak

Published: *Daily Express* between 13th May 1974 and 21st September 1974 (Series #3, strip 2542-2655)

Source: Original story

Plot Summary: MI6 receive a tip off about something called "Operation Nevsky." Following the lead Bond arrives in Sussex where he is surprised by a nude woman descending in a parachute. The woman and a Russian agent are killed in an exchange of gun fire. Shortly afterwards a renegade aristocrat claims to broadcast a message from King Arthur and ghostly knights are seen in Cornwall. It all turns out to be a SMERSH backed plot to kidnap the Secretary of State for Defense and hustle him away via submarine.

Notes: This is perhaps one of Lawrence's weakest stories despite two intriguing opening hooks, a naked girl in a parachute and King Arthur's ghost, It soon descends into formulaic nonsense and it is plagued with massive plot holes. Not least of which is why Bond and MI6 would get involved in the first place. As all the action takes place in the UK, it would have been handled by MI5. The rest hinges on coincidence and illogical actions by both Bond and SMERSH.

English Reprints

"The Nevsky Nude" has yet to be reprinted.

Translations

Denmark
- James Bond, Agent 007 #38 (1976)—"Sagen fra skyerne"

Finland
- James Bond, Agent 007 #3 (1976)—"Operatio Nevski"

- Agnetti X-9 #3 (1991)—"Operaatio Nevski"

Italy
- Albi Dell'avventura—Serie James Bond #? (Date?)—"Operazione Nevsky"

Norway
- Agent 007 - James Bond #4 (1982)—"Spøkelset fra skyene"
- James Bond #2 (1994)—"Himmelfallen"

Sweden
- James Bond, Agent 007 #37 (1976)—"Fallen fra skyarna"
- James Bond, Agent 007 #3 (1982)—"Fallen fra skyarna"

THE PHOENIX PROJECT

NEWSPAPER STRIP

Type: *Daily Express* comic strip
Writer: Jim Lawrence
Artist: Yaroslav Horak

Published: *Daily Express* between 23rd September 1974 and 18th February 1975 (Series #3, strip 2656-2780)

Source: Original story

Plot Summary: The Phoenix Project is a new suit of armor that will render the wearer impenetrable to bullets, grenades or fire. During a test it goes wrong and the wearer is killed. Investigations lead Bond to Istanbul and an arms dealer named Kazim. Bond manages to work his way into Kazim's inner circle before his cover is blown and he has to escape using a fully functioning version of The Phoenix Project armor.

Notes: Jim Lawrence once more touches on his science fiction roots with a story revolving around a suit of indestructible armor. The character of Bond seems to alter part way through the story with the first half featuring a tougher Connery-like Bond, who even questions M, while the second half he is more light hearted, in line with the Roger Moore interpretation which had debuted on the movie screen a few months before the strip appeared.

English Reprints

"The Phoenix Project" was reprinted in the 2007 Titan Books album *"The Phoenix Project."*

Translations

Denmark
- James Bond, Agent 007 #44 (1978)—"Projekt Fenix"

Finland
- James Bond, Agent 007 #5 (1977)—"Projekti Fenix"

Italy
- Albi Dell'avventura—Serie James Bond #? (Date?)—"Progetto Phoenix"

Norway
- Agent 007 - James Bond #2 (1980)—"Prosjekt Føniks"
- James Bond #2 (1992)—"Prosjekt Føniks"

Sweden
- James Bond, Agent 007 #42 (1976)—"Projekt Fenix"
- James Bond, Agent 007 #4 (1982)—"Projekt Fenix"
- James Bond, Agent 007 #8 (1990)—"Projekt Fenix"

THE BLACK RUBY CAPER

NEWSPAPER STRIP

Type: *Daily Express* comic strip
Writer: Jim Lawrence
Artist: Yaroslav Horak

Published: *Daily Express* between 19th February 1975 and 15th July 1975 (Series #3, strip 2781-2897)

Source: Original story

Plot Summary: Bond is sent after a bomber called Herr Rubin, aka Mr. Ruby, and tricks Ruby into believing that his girlfriend is helping Bond. Ruby escapes and resurfaces in Ghana where he has recruited a sculptor named Roscoe Carver, who had once been hunted by the FBI, to build a hollow statue in which Ruby can plant another bomb. Carver's daughter and a beautiful model team up to help Bond by luring Ruby into a trap where Bond kills him by pouring molten metal over him.

Notes: Lawrence spins a fairly complex tale here with numerous plot twists and turns. Female 00 agent Suzi Kew makes her second appearance in the strip, but is somewhat overshadowed by the stronger character of Damara Carver.

English Reprints

"The Black Ruby Caper" was reprinted in the 2007 Titan Books album "*The Phoenix Project*."

Translations

Denmark
- James Bond, Agent 007 #41 (1977)—"Kodenavn: Sorte storm"

Finland
- James Bond, Agent 007 #6 (1976)—"Koodinimi: Musta myrsky"

Italy
- Albi Dell'avventura - Serie James Bond #? (date?)—"Operazione Tempesta Nera"

Norway
- Agent 007 - James Bond #4 (1983)—"Kodenavn: Svart storm"
- James Bond #7 (1994)—"Kodenavn: Svart storm"

TILL DEATH DO US PART

NEWSPAPER STRIP

Type: *Daily Express* comic strip
Writer: Jim Lawrence
Artist: Yaroslav Horak

Published: *Daily Express* between 17th July 1975 and 14th October 1975 (Series #3, strip 2898-2983)

Source: Original story

Plot Summary: Bond is sent out to seduce Ardra Petrich the daughter of an ex MI6 agent in Eastern Europe, with the intention of getting her to return to Britain. Her married lover also believes that she knows her father's secrets and offers to sell her to the KGB.

Notes: Till Death inverts the complex story structure of the previous strip and is played more or less straight. One aspect of note in this strip is artist Horak's use of a Doppler effect concentric circles to indicate the passage of sound waves during the car chase. These, combined with abrupt changes in "camera" angle, give the chase a real dynamic feeling. From a story telling perspective this is one of the few times in any medium that we see the consequences of Bond's actions as his attempted kidnapping of Ardra leads to a diplomatic incident.

English Reprints

"Till Death Do Us Part" was reprinted in the 2007 Titan Books album "*The Phoenix Project*."

Translations

Denmark
- James Bond, Agent 007 #45 (1978)—"Ballade på Balkan"

Italy
- Albi Dell'avventura—Serie James Bond #? (date?)—"Finche Morte non ci separe"

Norway
- Agent 007 - James Bond #3 (1982)—"Intrige på Balkan"

Sweden
- James Bond, Agent 007 #44 (1976)—"Intrig på Balkan"

TORCH-TIME AFFAIR

NEWSPAPER STRIP

Type: *Daily Express* comic strip
Writer: Jim Lawrence
Artist: Yaroslav Horak

Published: *Daily Express* between 15th October 1975 and 15th January 1976 (Series #3 strip 2984-3060)

Source: Original story

Plot Summary: Bond is sent to locate agent Tim Hurst who is meant to be in possession of Torch-Time, a document time—tabling various subversive acts. The trail leads to a deserted beach in Acapulco where, instead of Hurst, he finds a woman buried in the sand up to her neck. Bond rescues the woman, Carmen Perez, who says she was lured to the beach by a known SMERSH agent. Hurst's body turns up in Mexico City along with an empty tape recorder. Various clues lead Bond to realize that Carmen is an enemy agent also after the tape.

Notes: Lawrence experiments with a 'fair play' mystery style story in which the observant reader could follow some visual clues to solve the puzzle as they read along. The result is a more straightforward mystery with a few twists along the way.

English Reprints

"Torch-Time Affair" was reprinted in the 2007 Titan Books album "*The Phoenix Project.*"

Translations

Denmark
- James Bond, Agent 007 #47 (1979) —"En enkelt Acapulco"

Finland
- James Bond, Agent 007 #5 (1977)—"Seikkailu Acapulcossa"

Norway
- Agent 007 - James Bond #2 (1980)— "Enveisbilett til Acapulco"
- James Bond #7 (1992)—"Enveisbilett til Acapulco"

Sweden
- James Bond, Agent 007 #46 (1977?)—"En enkel, Acapulco"
- James Bond, Agent 007 #1 (1994)—"En enkel, Acapulco"

HOT SHOT

NEWSPAPER STRIP

Type: *Daily Express* comic strip
Writer: Jim Lawrence
Artist: Yaroslav Horak

Published: *Daily Express* between 16th January 1976 and 1st June 1976 (Series #3, strip 3061-3178)

Source: Original story

Plot Summary: Bond teams up with Fatima Khalid, a Palestinian freedom fighter, to investigate the Elbis terrorist group who appear to be responsible for several aircraft midair explosions. The Elbis group is lead by a man known only as Huliraya. Huliraya means King Tiger and a string of tiger themed deaths lead Bond and Fatima to uncover the truth – Huliraya is in fact Dr. Julius No!

No plans to use a giant parabolic mirror that can focus the sun's rays to destroy a plane carrying the US Secretary of State. The ray-gun is mounted on board a super tanker, but Bond gets on board and destroys the tanker before the weapon can be fired.

Notes: This story is one of Lawrence's weakest plots. How Dr. No survived his earlier "death" is never explained. One vital clue is transmitted via a crumpled note left in a dead man's hand, and are we to believe that Dr. No would allow himself to be traced through a series of themed murders? Several elements of the story will be familiar to movie fans with the parabolic mirror gun capable of destroying the aircraft turning up in the movie version of *The Man With The Golden Gun*, and to some extent in *Diamonds Are Forever*. The super tanker based villain is used in *The Spy Who Loved Me*.

English Reprints

"Hot-Shot" has not yet been reprinted.

Translations

Denmark
- James Bond, Agent 007 #46 (1978)—"Dødsstrålen"

Below: opening title for "The Black Ruby Caper" newspaper strip, art by Yaroslav Horak, 1975

Norway
- Agent 007 - James Bond #5 (1980)—"I tigerens klør"
- James Bond #1 (1993) – "I tigerens klør"

Sweden
- James Bond, Agent 007 #48 (1977?)—"Dödsstrålen"
- James Bond, Agent 007 #6 (1993)—"Dödsstrålen "

NIGHTBIRD

NEWSPAPER STRIP

Type: *Daily Express* comic strip
Writer: Jim Lawrence
Artist: Yaroslav Horak

Published: *Daily Express* between 1st June 1976 and 4th November 1976 (Series #3, strip 3179-3312)

Source: Original story

Plot Summary: An old girl friend of Bond's is apparently kidnapped by "Martians" and killed before a ransom can be paid. As Bond investigates, one of his informants is killed and several other people are abducted by the strange looking creatures. Bond eventually traces the various clues to film producer Ferdinand Polgar. Bond befriends Polgar's girl friend who leads him to the producer's villa on Sardinia where the kidnap victims are being held.

Notes: Lawrence once again plays out a B-movie science fiction theme before spinning it into a fairly ordinary kidnap/rescue plot. The strips suffer from some internal inconsistencies that suggest they may have been rushed, or at least not thoroughly copy edited.

English Reprints

"Nightbird" has not yet been reprinted.
Note: Titan Books did advertise an album titled "*Nightbird*" in the back of their 2007 *Phoenix Project* album, but to date it hasn't been published.

Translations

Denmark
- James Bond, Agent 007 #49 (1979)—"Natfuglen"

Norway
- Agent 007—James Bond #2 (1982)—"Nattfuglen"

Sweden
- James Bond, Agent 007 #50 (date?)—"Nattfågeln"

APE OF DIAMONDS

NEWSPAPER STRIP

Type: *Daily Express* comic strip
Writer: Jim Lawrence
Artist: Yaroslav Horak / Neville Colvin

Published: *Daily Express* between 5th November 1976 and 22nd January 1977 (Series #3, strip 3312-3437)

Source: Original story

Plot Summary: The Secret Service are sent a film showing a gorilla attacking a woman accompanied by an "Ape of Diamonds" playing card. Another ape kidnaps an Arab dignitary in London and Bond is assigned to find out what's going on. The woman in the film is identified and Bond travels to Egypt to ask questions at the game park where she worked. Here he meets the woman's sister who admits she uses trained gorillas to assassinate people, and Bond offers her a job!!

Notes: This strange story would be the last Bond strip printed in the *Daily Express*, bringing to an end a near nineteen year run. The story is cut short in the *Daily Express* version at strip #3377 and comparison with the syndicated complete version shows that the dialogue for that last two days worth of strips was altered to try and make some sort of satisfactory conclusion. The complete story, to strip #3437, was syndicated for translation with strips #3381-3437 drawn by Neville Colvin rather than series regular Yaroslav Horak.

English Reprints

"Ape of Diamonds" has not yet been reprinted.

Translations

Denmark
- James Bond, Agent 007 #48 (1979)—"Dødelig commando"

Norway
- Agent 007 - James Bond #6 (1982)—"Dødelig oppdrag"

WHEN THE WIZARD AWAKES

NEWSPAPER STRIP

Type: *Sunday Express* comic strip
Writer: Jim Lawrence
Artist: Yaroslav Horak

Published: *Sunday Express* between 30th January 1977 and 22nd May 1977 (Series #4, strip 1-54)

Source: Original story

Plot Summary: Bond is sent to confirm that a Hungarian traitor died many years before. When the grave is opened Bond is surprised to see the body move just before a bomb destroys the grave site. It transpires that the Mafia is trying to convince the Hungarian government that the traitor is still alive and has smuggled the Crown of St. Stephen out of Hungary. The truth is that the real Crown is being held by the CIA in Fort Knox, but the CIA can't tell the Hungarians because SPECTRE has threatened to release a list of CIA agents in Hungary to the Russians if they do.

Notes: This is the only Bond comic strip to appear in The Sunday Express. Due to appearing in a weekly paper, this is the shortest Lawrence scripted Bond story at just 55 strips. The Sunday format also meant that each week three strips were printed instead of the single strip of the daily newspaper.

English Reprints

"When The Wizard Awakes" was reprinted in the 2007 Titan Album, *Death Wing*.

Translations

Denmark
- James Bond, Agent 007 #49 (1979)—"Troldmanden vågner"

Norway
- Agent 007 - James Bond #2 (1982)—"Trollmannen våkner"

- James Bond #2 (1994)—"Trollmannen våkner"

Sweden
- James Bond, Agent 007 #54 (date?)—"Trollkarlen vaknar"
- James Bond, Agent 007 #2 (1995)—"Trollkarlen vaknar"

SEA DRAGON

NEWSPAPER STRIP

Type: Newspaper comic strip
Writer: Jim Lawrence
Artist: Yaroslav Horak

Published: Although produced for the *Express* group of newspapers, Sea Dragon was never published in the UK papers. (Series #4, strip 55-192)

Source: Original story

Plot Summary: When oil magnate Sir Ivor Morlock is murdered in an explosion on his private boat in the Bahamas, Bond escapes with his life, but only just. The mystery deepens when a second member of Morlock's oil consortium is killed by a sea dragon!

Notes: Lawrence once again drifts into the realm of fantastic murderous beasts with this improbable tale. Major Boothroyd (Q) makes a rare and brief appearance.

English Reprints

Sea Dragon was included in the 2007 Titan Album, *Death Wing*. That was the first time it had been published in English.

Translations

Denmark
- James Bond, Agent 007 #51 (1980)—"Operation Big Mama"

Finland
- James Bond, Agent 007 #3 (1979)—"Operaatio Big Mama"

Norway
- Agent 007 - James Bond #1 (1979)—"Operasjon Big Mama"
- James Bond #1 (1992)—"Operasjon Big Mama"

Sweden
- James Bond, Agent 007 #58 (date?)—"Operation Big Mama"
- James Bond, Agent 007 #1 (1991)—"Operation Big Mama"

Turkey
- James Bond #? (date?)—"Deniz Ejderi"

DEATH WING

NEWSPAPER STRIP

Type: Newspaper comic strip
Writer: Jim Lawrence
Artist: Yaroslav Horak

Published: Although produced for the *Express* group of newspapers, "Death Wing" was never published in the UK papers. (Series #4, strips 193-354)

Source: Original story

Plot Summary: Bond catches a female spy trying to interfere with a Royal Air Force test. His investigations lead him to Matteo Mortellito, an aerospace engineer who has created the "Death Wing" flying sleds. Bond manages to work his way into Mortellito's organization aiming to prevent the sleds from being put to use.

Notes: Perhaps one of the most visually exciting of the Lawrence/Horak stories. The strip's concluding act is highly cinematic featuring an air battle above the streets of Manhattan.

English Reprints

"Death Wing" was included in the 2007 Titan Album, *Death Wing*. That was the first time it had been published in English.

Translations

Denmark
- James Bond, Agent 007 #53 (1980)—"Operation Deathwing"

Finland
- Agentti X-9 #1 (1993)—Deathwing—"Lentävä koulema"

Norway
- Agent 007—James Bond #1 (1982)—"Operasjon Deathwing"

Sweden
- James Bond, Agent 007 #61 (date?)—"Deathwing"
- James Bond, Agent 007 #5 (1992)—"Deathwing"

THE XANADU CONNECTION

NEWSPAPER STRIP

Type: Newspaper comic strip
Writer: Jim Lawrence
Artist: Yaroslav Horak

Published: Although produced for the *Express* group of newspapers, The Xanadu Connection was never published in the UK papers. (Series #4, strips 355-468)

Source: Original story

Plot Summary: Bond is sent into East Germany to extract undercover MI6 agent Heidi Franz. Franz's tells MI6 about a plan to capture a Russian dissident and MI6 informer known only as Marco Polo. The plot is somehow linked to the mysterious performer and his shadowy Xanadu organization.

Notes: The central gadget of this story is a steerable drill vehicle that appears to be lifted straight from the TV puppet series *Thunderbirds*.

English Reprints

"The Xanadu Connection" was included in the 2007 Titan Album, *Shark Bait*. That was the first time it had been published in English.

Opposite page: cover to Danish edition of "Hot Shot," 1978.

Translations

Denmark
- James Bond, Agent 007 #55 (1980)—"Operation Xanadu"

Norway
- Agent 007—James Bond #1 (1984)—"Operasjon Xanadu"

Sweden
- James Bond, Agent #63 (date?)—"Operation Xanadu"
- James Bond, Agent #1 (1993)—"Operation Xanadu"

SHARKBAIT

NEWSPAPER STRIP

Type: Newspaper comic strip
Writer: Jim Lawrence
Artist: Yaroslav Horak

Published: Although produced for the *Express* group of newspapers, Sharkbait was never published in the UK papers. (Series #4, strips 469-636)

Source: Original story

Plot Summary: Bond and KGB agent Katya Orlova team up to stop a renegade Red Navy officer and his pilots.

Notes: One of the longer strips often split into two separate parts when translated. It is also one of the most dialogue heavy strips with, unusually for a Horak drawn strip, fairly static artwork.

English Reprints

"Shark Bait" was included in the 2007 Titan Album, *Shark Bait*. That was the first time it had been published in English.

Translations

Denmark
- James Bond, Agent 007 #58 (1981)—"Operation lokkemad" (part 1)
- James Bond, Agent 007 #61 (1981)—"Operation KGB" (part 2)

007 JAMES BOND

NR. 46 • KR. 5,20

DØDSSTRÅLEN

Finland
- James Bond, Agent 007 #2 (1981)—"Operaatio hainsyötti" (part 1)
- Agnetti X-9 #4 (1991)—"Operaatio KGB" (full story)

Norway
- Agent 007—James Bond #5 (1981)—"Operasjon KGB" (part 1)
- Agent 007 - James Bond #2 (1983)—"Operasjon Shark Bait" (part 2)

Sweden
- James Bond, Agent 007 #67 (date?)—"Operation Shark Bait" (part 1)
- James Bond, Agent 007 #70 (date?)—"Operation KGB" (part 2)
- James Bond, Agent 007 #12 (1990)—"Operation KGB" (part 2)
- James Bond, Agent 007 #2 (1995)—"Operation Shark Bait" (part 1)

DOOMCRACK

NEWSPAPER STRIP

Type: *Daily Star* newspaper comic strip
Writer: Jim Lawrence
Artist: Harry North

Published: Appeared in the *Daily Star* between 2nd February 1981 and 19th August 1981. (Series #5, strips 1-174)

Source: Original story

Plot Summary: The Doomcrack is a sonic weapon with the ability to topple buildings. Bond is initially assigned to bring it back to Britain, but it is stolen and various international landmarks are threatened. Bond believes that SPECTRE is back in action. Bond is set up to look like he has been stealing secrets from MI6 so he can appear to have "turned." He eventually works his way on to SPECTRE's submarine base where he eventually meets Madame Spectra. Bond uses a new improved version of the Doomcrack weapon to destroy the submarine and escape.

Notes: This was the first James Bond strip to appear in the Express group tabloid paper the *Daily Star*. To mark the switch and to introduce Bond to his new readers, the first day three strips were run together (as they had been in the *Sunday Express*), after which the regular one strip per weekday formula was adopted. Artist Harry North was best known for his work on *MAD* magazine. Reportedly he got the "Doomcrack" assignments after Express editors were impressed by his work on *MAD's* parody of the Roger Moore movie *Octopussy*. Lawrence's tale is of a grander scope and escalates to Bond thwarting a global threat more in line with the movie plots than previous strips. That combined with North's art actually make this strip read more like a movie parody than a tight adventure story.

English Reprints

"Doomcrack" was included in the 2007 Titan Album, *Shark Bait*.

Translations

Sweden
- James Bond, Agent 007 #2 (1991)—"Doomcrack"

Below: daily from "Doomcrack," art by *MAD* magazine artist Harry North, 1981. Opposite page: cover to the Titan Books edition of *The Paradise Plot*, 2008.

THE PARADISE PLOT

NEWSPAPER STRIP

Type: *Daily Star* newspaper comic strip
Writer: Jim Lawrence
Artist: John McLusky

Published: Appeared in the *Daily Star* between 20th August 1981 and 4th June 1982 (Series #5, strips 175-378)

Source: Original story

Plot Summary: Two industrialists appear to be visited by their dead children and all the clues lead to a cult leader known as Father Star. Bond follows the trail to Star's "Project Polestar" based on a Caribbean island, and using the "I've been kicked out of MI6" ploy once again is accepted into the villain's organization. Bond learns that Star uses a nuclear powered airship to attack his enemies, has managed to gain control of a US spy plane by brain washing its pilot, and is building a private army!

Notes: This is perhaps one of the most convoluted and far fetched of Lawrence's plots. It's as if he knew the series was close to ending and tried to throw in every idea he still had in his note book. There is a brief (unnamed) cameo by Q'ute (Anne Reilly) from the John Gardner novels. Moneypenny's dialog at the strip's conclusion hints that James Bond may have been knighted recently. In the translated versions she directly refers to Bond as "Sir James." Paradise Plot featured a return of original Bond artist John McLusky after a gap of fifteen years. The change in the main characters features is startling after so many years of Horak's artwork. Starting with this story the Bond strips publishing frequency was reduced from six days a week to five.

English Reprints

"The Paradise Plot" was included in the 2008 Titan Album, *The Paradise Plot*.

Translations

Finland
- James Bond, Agent 007 #7 (1992)—"James Bond ja tähtien lapset"

Norway
- James Bond #3 (1994)—"Stjernesekten"

Sweden
- James Bond, Agent 007 #6 (1982)—"Stjärnornas barn" (part 1)
- James Bond, Agent 007 #7 (1982)—"Projekt Polstjärnan" (part 2)
- James Bond, Agent 007 #8 (1982)—"Order att döda" (part 3)

THE GOLDEN TRIANGLE

COMIC BOOK

Sweden

Type: Semic comic story
Writer: Johann Vlaanderen
Artist: Ramon Escolano Metaute

JAMES BOND
Agent 007
Text: Johann Vlaanderen Teckning: Escolano
DEN GYLLENE TRIANGELN
© BULLS/GLIDROSE PUBLICATIONS LIMITED 1982
HOTEL SIAM
CLUB
MR BOND, FÖRMODAR JAG?
GODDAG, MR GREENE, "M" PRATAR FORTFARANDE OM DEN GAMLA GODA TIDEN! SÅ ATT NI HAR DRAGIT ER TILLBAKA ---
VI VAR UNGA OCH GALNA PÅ DEN TIDEN!
MEN DET VAR LÄNGESEN--- HÄR I BANGKOK ÄR JAG BARA MR GREENE, EN RESPEKTABEL FINANSIÄR!
BOND--- JAMES BOND!
MAI LEY!
DAGS FÖR DEJ ATT GÅ, LILLA VÄN! IVÄG MED DEJ!
JB 5/82
3

Published: James Bond, Agent 007 #5 in 1982 as "Den gyllene Triangeln"

Source: Original story

Plot Summary: Bond is sent to Bangkok to uncover why heroin exports from the infamous Golden Triangle have suddenly increased. He is helped by an old friend of M.

Notes: The "Swedish Bond" debuted in a fairly pedestrian and predictable tale that didn't really need the character of James Bond to make it work.

Translations

Denmark
- James Bond, Agent 007, #65 (1982)—"Den gyldne triangle"

Finland
- James Bond, Agent 007 #4 (1982)—"Kultainen kolmio"

Norway
- Agent 007—James Bond #1 (1983)—"Den gyldne triangle"

DEATHMASK

NEWSPAPER STRIP

Type: *Daily Star* newspaper comic strip
Writer: Jim Lawrence
Artist: John McLusky

Published: Appeared in the *Daily Star* between 7th June 1982 and 8th February 1983. (Series #5, strips 379-552)

Source: Original story

Plot Summary: A series of mysterious deaths are linked to a fast acting virus that leaves the face swollen, and one of the corpses is found holding a Greek deathmask. The trail of clues leads Bond to Crete where he finds a secret cavern marked with the deathmask. The cavern blows up before he can investigate further. The deathmask is connected to the industrialist Ivor Nyborg. Nyborg has genetically engineered the new virus which he intends to spread around the world using his robotic plane, the Global Ghost, but Bond manages to gain control of the plane and crash it into Nyborg's headquarters.

English Reprints

"Deathmask" was included in the 2008 Titan Album, *Paradise Plot*.

Translations

Finland
- James Bond, Agent 007 #4 (1983) – "Tappajavirus"

Norway
- Agent 007 - James Bond #7 (1985) – "Dødsmasken"

Sweden
- James Bond, Agent 007 #4 (1983) – "Dødsmasken del 1"
- James Bond, Agent 007 #5 (1983) – "Dødsmasken del 2"

OPERATION JUNGLE DEVILS

COMIC BOOK

Sweden

Type: Semic comic story
Writer: Sverre Arnes
Artist: Ramon Escolano Metaute

Published: James Bond, Agent 007 #1 in 1983 under the English title "Operation Jungle Devils"

Source: Original story

Plot Summary: no information.

Translations

Denmark
- James Bond #1 (1983)—"Operation jungle djævlene"

Holland
- James Bond #7 (date?)—"Operatie 'Jungle devils'"

Opposite page: interior page from "The Golden Triangle," the first Semic original story, art by Ramon Escolano, 1982.

Published: James Bond, Agent 007 #2 in 1983 as "Slavhandlarna"

Source: Original story

Plot Summary: Bond is sent undercover to stop a slaving operation run by British mercenaries and sponsored by the KGB. To infiltrate the gang Bond is disguised as a half-black African mute.

Notes: If the idea of Bond disguising himself as a Japanese fisherman in *You Only Live Twice* was stretching credibility, this breaks it. However once you get past the patent absurdity of Bond's disguise, what remains is a strong Bond story that actual gives a little insight into his character.

Swedish Reprints
Reprinted in James Bond #3 (1994).

Translations

Denmark
- James Bond #2 (1983)—"Slavehandlerne"

Holland
- James Bond #2 (1984)—"Slavenhandelaars"

Norway
- Agent 007—James Bond #6 (1983)—"Slavehandlerne"

Spain
- James Bond #2 (1985)—"Traficantes de Esclavos"

CODENAME: NEMESIS

COMIC BOOK

Sweden

Type: Semic comic story
Writer: Jack Sutter
Artist: Josep Gual

Hungary
- James Bond #1 (1989)—"A dzsungel ördögei akció"

Norway
- Agent 007—James Bond #5 (1983)—"Operasjon Jungle Devils"
- James Bond #4 (1992)—"Jungelens djevler"

Russia
- James Bond #1 (1994)—title?

Spain
- James Bond #1 (1985)—"Operación Diablos de la Jungla"

THE SLAVE TRADERS

COMIC BOOK

Sweden

Type: Semic comic story
Writer: Jack Sutter
Artist: Ramon Escolano Metaute

Right: cover for "Codename Nemesis," from *James Bond* #3 published in Denmark, 1983. Opposite page: interior page from "Codename Nemesis."

120 the history of the illustrated 007

Published: James Bond, Agent 007 #3 in 1983 as "Kodnamn Nemesis"

Source: Original story

Plot Summary: Bond is assigned to investigae two highly placed traitors, one a known KGB mole and the other a neo-Nazi, before they are assassinated. The investigation turns out to be more complex than originally thought, especially when the chief assassination suspect turns out to be Felix Leiter.

Notes: One of the more complex Bond stories with a lot of espionage elements thrown in. The second half of the story reads more like an outline than a finished script and leaves you wondering if writer Jack Sutter tried to cram too much story into the 24 pages he had available.

Translations

Denmark
- James Bond #3 (1983)—"Kodenavn Nemesis"

Finland
- James Bond, Agent 007 #3 (1983)—"Koodinimi Nemesis"

Holland
- James Bond #1 (1984) – "Codenaam Nemesis"

Norway
- Agent 007 - James Bond #7 (1983)—"Kodenavn Nemesis"
- James Bond #4 (1991)—"Kodenavn Nemesis"

Spain
- James Bond #3 (1985)—"Juicio Final"

OPERATION: BURMA

COMIC BOOK

Sweden

Type: Semic comic story
Writer: Jack Sutter
Artist: Juan Sarompas

Published: James Bond, Agent 007 #6 in 1983 as "Operation Burma"
Source: Original story

Plot Summary: Bond is sent to Burma to investigate the double murder of a KGB agent and the female British agent assigned to watch him.

Notes: Once again writer Jack Sutter appears to have pacing problems with a lot of plot points crammed into the last few pages.

Translations

Denmark
James Bond #4 (1984)—"Operation Burma"

Holland
James Bond #3 (1984)—"Operatie Birma"

Norway
Agent 007—James Bond #7 (1984)—"Operasjon Burma"

LIQUIDATE BOND

COMIC BOOK

Sweden

Type: Semic comic story
Writer: Jack Sutter
Artist: Josep Gaul

Published: James Bond, Agent 007 # 7 in 1983 as "Likvidera Bond!"

Source: Original story

Plot Summary: Bond is sent to capture the insane 002 who, after being captured and tortured by the enemy, is now on the run threatening to kill those he believed betrayed him.

Notes: A different Bond tale with a good solid premise, unfortunately it suffers from a weak middle act. Some of the sequences echo parts of the *GoldenEye* and *Die Another Day* movies.

Translations

Denmark
- James Bond #5 (1984)—"Likvidér Bond"

Finland
- James Bond, Agent #4 (1984)—"Tappakaa Bond!"

THE WHITE DEATH

COMIC BOOK

Sweden

Type: Semic comic story
Writer: Sverre Årnes
Artist: Juan Sarompas

Published: James Bond, Agent 007 #8 in 1983 as "Den vita döden"

Source: Original story

Plot Summary: Bond is sent out to investigate an aid hospital located on "The River of Death" in the Brazilian rain forest, as the head doctor is suspected of being an ex-SS officer.

Notes: Despite a strong opening that hints at greater peril, this quickly turns into a predictable by the numbers Bond story. No mention is made of the fact that Bond previously visited *The River of Death* in that eponymously titled comic strip.

Translations

Denmark
- James Bond #6 (1984)—"Den hvide død"

Norway
- Agent 007—James Bond #3 (1984)—"Den hvite døden"

FLITTERMOUSE

NEWSPAPER STRIP

Type: *Daily Star* newspaper comic strip
Writer: Jim Lawrence
Artist: John McLusky

Published: Appeared in the *Daily Star* between 9th February 1983 and 20th May 1983 (Series #5, strips 553-624)

Source: Original story

Plot Summary: Two people who try and sell the same intelligence report to MI6 are murdered using vampire bats. Amazingly, Bond manages to deduce from this that Dr. Cat (from *River of Death*) has returned. Bond and Suzie Kew fall into an ambush at Dr. Cat's headquarters. Cat orders the captured Bond to strip but Bond manages to shoot him with a gun concealed in the medallion he is wearing around his neck!

Notes: Bond a medallion man? Once again Lawrence veers off into tired territory of humans using controlled animals to kill, amazing logic jumps by Bond during investigations and the escape from the impossible trap ending.

English Reprints
"Flittermouse" has yet to be reprinted in English.

Roemer- und Pelizaeus-Museum Hildesheim

James Bond. Die Welt des 007 · 19. Juni - 18. Oktober 1998

Translations

Finland
- James Bond, Agent 007 #2 (1984)—"Vampyyrien valtias"

Norway
- Agent 007—James Bond #5 (1984)—"Vampyrenes herskere"

Sweden
- James Bond, Agent 007 #1 (1984)—"Vampyrernas härskare"

Above: poster from the 1998 German Hildesheim Museum James Bond exhibit.

POLESTAR

NEWSPAPER STRIP

Type: *Daily Star* newspaper comic strip
Writer: Jim Lawrence
Artist: John McLusky

Published: Appeared in the *Daily Star* between 23rd May 1983 and 15th July 1983 (Series #5, strips 625-719)

Source: Original story

Plot Summary: Strange deaths and mysterious missile interceptions lead Bond to the North Pole and the Polestar

123 **The Missions**

scientific outpost. Bond infiltrates the post by posing as a renegade rocket engineer, but has to break cover when his companion is threatened.

Notes: This story has the dubious honor of being the last James Bond newspaper strip published in the UK. It was stopped abruptly mid—story at strip # 673, just as Bond reached the Polestar camp, bringing to an end twenty five years of Bond.

English Reprints

"Polestar" has yet to be reprinted in the English language.

Translations

Finland

- James Bond, Agent 007 #6 (1984)—"Operaatio Alaska Star"

Norway

- James Bond #8 (1984)—"Operasjon Alaska Star"

Sweden

- James Bond, Agent 007 #4 (1984)—"Operation Alaska Star"

THE SCENT OF DANGER

NEWSPAPER STRIP

Type: Newspaper comic strip
Writer: Jim Lawrence
Artist: John McLusky

Published: Although completed this strip was never published in the UK. (Series #5, strips 720-821)

Source: Original story

Plot Summary: No information available.

English Reprints

"The Scent of Danger" has yet to be published in the English language.

Translations
Finland

- James Bond #3 (1985)—"Kuoleman tuoksu"

Norway

- James Bond #3 (1985)—"En duft av død"

Sweden

- James Bond, Agent 007 #7 (1984)—"En doft av död"
- James Bond, Agent 007 #1 (1995)"En doft av död"

SNAKE GODDESS

NEWSPAPER STRIP

Type: Newspaper comic strip
Writer: Jim Lawrence
Artist: Yaroslav Horak

Published: Although completed this strip was never published in the UK (Series #5, strips 822-893)

Source: Original story

Plot Summary: A giant snake attacks Moneypenny and a village in Cornwall. Bond's investigations lead him to a girl called Freya who claims to be a reincarnation of the Norse goddess. Freya is in fact being controlled by a villain named Vidyala who plans to use his giant snake to attack the British Navy.

English Reprints
"Snake Goddess" has yet to be published in the English language.

Translations
Finland

- James Bond, Agent 007 #12 (1992)—"Maailmanloppu"

Norway

- James Bond #8 (1985)—"Operasjon Ragnarokk"

Sweden

- James Bond, Agent 007 #2 (1985)—"Operation Ragnarök"
- James Bond, Agent 007 #4 (1992)—"Operation Ragnarök"

DOUBLE EAGLE

NEWSPAPER STRIP

Type: Newspaper comic strip
Writer: Jim Lawrence

Artist: Yaroslav Horak

Published: Although completed this strip was never published in the UK. (Series #5, strips 894-965).

Source: Original story

Plot Summary: no information.

Notes: This was the final James Bond newspaper strip produced for the Express group of newspapers.

English Reprints
"Double Eagle" has yet to be published in the English language.

Translations

Norway
- James Bond #5 (1986)—"Operasjon Dobbelørnen"

Sweden
- James Bond, Agent 007 #8 (1985)—"Operation Dubbelörnen"

DEADLY DUPLICITY

COMIC BOOK

Sweden

Type: Semic comic story
Writer: Jack Sutter
Artist: Juan Sarompas

Published: Semic Album #2 in 1984 as "Dödligt dubbelspel"

Source: Original story

Plot Summary: Bond robbed a train in France and Felix Leiter also turns criminal only to apparently be killed when his get away plane crashes. Bond is rescued from prison by a gang of masked men, who turn out to be Leiter and a team of CIA agents. The crimes have been committed by doubles with the aim of getting the two top agents removed from duty. A psychic working with the CIA pinpoints the mastermind behind the plan as the mysterious Chan, who she claims is planning to destroy the world from his base on Mars!

Notes: Simply one of the most absurd Bond stories ever written. For some reason it was allocated twice the usual number of pages and published as a special "album."

Translations

Denmark
- James Bond Årsalbum (Album) 1985 – "Dødelig dobbeltspill"

Finland
- James Bond Album 1984—"Tappava juoni"

OPERATION: LITTLE

COMIC BOOK

Sweden

Type: Semic comic story
Writer: Jack Sutter
Artist: Juan Sarompas

Published: James Bond, Agent 007 #2 (1984) as "Operation Little"

Source: Original story

Plot Summary Bond is sent out to prevent the murder of the world's greatest assassin, known only as "Little." Little turns out to be a dwarf who lives in a Swiss castle and drives around on a toy train while using other remote control deadly toys to kill intruders.

Notes: The idea of a child like assassin using deadly toys isn't new (in fact one was mentioned in *The Living Daylights* movie), and neither is the concept of delivering the fatal blow via radio control. But this has to be one of the worst interpretations of the concept.

Swedish Reprint
James Bond #4 (1994).

Translations

Finland
- James Bond #5 (1984)—"Operaatio Little"

the history of the illustrated 007

THE MAD EMPEROR

COMIC BOOK

Sweden

Type: Semic comic story
Writer: Peter Sparring
Artist: Josep Gaul

Published: James Bond #3 (1984) as "Den galne kejsaren"

Source: Original story

Plot Summary: While in Nassau on vacation Bond is drugged and tricked into being beholden to a voodoo leader who calls himself "Emperor" Henry Christophe II. The "Emperor" wants Bond to assassinate the leader of Varadero, a political rival, so he can create a United States of the Caribbean. However there is another hand at work, the "Emperor" is controlled by an Argentinean general who wants Bond to get caught in the act so that it will discredit the British government.

Notes: This story is obviously influenced by the then-recent conflict between Britain and Argentina over the Falkland Islands. For some reason the location of Cuba was replaced by the fictitious country of Varadero, yet all other locations and countries are correctly name checked.

Translations

Finland
- James Bond, Agent 007 #3 (1984) –"Hullu keisari"

Norway
- Agent 007—James Bond #6 (1984) –"Den gale keiseren"

OPERATION: JUGGERNAUT

COMIC BOOK

Sweden

Type: Semic comic story
Writer: Jack Sutter
Artist: Juan Sarompas

Published: James Bond, Agent 007 #5 (1984) as "Operation Juggernaut"

Source: Original story

Plot Summary: While in America on the trail of a missing female Secret Service agent, Bond is pursued by a group of seemingly bullet proof soldiers. The pursuit continues until Bond takes refuge in a submarine. The submarine turns out to be a SPECTRE trap and the female agent and the soldiers are revealed as robots. Bond is rescued from the submarine by Felix Leiter and the two join up, once again, to prevent SPECTRE and its robot army from taking over the world.

Notes: This reads more like an Austin Powers story than a James Bond one. In one scene Bond and Leiter track down Blofeld by asking his address from a realtor who specializes in selling secret lairs to super villains! The artist was wrongly credited as Josep Gual in some printings.

Opposite page: U.S. 27 x 41 inch movie poster from *Never Say Never Again*, 1983. **Below:** first edition dustjacket for *Octopussy and The Living Daylights*.

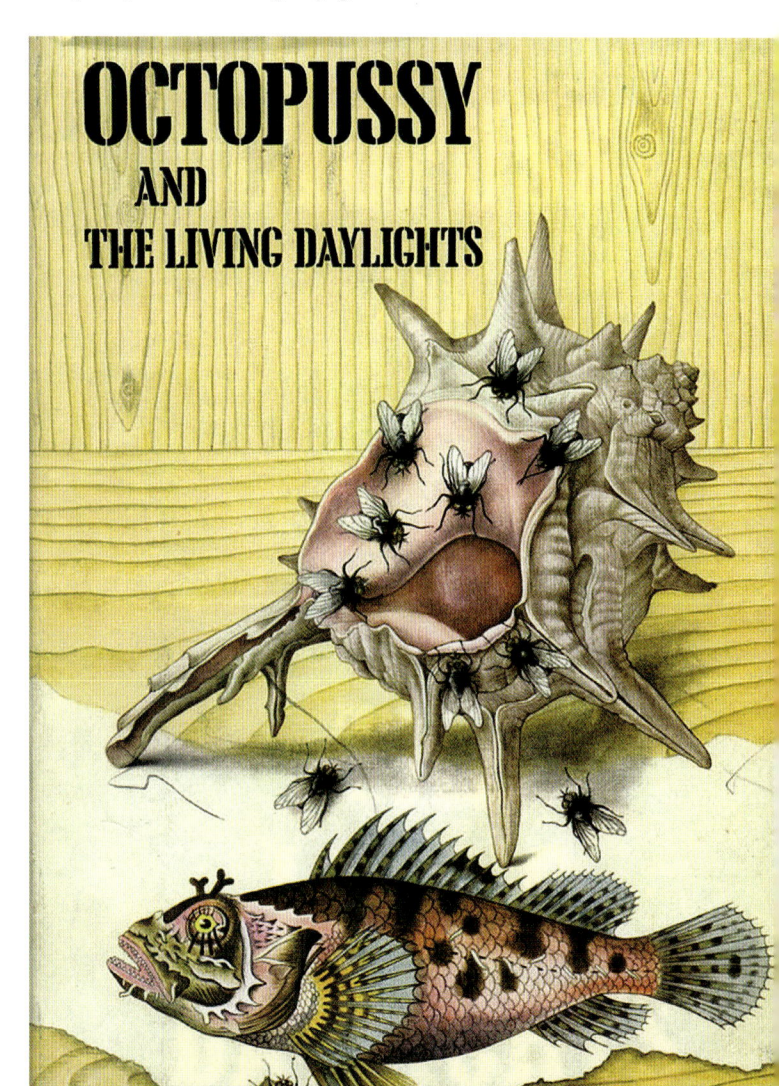

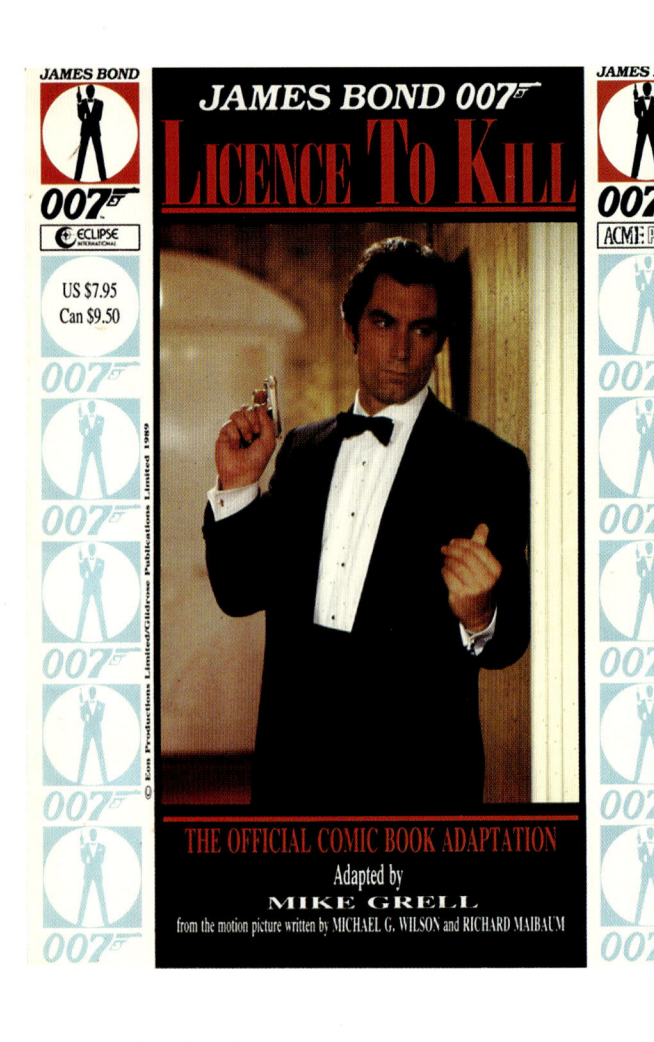

Swedish Reprints

James Bond, Agent 007 #1 (1995)

Translations

Norway
- James Bond #2 (1985)—"Operasjon Juggernaut"

OPERATION: UFO

COMIC BOOK

Sweden

Type: Semic comic story
Writer: Jack Sutter
Artist: Josep Gual

Published in James Bond, Agent 007 #6 (1984) as "Operation UFO"

Source: Original story

Plot Summary: After a series of mysterious flying saucer abductions, Bond goes undercover as "Professor Bond," and is soon kidnapped himself. 007 wakes up apparently on the moon and learns that he has been taken by a race called the Deokans who need the missing scientists to repair their mother ship so that they can continue on their way.

Notes: Apart from the patent absurdity of it all, the main problem with this story is that its inevitable conclusion is obvious right from the start. It's all a hoax, and it's so obvious that there is no tension in the script.

Swedish Reprint
James Bond, Agent 007 #4 (1994)

Translations

Holland
- James Bond #8 (1985)—"Operatie UFO."

Norway
- James Bond #1 (1985)—"Operasjon UFO"

OPERATION: BLUCHAR

COMIC BOOK

Sweden

Type: Semic comic story
Writer: Sverre Arnes
Artist: Josep Gual

Published in James Bond, Agent 007 #8 (1984) as "Operation Blücher"

Source: Original story

Plot Summary: A sunken World War II era German cruiser becomes the scene of a stand off between a group of British neo-Nazis and the Norwegian government. The neo-Nazis are after the gold bars they believe are on board and threaten to blow up the ship's oil tanks and pollute the waters if the authorities interfere.

Above: cover to the Eclipse Comics "Licence to Kill" movie adaptaton, 1989. Opposite page: U.S. 27 x 41 inch advance movie poster for *License to Kill*, 1989.

Notes: This is not a James Bond story. Bond is shoe horned into what was obviously an existing script by Norwegian writer Sverre Arnes. The fact that a movie called Blucher, written by Arnes, was later made in Norway seems to confirm that suspicion. The writer is wrongly credited as Jack Sutter, in some versions.

Translations

Finland
- James Bond, Agent 007 #4 (1985)—"Operaatio Blücher"

Hungary
- James Bond #2 (1989)—"A "Blücher" akció"

Norway
- James Bond #4 (1985)—"Operasjon Blücher."

Russia
- James Bond #2 (1994)—title?

NEVER SAY NEVER AGAIN

MOVIE ADAPTATION

Argentina

Type: Movie Adaptation - Color
Writer: unknown
Artist: unknown

Originally Published: D'artagnan Color #38 (April 1984) as "Nunca Digas Nunca Jamas"

Notes: Fittingly the last of the unofficial Argentinian movie adaptations is based on the "unofficial" Sean Connery *Thunderball* remake.

CODENAME: ROMEO

COMIC BOOK

Sweden

Type: Semic comic story
Writer: Sverre Arnes
Artist: Josep Gual

Published in James Bond, Agent 007 #1 (1985) as "Kodnamn Romeo"

Source: Original story

Plot Summary: When the head of the CIA visits London, Bond is assigned to track down a group of would-be assassins who use a radio controlled bomb called "Romeo" that is designed to home in on a small transmitter code named "Julia"(sic).

Notes: A generic action story that doesn't really need James Bond in it to make it work.

Translations

Hungary
- James Bond #3 (1989) –"Fedöneve: Rómeó"

Norway
- James Bond #5 (1985) –"Kodenavn Romeo"

THE GREEN DEATH

COMIC BOOK

Sweden

Type: Semic comic story
Writer: Jack Sutter
Artist: Juan Sarompas

Published in James Bond #3 (1985) as "Den gröna döden"

Source: Original story

Plot Summary: In order to make themselves look young, the rich and powerful are flocking to a mysterious island in the Caribbean. The payment for their revitalized youth is that they must share their secrets to the island's owner, the mysterious Domonique. Bond is sent to the island to charm Domonique, which he naturally does. Dominque then tells him of her plans to develop an army of super plants that will attack only men.

Notes: Another story that reads more like a parody than a straight James Bond adventure.

Swedish Reprint
James Bond, Agent 007 #2 (1995)

Translations

Finland
- James Bond, Agent 007 #5 (1985)—"Vihreä koulema"

Hungary
- James Bond #4 (1990)—"Zöld halal."

Norway
- James Bond #6 (1985)—"Den grønne døden"

DEATH IN TAHITI

COMIC BOOK

Sweden

Type: Semic comic story
Writer: Sverre Arnes
Artist: Juan Sarompas

Published in James Bond, Agent 007 #4 (1985) as "Döden på Tahiti"

Source: Original story

Plot Summary: A French cruise ship is hijacked by pirates who plant bombs on board and demand a ransom. When it is discovered that one of the passengers is a former Secret Service agent Bond is dispatched to effect a rescue.

Notes: Even Bond himself can see the flaws in this story as in the opening scenes he tells M that anyone could have done the mission. And he's right, this is another generic action hero plot with Bond squeezed in.

Opposite page left: cover to Issue #1 of the Eclipse Comics series *Permission to Die*, 1991, the first original Bond story created for the US Market, art by Mike Grell. Right: cover to Issue #2 of the Eclipse Comics series *Permission to Die*, 1991, art by Mike Grell. This page, right: cover to Issue #3 of the Eclipse Comics series *Permission to Die*, 1991, art by Mike Grell.

Swedish Reprint
James Bond, Agent 007 #3 (1996)

Translations

Finland
- James Bond, Agent 007 #6 (1985)—"Kouleman Tahiti

Hungary
- James Bond #5 (1990)—"Halal Tahitin"

Norway

- James Bond #1 (1986)—"Døden på Tahiti"

THE BRIDE FROM BALKAN

COMIC BOOK

Sweden

Type: Semic comic story
Writer: Bill Harrington
Artist: Josep Gual

Published in James Bond, Agent 007 #6 (1985) as "Bruden från Balkan"

Source: Original story

Plot Summary: Bond is sent to protect the British Ambassador to Bosnovia during the upcoming wedding of that country's crown princess to a playboy arms dealer. Once in Bosnovia Bond uncovers a plot involving the KGB and a criminal organization known as "The Black Hand."

Notes: Bond is the focus for this story and most of it revolves around his actions and deductions. The result is a fairly strong spy thriller.

Swedish Reprint
James Bond, Agent 007 #4 (1995)

Translations

Norway

- James Bond #3 (1986)—"Bruden fra Balkan"

CHINESE PUZZLE

COMIC BOOK

Sweden
Type: Semic comic story
Writer: Bill Harrington
Artist: Juan Sarompas
Published in James Bond, Agent 007 #7 (1985) as "Kinesiskt pussel"

Source: Original story

Plot Summary: Bond is sent to the Han-Su province in China where it turns out that a scientist is creating an army of humanoid robot warriors.

Notes: More robots!

Translations

Hungary
- James Bond #6 (1990)—"Kínai kirakós játék."

Norway
- James Bond #4 (1986)—"Kinesisk eske"

DATA TERROR

COMIC BOOK

Sweden

Type: Semic comic story
Writer: Sverre Arnes
Artist: Juan Sarompas
Published in James Bond, Agent 007 #1 (1986) as "Data Terror"

Source: Original story

Plot Summary: Numerous British companies suddenly find that all their computers have been wiped clean of information. Thinking that it might be foreign backed financial or industrial espionage, M assigns Bond to uncover the truth. The culprit is revealed as Billy Braxton, a crooked computer expert who has developed small "magnetic bombs."

Notes: A fairly well written detective story with a series of clues leading to a reasonable conclusion. The only problem is that James Bond isn't a detective. The idea of using magnetic pulses to destroy computer information was later used in the Pierce Brosnan movie *GoldenEye*.

Swedish Reprint
James Bond, Agent 007 #1 (1996)

Translations

Norway
- James Bond #6 (1986)—"Dataterror"

EXPERIMENT Z

COMIC BOOK

Sweden

Type: Semic comic story
Writer: Bill Harrington
Artist: Manuel Carmona

Published in James Bond #3 (1986) as "Eksperiment Z"

Source: Original story

Plot Summary: Bond is teamed up with a female agent from the Israeli Secret Service and sent to Brazil to investigate something known only as "Codename Z." They find an experimental hospital run by ex-Nazis who are implanting brain tissue, in the hope that it will grow and eventually take over the host's body. Bond is captured and the Nazi surgeons plan on implanting some of Adolf Hitler's brain tissue into 007!

Notes: The idea of Bond working alongside Israeli agent holds a lot of promise, but the plot quickly degenerates into farce. Bond does little except wait for the bad guys to reveal all via expository dialog. The idea of a secret Nazi run hospital deep in the Amazon jungles is overworked by this point having been featured in at least two other stories. New artist Manuel Carmona seems unsure of how to draw Bond as his rendering of Bond's features varies throughout.

Above: interior page from "Experiment Z," art by Manuel Carmona, 1986.

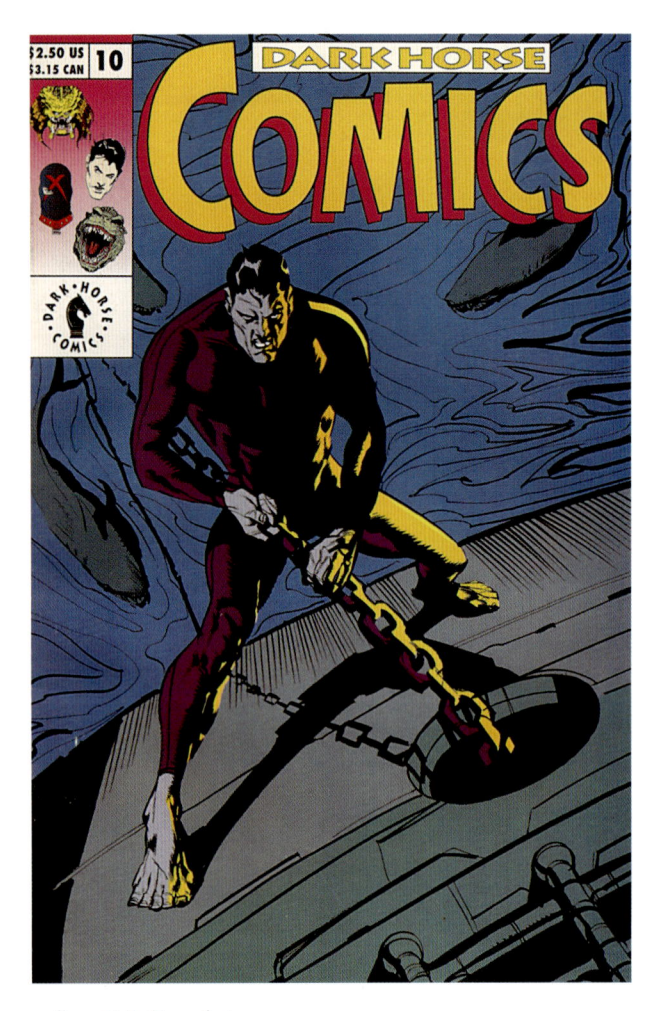

Swedish Reprints

James Bond, Agent 007 #32 (1994)

Translations

Norway

- James Bond #8 (1986) – "Eksperiment Z"

DEATH IN FLORENCE

COMIC BOOK

Sweden

Type: Semic comic story
Writer: Bill Harrington
Artist: Manuel Carmona

Published in James Bond, Agent 007 #5 (1986) as "Döden i Florens"

Source: Original story

Plot Summary: An undercover KGB agent wishes to defect and Bond is sent to Florence to contact the agent through his Italian actress girlfriend. Just after Bond arrives the KGB agent's body is found floating in the river and the microfilm of secrets that had been promised to the Secret Service is missing.

Notes: One of the better Semic stories that with a stronger ending could read something like a Fleming short story. Artist Carmona seems to have decided on what his Bond actually looks like.

Translations

Norway

- James Bond #2 (1987)—"Døden i Firenze"

DEADLY DOUBLE

COMIC BOOK

Sweden

Type: Semic comic story
Writer: Jack Sutter
Artist: Juan Sarompas

Published in James Bond, Agent 007 #7 (1986) as "Dödlig dubbelgångare"

Source: Original story

Plot Summary: The body of 009 is found in the middle of the Amazon. He is carrying a camera on which are photos of mutated animals and humans. Satellite imaging also shows a high level of radiation in the area. Bond is sent to investigate and discovers not only a "lost world" complete with a tribe of beautiful women, but an evil madman known as Faust.

Notes: Another Jack Sutter story that wanders firmly into the area of parody with every possible cliché thrown in to the mix to pad out a weak plot.

Swedish Reprint

James Bond, Agent 007 #4 (1996)

Translations

Denmark

- Agent X-9 #111 (1988)—"Dødsens farlig dobbeltgænger"

Norway

- James Bond, Agent 007 #4 (1987)—"Dødelig dobbeltgjenger"

GREEK FIRE

COMIC BOOK

Sweden

Type: Semic comic story
Writer: Bill Harrington
Artist: Manuel Carmona

Published in James Bond, Agent 007 #10 (1986) as "Greek Fire"

Source: Original story
Plot Summary: A bitter dispute with his main rival has almost bankrupted Greek shipping magnate Dimitri Kimopolous when the KGB make him an offer. They will ensure he wins a major Russian naval contract on condition that he hires James Bond as his new bodyguard and then frames Bond for the murder of his rival.

Notes: A return to some basic espionage and thriller type elements, but the basic premise is thin and doesn't really need James Bond to make it work.

Opposite page: cover from *Dark Horse Comics* #10, "Light of My Death," 1993. Below: detail of James Bond from the cover of *Dark Horse Comics* #11, art by Arthur Adams, 1993.

to be hanged. During the escape they seem to employ every type of special vehicle in the Q-branch arsenal. Once rescued, the math genius is launched into space to join an experimental community on board a space station. The story then shifts to an American prison where the evil mastermind Chan (previously seen in Deadly Duplicity) is being held. But according to the CIA's psychic specialist only his body is imprisoned, his mind is floating free "doing evil things." Chan's body is rescued from prison by a gang of mercanaries. He then proceeds to unleash his army of Dominique clones to rescue the real Dominique (from "The Green Death") as she is necessary to complete his plan to conquer the Earth.

Enter James Bond who after fighting dinosaurs, flying helicopters through underground tunnels and many other absurd things, manages to convince Chan that he has a small nuclear device implanted in his body and that it will go off if he is killed.

Notes: While some of Sutter's other scripts were tolerable as super-spy parody this one is simply almost unreadable. It is probably the candidate for the title of the worst James Bond story ever written. You have to wonder how, and why, this was ever approved by the Semic editorial team, or the Bond license holders. And it gets the full 48-page special album treatment! Just to add to the whole surreal nature of this story, the Millennium Falcon (yes, from *Star Wars*) even makes a brief cameo appearance.

Translations

Norwa

- James Bond #2 (1993)—"Siste par ut"

KILLING MUSIC

COMIC BOOK

Sweden

Type: Semic comic story
Writer: Bill Harrington
Artist: Manual Carmona

Published in James Bond, Agent 007 #1 (1987) as "Mördande musik"

Source: Original story

Plot Summary: Bond is sent to Amsterdam to meet a courier who is carrying Soviet submarine plans. Before they can meet the courier is murdered by a giant with a

---

Translations

Norway

- James Bond #5 (1987)—"Gresk ild"

LAST PAIR OUT

COMIC BOOK

Sweden

Type: Semic comic story
Writer: Jack Sutter
Artist: Juan Sarompas

Published in Semic Album #4 (1986) as "Sista paret ut

Source: Original story

Plot Summary: Bond rescues a math genius from the clutches of an unnamed Arab country where he is about

Right: Cover to *Dark Horse Comics* #25 which included "Minute of Midnight," art by Russ Heath. Opposite page: original artwork from "Minute of Midnight," Russ Heath, pencils and inks.

136 the history of the illustrated 007

TITLE: JAMES BOND
ISSUE/MONTH: PART 1
PAGE 6
ONE HOUR LATER:
UNITED PRODUCE COMPANY
WHAT DO YOU WANT? HOW DID YOU GET PAST THE SECURITY GUARD IN THE LOB--
UNDER-COVER.
THE NAME IS BOND...
JAMES BOND.
SO I SEE... AND I'M SHADOW BREIGHT.
REALLY? THEN YOUR PARENTS HAD A--
VERY GOOD TIME IN THE SIXTIES... BUT AT LEAST THEY DIDN'T NAME ME "SUNSHINE" OR "MOONBEAM."
PERHAPS WE COULD--
MR. SYKES IS WAITING FOR YOU, MR. BOND-- THIRD DOOR ON THE LEFT.
AND MORE'S THE PITY, BRIGHT SHADOW.

steel claw instead of a right hand. After chasing off the giant Bond finds the plans missing and an empty music box which seems to be a clue. The police arrive and arrest Bond for the murder, but the next day he is sprung by M who sends him to hunt down the missing plans and the clawed giant.

Notes: A fairly standard espionage tale that seems to make some references to a couple of the Bond movies, *Live and Let Die* (tall steel clawed villain) and *Octopussy* (chasing a precious object stolen at auction).

<u>Translations</u>

Norway

- James Bond #6 (1987)—"Drepende musikk"

THE SPY TRAP

COMIC BOOK

Sweden

Type: Semic comic story
Writer: Jack Sutter
Artist: Juan Sarompas

Published in James Bond #2 (1987) as "Spionfällan"

Source: Original story

Plot Summary: Bond is sent out to track down a piece of film footage which is reported to reveal the identity of the KGB's latest "super spy." Of course Bond must contend with his mysterious counterpart who is also trying to recover the film. Of course the super spy turns out to be the last person Bond was expecting—his current girl friend.

Notes: A somewhat subdued script from Jack Sutter, but he still manages to squeeze in multiple chase scenes as the two spies race across Europe in their quest.

<u>Translations</u>

Norway
- James Bond #8 (1987)—"Spionfellen"

THE AMAZONS

COMIC BOOK

Sweden

Type: Semic comic story
Writer: Bill Harrington
Artist: Josep Gual

Published in James Bond, Agent 007 #3 (1987) as "Amazonerna"

Source: Original story

Plot Summary: After concerns are raised that the KGB has infiltrated a peace camp in front of a British based USAF air station, Bond is dispatched to uncover the truth.

Swedish Reprint
James Bond, Agent 007 #4 (1995)

Translations

Norway

- James Bond #1 (1988)—"Amazonene"

DEADLY SAND

COMIC BOOK

Sweden

Type: Semic comic story
Writer: Bill Harrington
Artist: Juan Sarompas

Published in James Bond, Agent 007 #4 (1987) as "Dödande sand"

Source: Original story

Opposite page: pencil illustration by Mike Grell of his version of James Bond. Above: interior page artwork from "The Immortals," from *James Bond, Agent 007* #10, 1987, Semic, art by Martin Salvador.

Plot Summary: no information.

Swedish Reprint
James Bond, Agent 007 #3 (1994)

Translations

Norway

- James Bond #3 (1988)—"Dødelig sand"

TERROR TIME

COMIC BOOK

Sweden

Type: Semic comic story
Writer: Bill Harrington
Artist: Manual Carmona

Published in James Bond, Agent 007 #5 (1987) as "Tid för terror"

Source: Original story

Plot Summary: A terrorist group is using a sequence of art forgeries to finance their operations. Bond is called in after an ambassador is killed during the opening night of an art show featuring the forgeries.

Swedish Reprint
James Bond, Agent 007 #3 (1994)

Translations

Norway

- James Bond #5 (1988)—"Tid for terror"

THE THIRTEENTH JUDGE

COMIC BOOK

Sweden

Type: Semic comic story
Writer: Bill Harrington
Artist: Josep Gual

Published in James Bond, Agent 007 #6 (1987) as "Den trettonde domaren"

139   The Missions

Source: Original story

Plot Summary: When a British judge becomes the latest judge to disappear under mysterious circumstances, Bond is called in to uncover the truth.

Translations

Norway

- James Bond #7 (1988)—"Den 13. dommeren"

ESCAPE FROM VIETNAM

COMIC BOOK

Sweden

Type: Semic comic story
Writer: Bill Harrington
Artist: Manual Carmona

Published in James Bond, Agent 007 #9 (1987) as "Flykten från Vietnam"

Source: Original story

Plot Summary: While on assignment in Singapore searching for a missing agent, Bond becomes involved with a group of Vietnamese boat people.

Translations

Norway

- James Bond #8 (1988)—"Flukten fra Vietnam"

THE IMMORTALS

COMIC BOOK

Sweden

Type: Semic comic story
Writer: Bill Harrington
Artist: Martin Salvador

Published in James Bond, Agent 007 #10 (1987) as "De odödliga"

Source: Original story

Plot Summary: no information.

Swedish Reprint
James Bond, Agent 007 #1 (1996)

Translations

Norway

- James Bond #1 (1989)—"De udødelige"

ISTANBUL INTRIGUE

COMIC BOOK

Sweden

Type: Semic comic story
Writer: Bill Harrington
Artist: Manuel Carmona

Published in James Bond, Agent 007 #11 (1987) as "Intrig i Istanbul"

Source: Original story

Plot Summary: no information.

Translations
Norway

- James Bond #2 (1989)—"Intrige i Istanbul"

CUBA COMMANDOES

COMIC BOOK

Sweden

Type: Semic comic story
Writer: Jack Sutter
Artist: Juan Sarompas

Published in James Bond, Agent 007 #1 (1988) as "Kommando Kuba"

Source: Original story

Plot Summary: Bond is interrupted during a Caribbean vacation by the CIA who want his help tracking down three US soldiers who have gone missing in Cuba.

Swedish Reprint
James Bond, Agent 007 #2 (1995)

Translations

Denmark

- Agent X-9 #125 (1989)—"Cuba affæren"

Norway

- James Bond #3 (1989)—"Kommando Cuba"

LETHAL DOSE

COMIC BOOK

Sweden

Type: Semic comic story
Writer: Sverre Arnes
Artist: Josep Gual

Published in James Bond, Agent 007 #2 (1988) as "Dödlig dos"

Source: Original story

Plot Summary: After a number of retired agents die under mysterious circumstances, Bond visits a health clinic that seems to connect them all. Despite being framed for the murder of a nurse, he manages to stop plans to surgically implant a bomb in the chest of another ex-agent.

Swedish Reprint
James Bond, Agent 007 #4 (1996)

Translations
Denmark
- Agent X-9 #119 (1988)—"Dødelig Dosis"
Norway

- James Bond #5 (1989)—"Dødelig dose"

WITH DEATH IN SIGHT

COMIC BOOK

Sweden

Type: Semic comic story
Writer: Bill Harrington
Artist: Manuel Carmona

Published in James Bond, Agent 007 #4 (1988) as "Med döden i sikte"

Source: Original story

Plot Summary: Bond must cross Europe and get some stolen Soviet plans back to London while avoiding various traps and ambushes on the way.

Notes: This whole story is really nothing but one long chase sequence.

Translations
Denmark
- Agent X-9 #122 (1988)—"Med Døden i sigte"
Norway

- James Bond #6 (1989)—"Med døden i sigte"

ROBO-KILLER

COMIC BOOK

Sweden

Type: Semic comic story
Writer: Jack Sutter
Artist: Juan Sarompas

Published in James Bond, Agent 007 #7 (1988) as "Robo-Killer"

Source: Original story

Plot Summary: no information.

Translations

Denmark
- Agent X-9 #132 (1990)—"Robo-Killer"
Norway

- James Bond #3 (1990)—"Robo-Killer"

DANSE MACABRE

COMIC BOOK

Sweden

Type: Semic comic story
Writer: Bill Harrington
Artist: Josep Gual

142 the history of the illustrated 007

Published in James Bond, Agent 007 #8 (1988) as "Danse Macabre"

Source: Original story.

Plot Summary: no information

Translations

Norway

- James Bond #7 (1989)—"Dance Macabre"

OPERATION: UBOKI

COMIC BOOK

Sweden

Type: Semic comic story
Writer: Bill Harrington
Artist: Josep Gual

Published in James Bond, Agent 007 #11 (1988) as "Operation Uboki"

Source: Original story

Plot Summary: Bond and M become entangled in the political affairs of the African nation of Uboki.

Translations

Norway

- James Bond #8 (1989)—"Operasjon Uboki"

THE LIVING DEAD

COMIC BOOK

Sweden

Type: Semic comic story
Writer: Jack Sutter
Artist: Juan Sarompas

Published in James Bond, Agent 007 #12 (1988) as "Levande död"

Opposite page: interior page from *Permission to Die* #1, Art by Mike Grell, 1991.

Source: Original story

Plot Summary: In Thailand with orders to assassinate a drug lord, Bond is stunned to discover that the man's mistress is a Russian spy Bond had seen killed in West Berlin. The truth behind the spy's apparent resurrection from the dead forces M to dispatch Bond to the USA—with orders to assassinate the President!

Notes: The story also suffers from pacing issues, in particular in the execution of the Bond vs The President final act.

Translations

Norway

- James Bond #7 (1990)—"Levende død"

LICENCE TO KILL

MOVIE ADAPTATION

USA

Type: Movie Adaptation
Writer: Richard Ashford
Artists: Mike Grell (Breakdowns), Chuck Austen, Tom Yates, Stan Woch

Published in Licence To Kill (Eclpise Comics) — 1989

Source: Based on the 1989 Timothy Dalton movie *Licence To Kill*

Plot Summary: On the way to Felix Leiter's wedding, Bond and Leiter are diverted to participate in the arrest of drug dealer Sanchez. Later that day Sanchez is rescued while Sanchez's men kidnapped Leiter and kill his new wife. Leiter is fed to a shark and his maimed body dumped back at his house where it is later discovered by Bond. Bond sets out on a journey of personal revenge. M orders him to leave it to the local authorities and assigns Bond to a mission in Istanbul. Bond refuses, resigns and goes on the run.

Bond finds his way to the Republic of Isthmus where he works his way into Sanchez's employment by posing as a rogue agent and assassin looking for work. In Isthmus Bond uncovers that Sanchez is controlling the country through a puppet dictator and using a tele-evangelist and his cult as a front to manufacture and distribute drugs. Sanchez has also managed to obtain some stinger missiles and is threatening to shoot down an American airliner if the US Drug Enforcement Agency keep going after him. At the drug processing plant Bond manages to start a fire which quickly spreads. He escapes in a fuel tanker being used to carry the drugs and eventually crashes Sanchez off the road. Bond sets the gasoline soaked Sanchez alight with a lighter that Felix Leiter had given him for being the best man at his wedding.

Notes: The 1989 Eclipse adaptation of Dalton's debut *License To Kill*, while a fairly faithful adaptation, suffers from two major problems, both unfortunately common to media tie-ins. Firstly, the production was rushed to meet the movie release date so that writer Richard Ashford's tale ended up being handled by four different artists. Mike Grell did the breakdowns while final art chores were divided between Chuck Austen, Tom Yates and Stan Woch. The deadline rush probably also accounts for the fact that the last three pages of the story are rushed and the final scene from the movie is missing altogether. The second problem facing this particular adaptation was that they didn't have permission to use Timothy Dalton's likeness. As a result, Bond's appearance is inconsistent, his facial features changing slightly depending on which artist is drawing any given page.

Translations

Finland

- 007 ja lupa tappaa (1989)

France

- James Bond: Permis De Tuer (1989)

Germany

- James Bond: Lizenz zum Töten (1989)

Holland

- Licence To Kill (1989)

Norway

- James Bond: Med rett til å drepe (1989)

Sweden

- James Bond: Tid För Hämnd (1989)

PERMISSION TO DIE

COMIC BOOK

USA

Type: Comic Book - Eclipse
Writer: Mike Grell
Artists: Mike Grell

Published as a three issue mini-series (Eclpise Comics) —1989 – 1991

Source: Original story

Plot Summary: Erik Widziadlo, a wealthy scientist living in the USA, has offered the British Secret Service the plans to a new cheap system for launching payloads into space. The price: Rescuing his niece from Eastern block Hungary.

This mission falls to James Bond. Traveling to Hungary, Bond teams up with a band of gypsies, one of whom is Kerim Bey's daughter, but can Bond and the gypsies manage to rescue Widziadlo's niece when she is guarded by a whole army?

Notes: *Permission To Die* was a solo effort from writer/artist Mike Grell. The three issue mini-series was hampered by scheduling delays with a two year delay between issues two and three caused by financial problems with the printers. The plot's simple premise ends up as a fairly complex and multi-layered plot that is peppered with references to the Bond movies and the, then current, John Gardner Bond novels.

English Reprints

Reprinted in Trade Paperback in 1991

CODENAME: MR BLUE

COMIC BOOK

Sweden

Type: Semic comic story
Writer: Jack Sutter
Artist: Juan Sarompas

Published in James Bond, Agent 007 #1 (1990) as Kodnamn: Mr. Blue

Source: Original story

Plot Summary: no information.

Translations

Norway

- James Bond #9 (1990)—"Dekknavn: Mr. Blue"

GOODBYE MR. BOND

COMIC BOOK

Sweden

Type: Semic comic story
Writer: Bill Harrington
Artist: Juan Sarompas

Published in James Bond, Agent 007 #5 (1990) as "Farväl, Mr. Bond"

Source: Original story

Plot Summary: An injured Bond is resting at another agent's home when he gets caught up in a plot to replace all the world's top agents with robotic doubles.

Notes: Robots and body doubles! All this needed was an Amazon island with a secret hospital staffed by Nazis and it would have reworked all the Semic clichéd plots into one story.

Translations

Norway

- James Bond #1 (1991)—"Farvel, Mr. Bond"

OPERATION: YAKUZA

COMIC BOOK

Sweden

Type: Semic comic story
Writer: Ian Mennell
Artist: Juan Sarompas

Published in James Bond, Agent 007 #10 (1990) as "Operation Yakuza"

Source: Original story

Plot Summary: no information.

Translations

Norway

- James Bond #5 (1991)—"Operasjon Yakuza"

THE POISON FACTORY

COMIC BOOK

Sweden

Type: Semic comic story
Writer: Ian Mennell
Artist: Juan Sarompas

Published in James Bond, Agent 007 #6 (1991) as "Giftfabriken"

Source: Original story

Plot Summary: no information.

Notes: This story is actually a two-parter, but was printed in a single issue. The second part is titled "The Crawling Death." This is the last original Bond story published by Semic.

SERPENT'S TOOTH

COMIC BOOK

USA

Type: Comic Book - USA - Dark Horse
Writer: Doug Moench
Artists: Paul Gulacy

Published as a three issue mini-series (Dark Horse Comics) - 1992-1993

Source: Original story

Plot Summary: Flying Saucers kidnap a native woman in Peru, a scientist is kidnapped in London and a British nuclear sub is attacked while under the artic ice sheet. 009 is sent to investigate and ends up in Peru where he is killed. Bond is assigned to finish 009's work and recover the missing nuclear missiles from the submarine. All clues seem to lead to a man called Indigo, who looks like a human lizard.

Notes: *Serpent's Tooth* is regarded by some Bond scholars and fans as approaching the level of parody. Moench seems to have thrown in every Bond cliché and it's easy to spot several scenes lifted almost straight from various movies. The sense of the ridiculous is not helped by a plot featuring flying saucers and a bad guy who looks like a human lizard. However Gulacy's distinctive art and his stylized take on the world of Bond make this an interesting interpretation. Despite its flaws for the Bond purist, it is a fun fast paced read and perhaps the slickest looking Bond adventure. Maybe it's for this reason that it is perhaps the most well known, and most widely reprinted, of the various US Bond series.

English Reprints
Reprinted as Trade Paperback in 1994

Translations

Denmark

- James Bond Slangens Liga #1-3 (1995)—Note this is a black & white reprint.

France

- James Bond 007—La Dent du Serpent #1-3 (1995)

Germany

- Ian Fleming's James Bond 007 #1 (1993)— "Der Zahn Der Schlange" (Part 1)

- Ian Fleming's James Bond 007 #2 (1993)— "Blut in Eden" (Part 2)

- Ian Fleming's James Bond 007 #3 (1994)— "Der Fall von Eden" (Part 3)

Italy

- Hyperion—Oddisea Nel Fantastico #6-8 (1993) —title?

Norway

- James Bond #4—6 (1993)—"Slangens hugg del"

Sweden

- James Bond, Agent 007 #3 - 5 (1993)— "Ormens tand"

SILENT ARMAGEDDON

COMIC BOOK

USA

Type: Comic Book—USA—Dark Horse
Writer: Simon Jowett
Artists: John Burns

Planned as a planned four issue mini series in 1993 (Dark Horse Comics)—only the first two issues were published

Source: Original story

Plot Summary: The US Department of Defense computers have been hacked by a system called Omega and had their missile targets altered. Omega is the ultimate computer hacking program and can penetrate any security system. Omega's creators discover that a new artificial intelligence project is being developed that could put an end to Omega. They turn to the criminal organization known as Cerberus for protection. Cerberus attacked the labs where the AI is being developed leaving a teenage girl math genius as the sole survivor. Bond must convince the young teenager to reveal what she knows about the AI project while protecting her from a Cerberus strike team lead by Erik Klebb, the son of Bond's nemesis in *From Russia With Love*, Rosa Klebb.

Dark Horse Comics gave the following description of the events in the unpublished issues 3 and 4 when they were originally solicited:

> # 3 - A deadly computer virus demonstrates its lethal potential through automatic teller machines, hospital equipment, and prison cell locks in New York City. James Bond and Terri are determined to find out whether the Omega computer program is responsible for the mayhem, but the son of an old nemesis is even more determined to see Bond dead!

> #4 - All hell breaks loose as Bond attacks the heart of Cerberus' operation, deep beneath the streets of Hong Kong's Hidden City. He must destroy the ultimate computer virus, OMEGA, before Cerberus can use it to destroy the world. And his only allies are a band of untrustworthy mercenaries and a teenage girl!

> This grittiest Bond adventure yet takes 007 into a new universe of adventure, since to destroy OMEGA he has to face death in the world of Virtual Reality.

Notes: Artist John Burns was well known for illustrating newspaper strips such as *Modesty Blaise* and others that often featured curvaceous women losing various articles of clothing. He had also produced several beautifully rendered TV tie-in strips for various British comics magazines such as *TV-21, Look-In* and *Countdown*. His style seemed ideally suited to the smooth, sophisticated world of Bond. Unfortunately, the series was cancelled after the first two issues with Dark Horse citing a six month delay in art for issue 3 from Burns as the cause. Perhaps the switch from producing a few pages a week for the British style comics to the twenty-plus pages a month demanded by American comics was too much. Looking at the first two issues you can see the reason for the delay in Burn's artwork as each page is a fully painted delight combining Burns excellent panel layouts, deceptively simple inking and trademark color washes. For fans of Burns' art style these two issues are worth looking out for. Black and white images of the planned covers for the missing issues 3 and 4 have emerged online.

Translations

Norway

- X-9 Special #7-8 (1995)—"Dødelig smitte"

LIGHT OF MY DEATH

COMIC BOOK

USA

Type: Comic Book—Dark Horse
Writer: Das Petrou
Artists: John Watkiss

Published in four parts in the anthology title Dark Horse Comics #8-11 (1993)

Source: Original story

Plot Summary: A Secret Service agent is killed while conducting a clandestine meeting on board a cable car in the French Alps. Bond is sent to find the killer and is reunited with new Secret Service employee Tatiana Romanova. The trail leads from France to Hong Kong and finally to Egypt where they come to face with the assassin.

Notes: This is one of the more unusual Bond stories for a variety of reasons. First, it includes the return of a character from the Fleming novels in Tatiana Romanova who featured in *From Russia With Love*. Secondly, this is the only serialized original Bond tale published in the traditional US comic book format. All the other Dark Horse series had been published in the high-gloss square

bound "prestige" format. The story suffers slightly form trying to fit in a globe-trotting adventure with action, romance and a plot twist into such a confined space. Having said that, Petrou manages to weave a compelling, if slightly rushed, tale with plenty of subtle Bond references to keep the observant fans happy. This story is notable for being the only Bond "period piece" in that it is firmly set in 1961 as opposed to the ubiquitous "now" of all other Bond stories, be they movies, novels or comics. This unique Bond story has yet to be collected in a stand alone format, which is a shame as it deserves a wider audience.

Translations

Sweden

- James Bond, Agent 007 #3 (1994)—"Dödligt ljus"

MINUTE OF MIDNIGHT

COMIC BOOK

USA

Type: Comic Book— Dark Horse
Writer: Doug Moench

Above: first edition dustjacket from *You Only Live Twice*.

Artists: Russ Heath

Published in Dark Horse Comnics #25 in 1994

Source: Original story

Plot Summary: A wealthy villain called Lexis has organized a meeting of various terrorist leaders in Washington DC, but unknown to them the meeting has been secretly taped by a homeless bum. The homeless guy is later attacked by a street gang but manages to easily beat them off. The "bum" is, of course, James Bond. On his flight back to the UK, he is gassed and thrown out of the plane but manages to survive and return home intact. On his return M orders Bond to assassinate Lexis.

Notes: Instead of the usual anthology format, this final issue was in "flip book" format with the James Bond story, *Minute Of Midnight*, occupying the back half. The story is presented in three parts although the last scene which sets up a plot to kidnap M suggests that it was designed to run over several more installments across future issues of Dark Horse Comics. But, it was brought to a rapid conclusion with the title's cancellation.

Translations

Norway

- X-9 Special #9 (1995)—"Operasjon Miasme"

SHATTERED HELIX

COMIC BOOK

USA

Type: Comic Book—Dark Horse
Writer: Simon Jowett
Artists: David Jackson, David Lloyd.

Published as a two issue mini series (Dark Horse Comics) in 1994
Source: Original story

Plot Summary: Bond and a detachment of US Marines fail to stop an attack by the criminal organization Cerberus on a bio-dome known as The Ark in Arizona. The aim of the attack was so that Cerberus could kidnap Dr. Philip Boyce, the sole survivor of a secret CIA laboratory located in Antarctica. The laboratory had produced a lethal mutagen that had killed the rest of the scientists working on it. Cerberus need Boyce to find the lab and recover the mutagen for their own plans. Bond and his team of Marines head for Antarctica to stop them.

Notes: A return to the world of Bond for writer Simon Jowett, this time teamed with artists David Lloyd and David Jackson. The two issues of *Shattered Helix* were intended as a direct sequel to the incomplete *Silent Armageddon* but, beyond a few off hand references to events from the unpublished concluding issues, manages to stand alone as a tightly plotted self contained story. The story follows the model of the early Bond novels and movies by making good use of interesting locations to help drive the plot. The fast paced narrative and cinematic art style propel the story forward in an

Left: Bond in action from a page of the Dark Horse Comics series "The Quasimodo Gambit," 1996, art by Gary Caldwell. Opposite page: Below: James Bond in action in the Topps Comics "GoldenEye" movie adaptation, 1996, art by Claude St. Aubin.

HOW MANY SECONDS ELAPSED?
THIRTY? FORTY?
MOVE FAST, 007!
KRAK
KRASH
NOT MUCH OVER TWO MINUTES AND THIS ROOM IS GOING TO BE A TOXIC INFERNO--
--AND THE INCINERATED BODIES WILL BE THE LUCKY ONES!
OUR UMOV IS WRONG. THERE IS ONE FAST EXIT, THE CONVEYOR BELT THAT USUALLY CARRIES CONTAINED DEATH--
--NOW OFFERING LIFE!

entertaining manner that helps you overlook some basic plot holes – such as why Bond would be working with the US marines in the first place.

Translations

Sweden

- James Bond, Agent 007 #4-5 (1995)—"Dödlig smitta"

THE QUASIMODO GAMBIT

COMIC BOOK

USA

Type: Comic Book—Dark Horse
Writer: Don McGregor
Artists: Gary Caldwell

Published as a three issue mini series (Dark Horse Comics) in 1995

Source: Original story

Plot Summary: In Jamacia, Bond gets mixed up in the plans of an ex-mercenary turned religious fanatic and a gang of gun runners.

Notes: The last Dark Horse Bond story. The story is told in a very text heavy style with a lot of information crammed into each panel. The fact that some pages run to 24 panels per page adds to the feeling that perhaps this story would have worked better as a novel than a comic book.

English Reprints
The Quasimodo Gambit was also released in trade paperback format.

GOLDENEYE

MOVIE ADAPTATION

USA

Type: Movie Adaptation
Writer: Don McGregor
Artists: Claude St. Aubin
Published: Originally planned as a three issue series in 1996 (Topps Comics)—only one issue was published

Source: Original story

Plot Summary: The story opens "nine years ago" and shows an attack on a Russian chemical weapons plant by Bond and 006 (Alex Trevelyan) during which 006 is apparently killed and 007 escapes. Nine years later

Bond is in Monaco and witnesses the theft of a new experimental helicopter that is later used in an attack on the weapons bunker that controls the space weapon known as GoldenEye. Bond flies to St. Petersburg where he learns that the attack was probably backed by a mysterious "Cossack" named Janus. Janus is revealed as the scarred and bitter Alex Trevelyan. Bond traces Trevelyan to Cuba where his organization has built a secret station to control a second GoldenEye weapon which he plans to use to wipe out all electronic data in the city of London, thereby causing financial chaos in the west and making himself "richer than God."

Notes: New license holder Topps, decided to return to the adaptation format. But, Pierce Brosnan's debut as Bond in *GoldenEye* turned out to be 007's swansong in US comic book form as only the first issue of the planned three was published. In fact, at the time of writing, it still holds the dubious distinction of being the last new James Bond comic published. No clear reason for the withdrawal of issues 2 and 3 has ever been published, although some speculate that a disagreement between Topps and the license holders over the intended audience for the book may have been an issue. Others suggest concerns about the overt sexual nature of the planned cover for issue 2 and art that show the female villain, Xenia Onatopp clearly getting sexually aroused when killing. From the evidence of the first issue, this could have been the best Bond movie adaptation yet as the artist, Claude St. Aubin, moved away from the convention of trying to recreate the exact movie scenes in favor of retelling the story using comic book techniques. There is also a 00 issue of *GoldenEye* with black and white interior art which was produced as a special for the 1995 James Bond convention in New York.

The GoldenEye Mini-Interview

The following "interview" is drawn from various email response between the author and Claude St. Aubin (artist), Dwight Zimmerman (editor) and Jim Salicrup (editor in chief) who all worked on the Topps adaptation of *GoldenEye*.

Claude, it's been said that your approach to the Topps *GoldenEye* adaptation was one of the more innovative movie adaptations. It appears that instead of just trying to recreate movie scenes as panels, you reinterpreted the story using comics storytelling techniques. Was this a deliberate attempt on your part to use the differences between the two media to tell the story the best way you could?

Claude St. Aubin - Yes. A movie and a comic book are two different mediums. One is in constant "3D" motion, and the other is a " 2D freeze frame" that you can take with you anywhere. I had to take that in consideration. With a comic, you have to select your best scenes and make as much impact you can because it is stuck there for ever. You do not need to rewind or fast forward. You need to take the reader(s) and lead him into a story sequences that keeps him interested and entertained. You have time to think when you read a comic book. But with a movie the motion and sound does the job automatically and if you have a great subject and direction, you will enjoy it as much in a different way than with a comic with no motion and sound. You need to compensate the lack of it when you read a comic.

How far in advance of the movie's release did you start working on the adaptation?

Claude St. Aubin - If I remember correctly, we did the comic adaptation a few months before the movie release. Like three or four months if not less than two months ahead.

What source did you use for the adaptation, the script, or did you have access to an early print of the movie itself?

Claude St. Aubin - We didn't get very much visual references such as stills or prints. I remember being concerned on how little visual references were provided to do the projects. We did get some stuff, pretty much what had already been floating around since the promo of the film but not much more of what was really needed to do the adaptation as best we could.

We had to improvise and create a lot of the scenes from our heads and hope for the best. That was an unfortunate side of this project. BUT we did get a lot of support and help from Dwight. He made things happened and was very helpful with the situation we found ourselves in by having to create or imagine what was supposed to be instead of what was re: scenes, places and locations of the film.

Did EON Productions supply you with reference photographs such as production stills?

Claude St. Aubin - We did get photocopies of certain scenes and the main visual promos. EON was keeping as much secrecy and confidentiality as possible before the movie release. Which in my view was silly if they wanted the comic book adaptation as accurate and exciting as possible in order to promote the film with what we were trying to do with the comic.

Opposite page: British 30 x 40 inch movie poster from *GoldenEye*.

Did working on such a tightly controlled licensed character present any particular challenges from the editorial / publishers perspective?

Dwight Zimmerman - As I recall, our experience with the licensors of *GoldenEye* was very good. There were no particular extreme challenges. They were very good to work with.

Jim Salicrup - Not really. I'm a lifetime fan of James Bond, as is writer Don McGregor, and we wanted to be as true to Bond as possible.

Topps pulled the book after the first issue. Rumors as to why vary. Do you know the reason?

Claude St. Aubin - If I remember correctly, they took too long to approve the pages and it kind messed up the schedule. I think that's one of the reasons it was shelved.

Dwight Zimmerman - Unfortunately, my memory is rather vague on this. The only real reason it would have been pulled would have been lack of sales. So, I can only say that when we got the advance orders for the second issue, the decision was made to cancel the project because the orders were so small. Keep in mind that this was a time when the industry was entering its down period, so the low orders for GoldenEye were an advance signal that things were going to go bad.

Jim Salicrup - Yes, I certainly do know the reason. Unfortunately, I'd prefer not to get too specific here and simply say that we had a disagreement over which audience our comic book adaptation was intended for. We were aiming for the same audience that would go see the movie and they thought it should be adapted in a way that would be suitable for very young children. With all due respect for their position, doing such a juvenile adaptation of *GoldenEye* was not what we had signed on to publish, so we pulled the plug.

I have seen a small image of the cover from the aborted second issue, but never any of the interior art. Did you complete the whole series?

Claude St. Aubin - Yes, all three stories were drawn and inked. I don't know if all three went to color let alone printing, before it was cancelled.

Dwight Zimmerman - To the best of my memory, we did not. Claude would be able to tell you what he did for

Left: Bond is refused entry into S.H.I.E.L.D.'s secret HQ in *Strange Tales* #164, "Nick Fury Agent of S.H.I.E.L.D.," 1968. Opposite page: page from *THWAK* #5, 2003, from the story "Live and Let Spy," art by Dave Newton.

152   the history of the illustrated 007

art on the penciling side. We would have completed the script, but I don't think we finished production.

Jim Salicrup - Certainly that issue was completed. The rest was in various stages of completion when the decision was made not to publish.

(Author's note—There are reports that some copies of issues #2 and #3 are in circulation as writer Don McGregor is said to have had an extremely limited run printed up at his own cost. At the time of writing I haven't been able to confirm this.)

MAD, CRACKED AND SILLY BONDS

It doesn't matter in what medium Bond stories have been told, books or movies, they have been parodied. The same is true of comic books. Although, as has been noted in various entries in the previous chapter, it could be argued that many of the "official" Bond comics stories were parodies in their own right.

So how do we define a parody? The dictionary defines it as "a humorous or satirical imitation of a serious piece of literature or writing." For the purposes of this section I'd add the word "deliberate" to that definition. For me, a Bond parody is one that deliberately sets out to twist the familiar tropes of a Bond story for humorous effect. This section also includes comics where the Bond central themes have been lifted and applied wholesale (and not very subtly) to a whole new character, e.g. Jane Bond, the female spy for the British girl's comic Tina.

The most consistent Bond spoofs appeared in MAD magazine with several of the movies, plus numerous Bond clichés being fair game for examination. As noted earlier in the book, artist's Harry North's work on the parody of the Roger Moore movie, *Octopussy*, even landed him a job drawing the "serious" Bond for the *Daily Express* newspaper strip.[1]

The list below is not believed to be exhaustive, small cameos and parodies are hard to track down. Unless one has the unlimited time and money to read every comic book produced some are bound to be missed. These are the ones that I know about.

DIRECT PARODIES

CRACKED # ? (Globe/1977)—"The Spy Who Snubbed Me" – movie spoof

CRACKED #? (Globe /1979)— "Moonwrecker" movie spoof

CRACKED #306 (Globe/1996)—"Plasticeye" movie spoof

CRACKED Collectors Edition (Globe/2000)—"007's Latest Supercool Spy Gadgets"

CRACKED #342 (Globe/2002)—"The World is Not Enough" with Homer Simpson as James Bond.

CRAZY #? (Marvel/1973)—"Laff and Let Die" movie spoof

CRAZY #2 (Marvel/1974)—"Live and Let Spy" - spoof

Mad Magazine #94 (1964)—"It's True! Bonds Do Have More Fun Department: 007"—A MAD Musical

MAD Magazine #165 (1974)—#8 "James Bomb" Bomb Movies includes Dr No-No, From Russia With Lunacy, Goldfinger Bowl, Thunderblahh, You Only Live Nice, On His Majesty's Secret Shamus, Dollars are Forever, Live and Let Suffer

MAD Magazine #199 (1978)—"The Spy Who Glubbed Me"—movie spoof

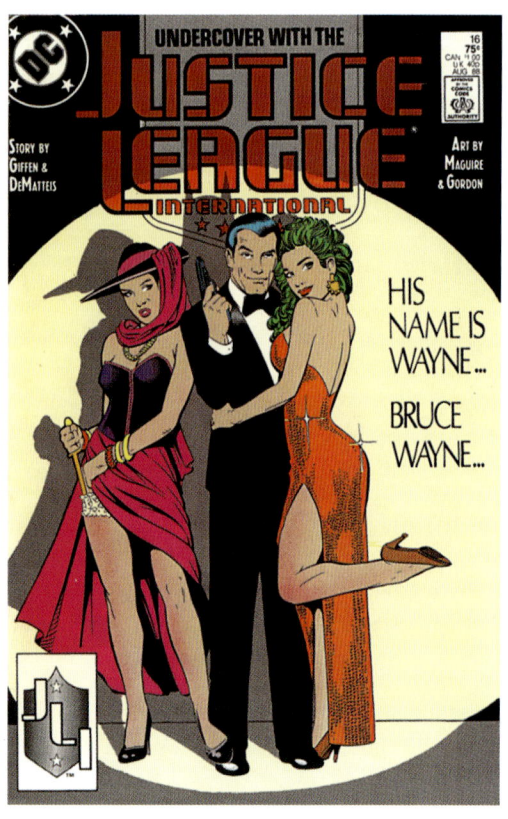

MAD Super Special #27 (1978)—reprints 8 "James Bomb" Bomb Movies

MAD Magazine #213 (1980)—"00$ Moneyraker" – movie spoof

MAD Magazine #229 (1982)—"For Her Thighs Only" —movie spoof

MAD Magazine Hot Air Mad Summer Super Special #63 (1988)—*For Your Eyes Only* spoof—reprints "For Her Thighs Only"

MAD Magazine #293 (1990)—"License To Kill" spoof

MAD Magazine #340 (1995)—"If James Bond Were Updated for the Politically-Correct '90s"

MAD Magazine #365 (1998)—"James Bond Villains Pet Peeves"

Super CRACKED #3 (Globe/1989)—"The Moon Ate A Big Pink Kumquat" (captions to Bond film stills,) "The Real Secrets Behind Agent 0007," "Fhive For The Fhun It!" (more captions), and "007 Devices That Bombed"

THWAK #5 (2003)—"Live and Let Spy"

COPY CATS AND ODD APPERANCES

Animaniacs #14 (DC Comics / 1996)—Contains "A Spy On The Wall," featuring James Bomb, Agent 007 7/8

Asterix and the Black Gold (date?)—Asterix meets Dubbleosix, a druid-spy modeled after Sean Connery

The Barbie Twins Adventures #1 (Topps/1995) — Cameo of an aged James Bond in a bondage (get it?) scene. (Note: An earlier ashcan edition of this story "Prelude To A Mission" was published by Studio Chikara.)

The Blonde Avenger (Blitz Weasel Studios/1996)—Contains "The Spying Game" featuring Jayne Blond, Ms. Momoney, Auntie M, Ernst T. Blojob and SPHINCTRE

Buster (1965 - 67)—UK humor weekly comic featuring "James Pond Agent 008 ½ — licensed to laugh"

Danger Girl (Image / DC Comics /1998-2007) — A team of attractive girl spys whose boss looks suspiciously like

Top: panel from *A League of Extraordinary Gentlemen: Black Dossier*, art by Kev O'Neill. Bottom: cover from *Justice League International* #16, art by Kevin Maguire.

Sean Connery and may in fact be a well known retired secret agent

James Bond 007 Adventure Storybook (Playvalue Books/date?)—Two children's story books done in comics format

Justice League International #16 (DC Comics / 1988)—Cover with Batman posing as Bond—"His name is Wayne …. Bruce Wayne"

League Of Extraordinary Gentlemen: The Black Dossier (DC/ABC Comics /2007)— A secret agent called Jimmy with a taste for vodka martini's and good looking women is a recurring character all the way through this remarkable volume

L.E.G.I.O.N. '94 Annual (DC Comics /1994)—Legion of Super Heroes spoof "The Man From L.E.G.I.O.N. 007"

Married With Children #? (NOW Comics/1994)—Contains "Double-OH-Bundy," 007 spoof

Nick Fury Agent of SHIELD #162 (Marvel / 1967) – Bond is named—checked when Fury is issued an invisible car

Nick Fury Agent of SHIELD #164 (Marvel 1968)—Bond is refused entrance to SHIELD's headquarters

Rick O'Shay (Chicago Tribune/1967)—Comedy Western newspaper strip that included a character named James Bounder, Agent 006 7/8 who worked for "O" and his secretary Miss Legal Tender

Secret Agents #1 (Personality Comics/1991)—Sean Connery

Secret Agents #2 (Personality Comics/1991)—Roger Moore

Secret Agents #3 (Personality Comics/1992)—Timothy Dalton

Secret Agents #0 (SPIES Comics/1994)—George Lazenby

SPIES Comics #1 (SPIES Comics/1994)—Pierce Brosnan

Tina / Princess Tina (1967—70)—"International" girls comic featuring Jane Bond, Secret Agent

Right: cover from the 1964 Signet paperback edition of *On Her Majesty's Secret Service*.

Notes

[1] An "Octopussy" strip appeared in the South American newspaper *EXTRA* that was clearly based on the movie, but it is not known if this was an official licensed adaptation or not.

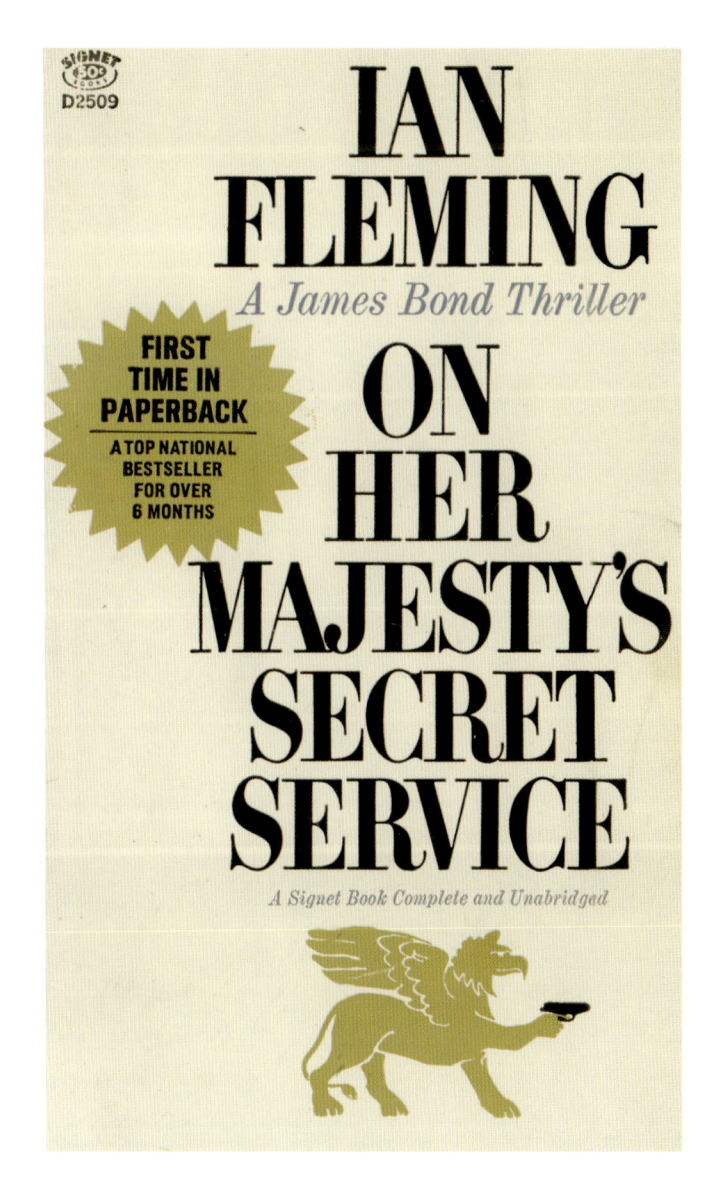

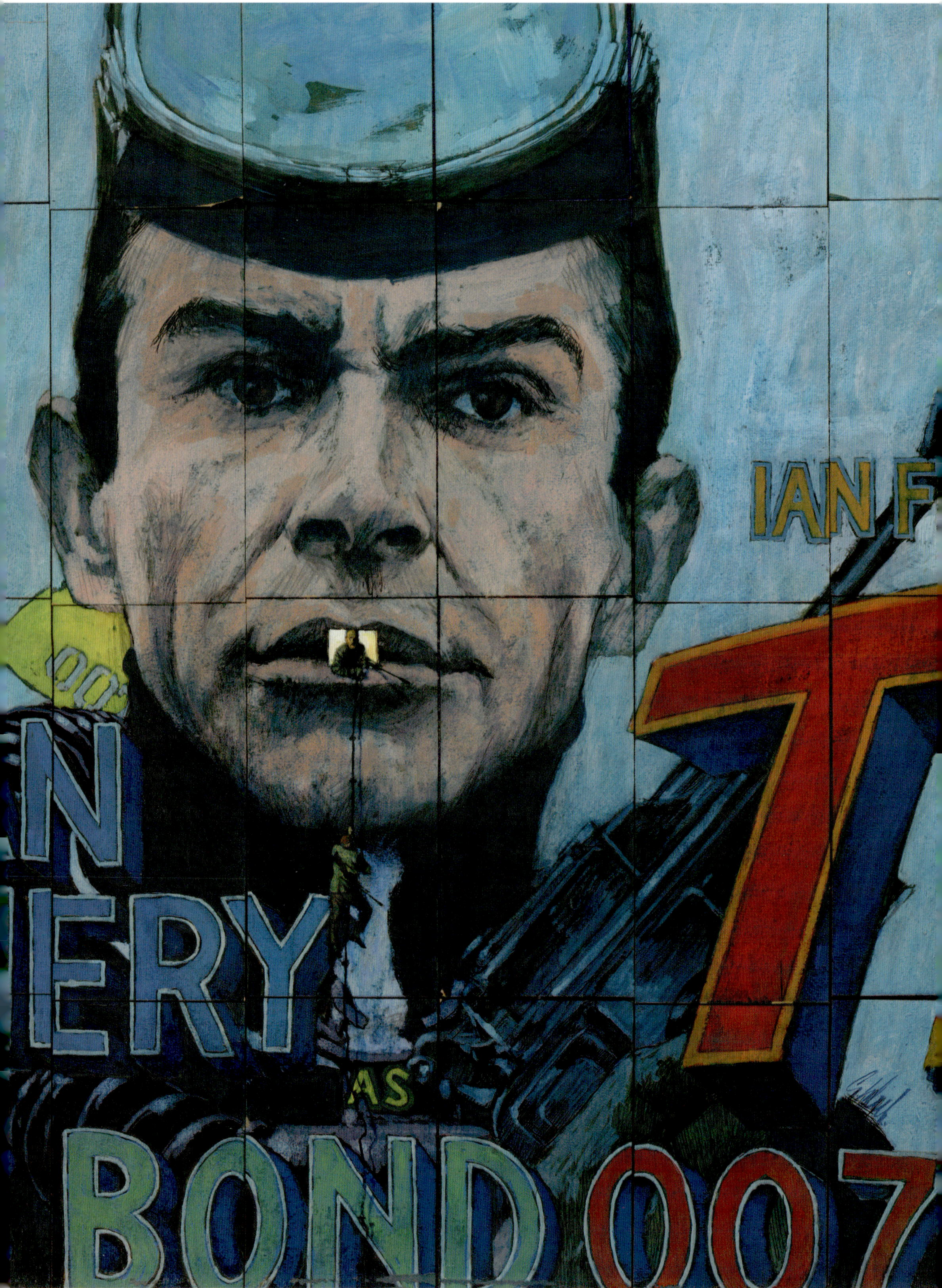
IAN F
N
ERY
AS
BOND 007

chapter 4
Talking Bond

During the preparation and research for this book I was lucky enough to make contact with several of the creators who worked on various James Bond comics. I started each interview with the same basic ten questions.

1. How did you become involved in doing a James Bond comic?

Claude St.Aubin (artist) - At Topps, I had already done some movie adaptations for other licensed products which they had acquired and I was a natural I guess to ask if I wanted to do the James Bond *GoldenEye* movie adaptation for the comic book version.

David Lloyd (artist) - It was a commission like any other. Dark Horse had an office in the UK at that time, and Dick Hansom, their editor, asked me if I'd be interested in doing one of the Bond books. I was very interested, but at the time I couldn't do the whole kit and caboodle. So I suggested I did breakdowns, layouts, rough

Opposite page: unused *Look* magazine cover publicizing *Thunderball*, 1965, artwork by James Deel. A cover using photographs from *Thunderball* was used instead.

pencils and final color work - with the finished pencils and inks being done by a colleague of mine, David Jackson. I suggested this because I knew David was good and capable of doing it – he's a real professional who I'd worked with before in a similar way. I agreed to do the two covers, though.

Simon Jowett (writer) - Through the sheer good luck of talking to Acme publisher and editor Dick Hansom in the convention bar at UKCAC, the annual London comic convention. This must have been in the summer of 1991? Dick mentioned in passing that he was putting together a line of Bond comics with Dark Horse and, during what was a fairly typical, alcohol-laced convention conversation, I happened to mention that the most effective and potentially devastating form of espionage would be to exert unseen influence over the world's proliferating information systems. To be able to alter the information on the screens of the world's stock markets, for example, then vanish into cyberspace would give one an incredible amount of power. And if that person had malice in mind... This wasn't intended as any kind of pitch, but Dick was interested enough to ask if I'd be interested in working that idea up into a story and writing an outline. The story became "Silent Armageddon." And the outline sat on a desk at Dark Horse for six months, until the rejection of a pitch by a more established writer meant there was a hole in the publishing schedule and Dick was able to remind Dark Horse that they already had a potential replacement awaiting their attention. It's ironic that the project should get the go-ahead because of a hole in the schedule, given that the artist went on to deliver the art for issue three late and to not deliver any art at all for issue four, thereby blowing the new schedule and, effectively killing off the entire line.

Dan Abnett (writer) - I was a regular freelancer for Marvel UK, and when the gig (James Bond Jr.) came up, I was approached by the editors to see if I'd be interested. I'd had plenty of experience writing ˜junior" licenses like *Thundercats, Ghostbusters* and so on, so it seemed like fun, especially as it was a chance to write US style stories, longer in page count than the usual UK stuff (I seem to remember Marvel UK was generating the material for its US parent).

Mike Grell (writer/artist) - I received a phone call from the folks who have the comic books rights and they were interested in having me do an original comic book story for James Bond. That was hard on heels of my stint on the *Green Arrow: The Longbow Hunters* and following a book I did called *Sable*.

Doug Moench (writer) - Like most people my age I grew up with Bond. One day out of the blue I got a call from (artist) Paul Gulacy and he said "This is it" I said "What?," and he said "We're doing Bond," said "They are doing Bond in comics now and they want us to do it." He was over the moon and, I guess because he and his wife were friends with Mike Richardson (the head of Dark Horse Comics) at the time, and his wife and had dinner (with *Mike*) and he'd mentioned that Dark Horse were doing (*Bond*) comics and Paul said "I gotta draw it." That was fine with me.

2. Were you a James Bond fan, or was this just another assignment for you?

Claude St.Aubin - I am, and still am, a big James Bond fan. So is my son. I was very thrilled when Topps asked me to do the project. AND to add my two cents, Sean Connery is to me the definite James Bond.

David Lloyd - I was definitely a fan. *From Russia With Love* was a major movie experience for me. A major experience – period. Saw *Dr*

Left: David Lloyd artwork for a limited edition book plate. Opposite page and for the remainder of this chapter, black-and-white and color original artwork from "Shattered Helix."

158 the history of the illustrated 007

No after that, out of sequence. In '64, I got free admittance to see *Goldfinger* because my Mum worked in a restaurant attached to the cinema. A real treat. I was reading *Live And Let Die* at around the same time. Great memories branded deep into my consciousness, and renewed through much TV re-visiting over the years. The books were less important to me than the movies, I have to say. And Sean Connery was the only real Bond as far as I was concerned.

Simon Jowett - I don't know that I'd call myself a fan. I remember enjoying the Connery Bonds as a child, and having a curious fascination for the covers of the early PAN editions of the novels I found on my parents' bookshelves.

Dan Abnett - Definitely a James Bond fan. Big treat as a kid to watch the Bond films on telly. I had a Corgi DB5 and everything.

Mike Grell - Absolutely, My eldest brother was the person who first turned me on to the novels before the first movie came out, *Dr No*. He was an avid reader, he would read the books and then tell me the story and I got so interested in his story telling that I decided to pick them up for myself and when the films started coming out I was first one in line.

Doug Moench - My favorite was *On Her Majesty's Secret Service*, although maybe because it was the first one I read, then I went back and read them (the Bond novels) in order but that one I guess just really lit me up. I prefer the novels to the movies. I know they are the same characters and everything but... they are so different. I love the movies as movies, but as far as the James Bond character goes I am always going to go back to the books. I was only 13 maybe when the *Dr No* movie came out and my father drove me to see it, it was a big deal, but I remember liking the books more than the movies.

3. How did you feel about tackling such a pop culture icon?

Claude St.Aubin - I was excited and very nervous at the same time. You always feel small and inadequate. Perhaps I was at that. But to be able to draw this legend and make him come alive in two dimensions (on paper) was a challenge and a privilege.

David Lloyd - Looked forward to doing it. Simon Jowett's script was great and captured the atmosphere and style of the Bond world. David Jackson was a Bond fan – with Connery as his particular favorite as well. And my method of working on the book was supported by the editor. So, no problem. I was enthused.

Simon Jowett - This was only my third or fourth professional commission as a comics writer, so I was as excited about that, as I was about it being an original Bond commission. Looking back, I'm amazed that Dick trusted a newbie like me with four issues of Bond. Luckily, Dick, Dark Horse, the US publisher, and Glidrose liked what I was doing enough to

160 the history of the illustrated 007

ask me if I had an idea for a two-part follow-up, which became "Shattered Helix."

Dan Abnett - I don't remember any anxieties. As I said above, I had a pretty good grounding in working on franchises, and was used to learning the style bible etc to get a firm grip on the property.

Mike Grell - I was very well upon legend and lore and it was something that I had just enough of an ego to tackle it without being too daunted. I thought it would be a lot of fun and it was. There were some challenges involved, for instance I was not allowed to use the characters that had been created specifically for the movies I was not allowed to use Q but that was fine.

4. How did you approach writing / drawing Bond? Did you go back to Fleming's works, draw inspiration from the movie Bond, look at previous comics interpretations, or just decide to do your own take on the character?

Claude St.Aubin - I only did the drawing. I was not consulted with the writing part of it. I was given a few (not too many) movie still photocopies, that was basically used to promote the movie. I could have used a lot more of them but the movie (if I remember correctly) hadn't been released yet so secrecy and confidentiality was what made it hard to get the right kind of references to be able to reflect better the movie itself for the comic book. I didn't have any previous comics interpretations or other James Bond material to work with and from. At the beginning I was trying to get close to the resemblance of the actors. I had to change that to make them more generic so as not to infringe on copyrights of the main players. So, yes, I made it my own character based on Pierce Brosnan who played James Bond at that time.

David Lloyd - Simon had done his job well, script-wise, and I had the movies to inspire me artistically in my area of the work. What I added to it of my own was a lively layout, but a controlled one. And I knew David would do something very solid and realistic in the pencils and inks - so the two would balance out into something that was conservative and actionful (sic) at the same time. The best Bonds for me were always the ones that weren't over the top in any department, but were a careful mix of the prosaic and the fantastic. In actually drawing Bond himself, the basic look was built from the kind of facial features Connery possessed, but it was meant to evoke the spirit of him rather than depict him.

Simon Jowett - The current Bond at the time I was writing was Timothy Dalton, so I rented both his films on VHS and watched them. I thought their gadget-light approach was a welcome change after the increasingly gadget-heavy Moores and I think that probably influenced my approach to a degree, but that was as far as I went in getting reacquainted with the character and the franchise. Beyond that, I had a vague memory of the books and the Connery movies. To be honest, I wasn't interested in writing a continuity-heavy piece of fan service. I was more interested in working out how to best tell the story (see my previous answer about this being only my third or fourth - and certainly the largest - professional commission). When "SA" was nominated for an Eagle Award (the annual British comic industry awards) in, I think, 93, in competition with another of the Dark Horse Bond mini-series, I was told by a member of the decision-making committee, that although "SA" was considered the better story, it wasn't considered a 100% Bond story. And I'm happy to go along with that.

Dan Abnett - It (James Bond Jr.) was very much its own thing, but I'm sure my imagination was informed by my knowledge of a proper canonical Bond.

Mike Grell - I went back to a couple of other original versions of James Bond, for instance there is a tendency along the various generations to model Bond after the various actors who have played Bond at the time but I was specifically told that I could not use any of the film actors. That didn't create a as much of a problem as it might have been because I went to Ian Flemings' original model, actor Hogey Carmichael. I found great shots of him and all I did was change the hair a bit and gave him a black comma over one eye, gave him a scar that ran down his eyebrow and thru his eyebrow so that it wouldn't be too noticeable by the bad guys and I chopped half an inch or so off his nose and the rest I pretty much based on Carmichael.

Doug Moench - Although I prefer the books I used the movies (in *Serpent's Tooth*) as that's the genre most comic book fans would be looking for. That's really what (artist) Paul (Gulacy) loves. With *Minutes to Midnight*, which was planned to be the start of a new James Bond series in the Dark Horse anthology book, I wanted to do a version closer to the novels.

5. What do you think are the characteristics of Bond that make him such an enduring icon?

Claude St.Aubin - I think (for the male species anyway) it's a bit like the Superman wannabe. Someone you'd like to be so that you'd always come up on top no matter what. James Bond is an expert with any kind of gadget (like a lot of people I still have a problem to connect all the gizmo when we buy for an example DVD and to try to hook it up correctly etc... let alone to program them to do anything these things are supposed to do). He can take on anybody, he's a one man army. Able to problem solve in a matter of fraction of a second under intense pressure and make the right decision. Attractive to women, who wouldn't want to be! A man of action and of the time. The typical hero of the hour! Yep, we always want to think or even see ourselves like that, but when you look into the mirror, we get a reality check and bingo... we know why we like to see James Bond in movies.

David Lloyd - From a movies point-of-view he came along at exactly the right time to form a perfect mix of heroic characteristics for a wide range of ages and tastes. Heroes before him were gallant or honorable or simple or humble

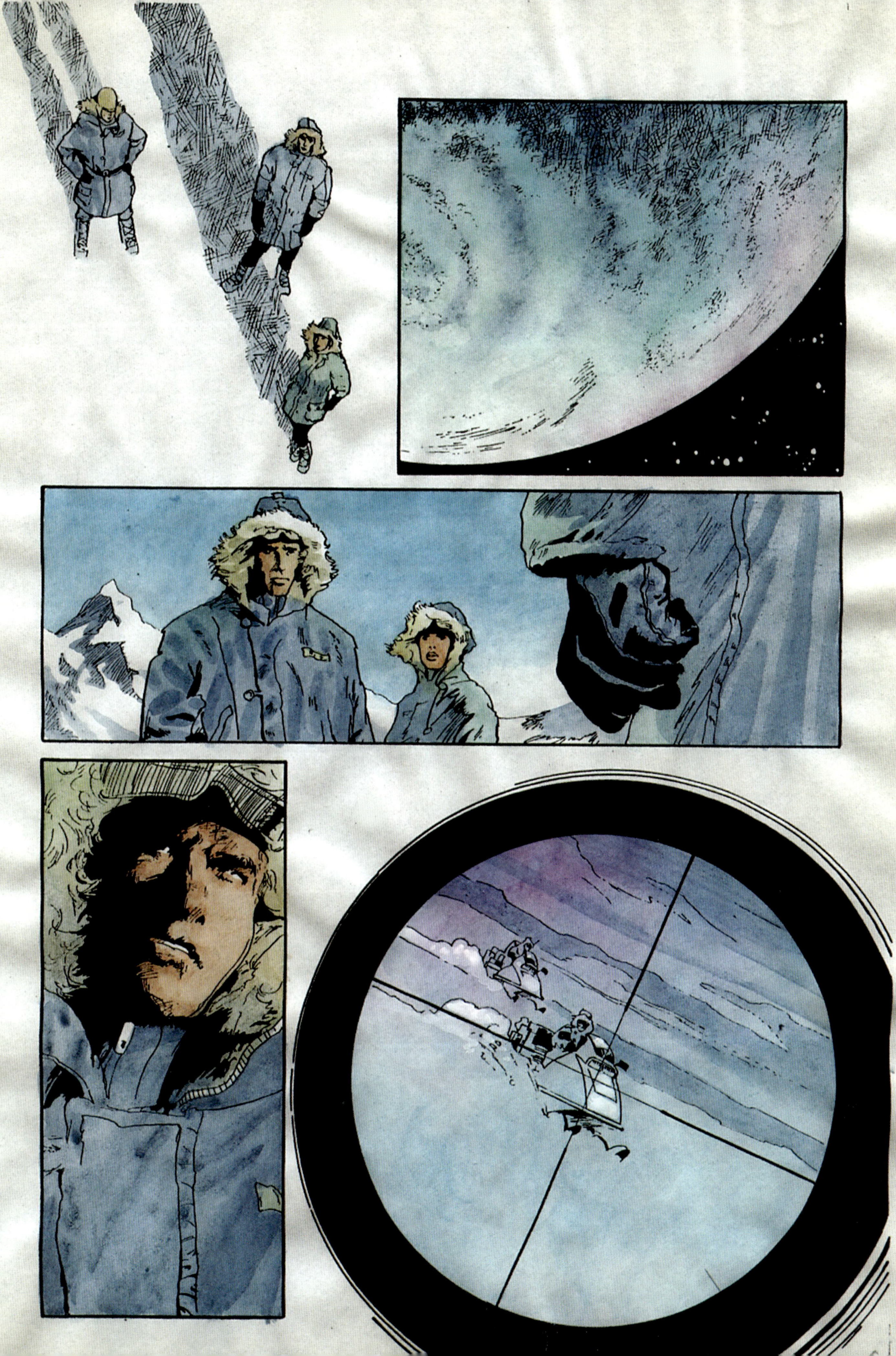

or gentle or fair-minded or never seen to have sex; or were a mix of all those qualities. James Bond was the opposite, so he appealed to everyone who lived in the real world and knew in their hearts what it really took to get things done. I think the growing 'spy as superman' identity from the early days was an unfortunate development but understandable considering the zeitgeist at the time. As time went by I think the content of the movies became a more important draw than the main character, sadly.

Simon Jowett - I wish I had some profound insightful answer to this question. But, if I knew the answer, I'd be busy building exactly those characteristics into a character of my own devising and preparing to buy my first island. Was he simply in the right place at the right time, culturally speaking? I think his being picked up by Hollywood, which had a vested interest in keeping him current, has much to do with his longevity. The books can be surprisingly somber, almost melancholy at times, and Bond is more brutal and flawed than he appears in the movies. I wonder if the movies' addition of glamour to the grit made Bond an acceptable fantasy figure as the 60s took off to replace the old-school, square-jawed heroes in the G-Men, Bulldog Drummond and Dick Tracy mould. I usually find that a weird kind of nostalgia – perhaps for the kind of games little boys play – is part of the mix when people talk about Bond. I suspect Bond still provides a grubby little thrill for men (and women) in our more politically-correct times.

Mike Grell - Absolutely, from a male reader's standpoint Bond is the suave sophisticated debonair lady's man. A dangerous individual who does the sort of things armchair quarterbacks, like me, like to envision they do in such situations. The kind of man every man wants to be, and every lady wants to be with. With Daniel Craig's portrayal, you see really inside the character and discover that he is not particularly likable, he is doing an unsavory job in the best way he knows how and it has an affect on him and his personal life and certainly with everyone that comes his way until Tracy (*Bond's wife*). That is a very important step and I would be interested to see at some stage in the game if they (the movie production company) remade *OHMSS* (*On Her Majesty's Secret Service*).

Doug Moench - James Bond is one of those characters that along with Sherlock Holmes, seems to transcend the medium as they are universal. I think JFK (US President John F. Kennedy who included *From Russia With Love* on his list of favorite books) may have helped. He made it popular in USA. The combination of the love and death stuff, the cold war, chance to fight the bad guys. The way Fleming made him it seemed a little more sophisticated than the usual mix of sex and violence, what he ate and drank, the way he dressed. He was worldly, globetrotting glam. The sense of place, that was as much a part of the plot as anything.

6. One of the Bond continuation novel authors once told me that he considered Bond as more of a plot device than a character - is that something you'd agree with?

Claude St.Aubin - Perhaps it has come to that now, I really don't know. You see, when you read the earlier novels, it doesn't give that impression. I see a character faced with a different situation and villain(s) with every novel. If you are not familiar too well with the James Bond sensation, you would probably see him more as a character hero than a device.

David Lloyd - I think that is the way it turned out, yes.

Simon Jowett - I can see why he might say that. Fleming famously referred to Bond as a "blunt instrument" and a "cardboard booby." More a living weapon than a fully-formed character, Bond is designed to cause a reaction when added to a situation. I wonder if calling Bond stories "spy stories" isn't a bit of a misnomer. Maybe they would be better described as "assassin stories." "Shag 'em or shoot em" maybe? The Italian "Kiss, kiss, bang bang" certainly sounds like a more accurate description of them than *The Spy Who Came In From The Cold*. One of my intentions when planning "Silent Armageddon" was to mess with the formula slightly – by placing Bond in an unfamiliar paternal role and making the "Bond girl" a 13-year old math prodigy, disabled by polio. I had fun writing a couple of small scenes where Bond struggles to establish some kind of rapport with a stroppy teen who could wipe the floor with him at chess, but eventually has to admit defeat.

Mike Grell - In films perhaps yes, but in the books no. Bond in the books was definitely a character, the central pivotal character and most everything was from his perception, if you look at the way the villains are portrayed and the women are portrayed from Bond's perspective too. Once you get to the *Spy Who Loved Me* another very interesting character study, book written from the point of the woman. Fleming would spend three or five pages on something that had nothing do with the plot, meal or golf, but all to do with the character. Agatha Christie said when you read a book you get 10% plot, 20% characterization and 70% of whatever knows best and I am sure that is what Fleming was doing.

7. Bond stories always seem to be set in the present, was this something you kept in mind when working on your comics?

Claude St.Aubin - Very much so. With keeping in touch with the newest "high tech gizmo" and the latest technology to take over or threaten the world, it has to be set in the present with (as an audience) the discovery of what kind of application it will be used for on both sides.

David Lloyd - Didn't have much choice, there. I was hired to draw, not to conceptualize. Licensed things - franchises - have fences of rules set out for the laborers who produce the material for them. It has to be set in the present, so naturally you keep it in mind re props, costume, etc. If you're asking me how I'd do Bond given a free hand, I guess I'd want to do something directly from a Fleming original – but that would only be to see what I could do with it, not because I'm any kind of Fleming purist.

Simon Jowett - Yes, insofar as it is an accepted convention, though I opened Silent Armageddon in the past, during the Cold War, to give a sense that the story I was telling had begun long before Bond – or the world – was aware of it.

Mike Grell - It's easier to create a current story however that jumped up and bit me in the backside eventually, the American publisher (Eclipse) was having some serious problems with their printer, financial difficulties that took them forever to sort out. *Permission to Die* was based on the concept of an escape from behind the Iron Curtain and by the time the third issue came out the curtain had collapsed, and the borders had all opened up. It was in the can for nine months before it was published. The first two issues came out close together as planned but that third wrap up issue came out so much later that in fact people thought that the first two issues were a complete story and they were very surprised by the time the third one came out.

Doug Moench - How can you do a story in the cold war when the cold war is over, set in the past?? I'm pretty sure they want James Bond up to date.

8. What approach did you take to designing Bond's world?

Claude St.Aubin - I had to be as true as possible to the movie itself. The comic book version had to be an adaptation of the movie. So whatever main elements, designs etc., important to the movie, it had to be translated pretty much as is and adapted to the comic book medium, so it would work. The cars used, planes, architectures clothes etc... Otherwise it would have been too different and could not have been titled *GoldenEye*.

David Lloyd - It was all in the script. I needed only to visualize it in a basic manner. You should ask David Jackson some of this. Cinematic sweep, is one phrase I could use to describe my rough designs, I suppose. But this is an unconscious application of style that probably arose through wanting to ape the best of Bond cinema in the work generally. I am noted in this business for cinematic storytelling, though, so it was an expected outcome.

Simon Jowett - Both my stories took their inspiration from existing science - of computer networks, artificial intelligence, bio-weapons and climate change – so my instinct was to place them in a more naturalistic world than the gadget-heavy one of the later Connery and all the Moores. If your characters can hollow out volcanoes to hold their secret bases and kidnap Space Shuttles in mid-flight, a self-aware computer virus seems less of a leap, somehow. Having the CIA fund the construction of a super-secret bio-weapons lab in the Antarctic was a bit of a stretch, but certainly no more of a stretch than the sub-swallowing ships and shuttle-kidnapping satellites of the movies.

Mike Grell - I mixed in as much as possible, I had a great appreciation for the design work that was done in the films, and I also have an appreciation for what Fleming created. I tried to do the best I could to combine the two. I did a montage page as an homage to the films, that featured the girl from *Goldfinger*, the Aston Martin. I did change the pistol to an Ash, I got great cooperation from the Ash Corporation who were more than eager to help out. I believe I modeled the various offices as they were pretty well described (in the books), If you go into Moneypenny's there's a doorway leading to M's office, that door had better be red, that sort of thing. When it came to designing the rest of it I am certainly a fan of the set designs that they created for the Bond films, and when I got to the final wrap story I was able to unleash a lot of that.

Doug Moench - (artist) Paul (Gulacy) and I discussed things in general, car chases, boat chases, snow, tropics, bikinis, gambling scene, everything that JB should be plus the Aston Martin. In general we decided to go whole hog.

9. Fleming's novels were as much about place as about plot - is this something that you took into account?

Claude St.Aubin - Definitely. All places, locations, if anything, the comic book had to mirror the movie.

David Lloyd - Well, I took into account the need to make the locations convincing. The arctic atmosphere that marked much of the story was carefully evoked through the use of color and space, while the hothouse atmosphere of the cultivated jungle world was brought to life similarly. The printing of the book wasn't all it could have been in bringing this perfectly to the reader, but that's another story.

Simon Jowett - In retrospect, very much so. The moment I read about Hong Kong's Hidden City (a vast multi-level slum district since demolished and built over) I thought it would make a great location for a story. As I developed and outlined "Silent Armageddon" I realized that it would make a good fit for the birthplace of my crippled math prodigy ... and as a secret base for the new international crime syndicate I was also in the process of developing. The two main locations in "Shattered Helix"—the multiple constructed environments within an experimental biosphere, itself constructed in the Arizona desert and the frozen desert of Antarctica—were chosen as much for their stark contrast as for what they added to the story thematically. Serena Mountjoy, She's a much more conventional Bond Girl, has a close familial and psychological link with Antarctica, which Bond is more than willing to exploit. And, given that my villains want to retrieve and "weaponize" a deadly virus, it seemed to make sense to have them travel to the Earth's last unspoiled wilderness to do it.

10. Did working on such a tightly controlled licensed character present any particular challenges?

Claude St.Aubin - If I remember correctly, they took too long to approve the pages and it kind messed up the schedule. I think that's one of the reasons it was shelved.

David Lloyd - It would have if I'd had my own ideas for portraying the character that were antipathetic to what I was being asked to do, but I was totally in sympathy with the story I was being asked to work on. It was a good script.

Simon Jowett - Only one - and I'd not really call it a challenge. Contractual and legal issues (dating back, I think, to the legal tussles between Fleming and Eon and Kevin McClory over *Thunderball*) meant that SPECTRE was off-limits, so I had to come up with my own international crime syndicate: CERBERUS, whose operations are divided into three areas of specialization: extortion, espionage and execution. Each area is controlled by one of the organization's three leaders: the "three heads of Cerberus," one of whom is dead by the end of "Silent Armageddon." One of the survivors appears obliquely in "Shattered Helix," which was set after the events of "SA" (although both parts appeared in the artist-enforced hiatus after issue 2 of "SA") and the organization was to take centre stage in a third multi-part story I had begun to plot out at the time the line was cancelled. Beyond that, I had no real problems. Glidrose seemed very happy with my scripts - they were particularly complimentary about the script for the first episode of "Shattered Helix" – and I was surprised and delighted when they let me introduce Rosa Klebb's bastard son, Erik – the result of a drunken, bathtub vodka-fuelled encounter between the famously Sapphic Kleb and an unnamed army officer during an operation in one of the USSR's more remote outposts. I like to think that she was later called upon to dispatch him with her shoe-spike. And that, of course, she didn't hesitate.

Mike Grell - No, apart from the limitation I mentioned earlier (not being able to use any of the characters from the movies), they (the Bond license holders) were very cooperative. They did edit out one phrase in a script description as the phrase I used meant something else in British English.

Doug Moench - No, nothing. The only feedback I received was one of the best compliments I ever got. Mike Richardson (head of Dark Horse Comics) called me to say he had just got out of a meeting with one of the top people at Glidrose (the Bond literary rights holders) who'd said the *Serpent's Tooth* was "the single best James Bond story ever."

12¢
SHOWCASE
SUPERMAN DC NATIONAL COMICS
APR. NO. 43
APPROVED BY THE COMICS CODE AUTHORITY
presents
DOCTOR NO
by IAN FLEMING
ANOTHER MOMENT, DOCTOR NO, AND I'LL JAM YOUR SIGNALS THAT WOULD'VE MADE THE AMERICAN ROCKET GO WILD!
BUT YOU HAVEN'T ANOTHER MOMENT, BOND. THIS IS YOUR LAST!
BASED ON THE NOVEL AND NOW A UNITED ARTISTS FILM THRILLER!

chapter 5
A Bibliography and the Films

Books

- Amis, Kingsley, **The James Bond Dossier,** 1966, Signet—p. 2960

- Biederman, Danny, **The Incredible World of Spy-Fi ,** 2004, Chronicle   0-8118-4224-X

- Bouzereau, Laurent, **The Art of Bond** , 2006, Abrams   ISBN 0-8109-5488-5

- Chancellor, Henry, **James Bond: The Man And His World,** 2005, John Murray   ISBN 0-7195-6815-3

- Chapman, James, **A Licence To Thrill: A Cultural History of James Bond,** 2000, Columbia   ISBN 231120486

- Fleming, Ian, **Casino Royale,** 1988, Coronet ISBN 0340425679

- Fleming, Ian, **Live and Let Die,** 1988, Coronet   ISBN 0340425709

- Fleming, Ian, **Moonraker,** 1988, Coronet ISBN 0340425660

- Fleming, Ian, **Diamonds Are Forever,** 1988, Coronet ISBN 0340425644 Coronet

- Fleming, Ian, **From Russia With Love,** 1988, Coronet ISBN 0340425628

- Fleming, Ian, **Dr. No,** 1988, Coronet ISBN 0340418990

- Fleming, Ian, **Goldfinger,** 1988, Coronet ISBN 0340425687

- Fleming, Ian, **For Your Eyes Only,** 1989, Coronet   ISBN 0340425725

- Fleming, Ian, **Thunderball,** 1989, Coronet   ISBN 034042561X

- Fleming, Ian, **The Spy Who Loved Me,** 1989, Coronet,   ISBN 0340425695

- Fleming, Ian, **On Her Majesty's Secret Service,** 1989, Coronet ISBN 0340425652

- Fleming, Ian, **You Only Live Twice,** 1989, Coronet ISBN 0340425636

- Fleming, Ian, **The Man With The Golden Gun,** 1989, Coronet ISBN 0340425717

- Fleming, Ian, **Octopussy and The Living Daylights,** 1989, Coronet ISBN 0340413654

Cover from DC Comics' *Showcase* #43, 1963, reprinting the English *Classics Illustrated* version of *Dr. No*.

- Gammidge, Henry; McLusky, John; & Simpson, Paul, **James Bond: On Her Majesty's Secret Service,** 2004, Titan Books ISBN 1-84023-674-4

- Gammidge, Henry; McLusky, John; Simpson, Paul & Pavlov, Vlad, **James Bond: Goldfinger,** 2004, Titan Books ISBN 1-84023-908-5

- Gammidge, Henry; McLusky, John & Simpson, Paul, **James Bond: Dr. No,** 2005, Titan Books ISBN 1-84023-089-1

- Gardiner, Philp, **The Bond Code: The Dark World of Ian Fleming and James Bond,** 2008, Career Press ISBN 978-1-60163-004-9

- Gifford, Denis, **The International Book of Comics,** 1984, Deans ISBN 0-603-03574-4

- Gifford, Denis, **Encyclopedia of Comic Characters,** 1987, Longman ISBN 0-582-89294-5

- Gravett, Paul, **Great British Comics,** 2006, Aurum ISBN 1-84513-170-3

- Haining, Peter, **James Bond: A Celebration,** 1987, Planet ISBN 1-8522-7020-9

- Hern, Anthony; Gammidge, Henry; McLusky, John; & Simpson, Paul, **James Bond: Casino Royale,** 2005, Titan Books ISBN 1-84023-843-7

- Kronenberg, Michael & Spurlock, David, **Spies, Vixens and Masters of Kung Fu,** 2005, Vanguard 1-887591-74-5

- Lane, Andy & Simpson, Paul, **The Bond Files,** 2000, Virgin ISBN 0-7535-0490-1

- Lawrence, Jim; Horak, Yaroslave & Simpson, Paul, **James Bond: The Man With The Golden Gun,** 2004, Titan Books ISBN 1-84023-698-6

- Lawrence, Jim; Horak, Yaroslav & Simpson, Paul, **James Bond: Octopussy,** 2004, Titan Books ISBN 1-84023-743-0

- Lawrence, Jim; Horak, Yaroslav & Simpson, Paul, **James Bond: The Spy Who Loved Me,** 2005, Titan Books ISBN 1-84576-174-X

- Lawrence, Jim; Horak, Yaroslav; Page, James; Wheatley, James; Barretway, Mathais & Hagen, Dan, **James Bond: Colonel Sun,** 2005, Titan Books ISBN 1-84576-175-8

- Lawrence, Jim; Horak, Yaroslav; Page James & Leigh, David, **James Bond: The Golden Ghost,** 2006, Titan Books ISBN 1-84576-261-4

- Lawrence, Jim; Horak, Yaroslav; Page, James & Wheatley, James, **James Bond: Trouble Spot,** 2006, Titan Books ISBN 1-84576-269-X

- Lawrence, Jim; Horak, Yaroslav; Page, James & Wheatley, James, **James Bond: The Phoenix Project,** 2007, Titan Books ISBN 1-84576-312-2

- Lawrence, Jim; Horak, Yaroslav; & Porter, Alan J., **James Bond: Death Wing,** 2007, Titan Books ISBN 1-84576-517-6

- Lawrence, Jim; Horak, Yaroslav; & Porter, Alan J., **James Bond: Shark Bait,** 2008, Titan Books ISBN 1-84576-591-5

- Lawrence, Jim; McLusky, John; & Porter, Alan J., **James Bond: The Paradise Plot,** 2008, Titan Books ISBN 1-84576-716-0

- Miller, John Jackson; Thompson, Maggie; Bickford, Peter & Frankenhoff, **The Standard Catalog of Comic Books,** 2002, Krause ISBN 0-87341-916-2

- Pearson, John, **The Life of Ian Fleming,** 1967 Bantam

- Picher, Tim & Brooks, Brad, **The Essential Guide To World Comics,** 2005, Colins & Brown ISBN 1-84340-300-5

- Plowright, Frank (Ed), **The Slings & Arrows Comic Guide (2nd Edition),** 2003, Slings & Arrows ISBN 0-9544589-0-7

Opposite page top: cover from the 1955 Signet pocket book edition of *Moonraker*. Bottom: cover from the 1956 Signet pocket book edition of *Diamonds Are Forever*.

- Rovin, Jeff, **Adventure Heroes: Legendary Characters from Odysseus to James Bond,** 1994, Facts On File ISBN 0-8160-2886-9
- Winder, Simon, **The Man Who Saved Britain: A Personal Journey into the Disturbing World of James Bond,** 2007, Picador ISBN 0-312-42666-6

Movies

- Casino Royale (1954)
- Dr. No (1962)
- From Russia With Love (1963)
- Goldfinger (1964)
- Thunderball (1965)
- You Only Live Twice (1967)
- Casino Royale (1967)
- On Her Majesty's Secret Service (1969)
- Diamonds Are Forever (1971)
- Live and Let Die (1973)
- The Man With The Golden Gun (1974)
- The Spy Who Loved Me (1977)
- Moonraker (1979)
- For Your Eyes Only (1981)
- Octopussy (1983)
- Never Say Never Again (1983)
- View To A Kill (1985)
- The Living Daylights (1987)
- Licence To Kill (1989)
- GoldenEye (1995)
- Tomorrow Never Dies (1997)
- The World Is Not Enough (1999)
- Die Another Day (2002)
- Casino Royale (2006)

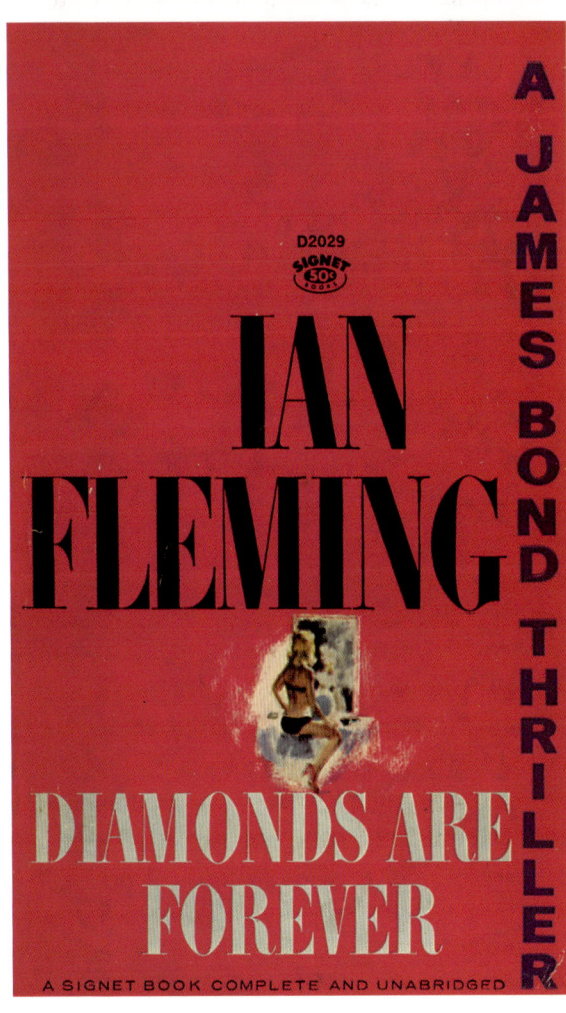

Acknowledgments

A book of this sort, by its very nature, can only be produced with the input and assistance of many people. This one is no exception. In particular I'd like to mention Johnny Oreskov without whose groundbreaking work on his James Bond Comics website, and his willingness to scan artwork from his own collection, this book would never have existed. I'd also like to thank Anders Frejdh for taking the time to share artwork from his collection.

A special thanks go out to the various James Bond writers, artists and editors who agreed to be interviewed, Claude St. Aubin, Dan Abnett, David Lloyd, Doug Moench, Dwight Zimmerman, German Gabler, Jean-Pierre Rutter, Jim Salicrup, Mike Grell, Paul Gulacy and Simon Jowett

Special thanks to Mike Aragona for his ceaseless cheerleading and support for all my projects and his invaluable editorial insights. Also thanks to Bob Greenberger, Daniel Herman, Dave Justus, Matthew Bradford, Matthew Sturges, Paul Benjamin, and Scott Kress, who all provided valuable feedback, encouragement and assistance at various points during this project.

Most of all I'd like to thank my wife Gill for both her proofreading skills and her immense patience with a husband who spent several months totally immersed in the world of James Bond.

COPYRIGHT HOLDERS

The publishers have made every effort to credit the artists and/or copyright holders whose work has been reproduced in this book. We apologize for any omissions, which will be corrected in future editions.

All images are copyright their respective creators or owners, listed below:

ALFA
America's Best Comics
Danjaq SA
Dark Horse Comics
DC Comics
Diamond Comics (India)
Eclipse Comics
EON Productions

Express Newspapers
Fleetway
Glidrose
Ian Fleming Publications Ltd
International Productions
Mike Grell
Paul Gulacy
David Lloyd
Marvel Comics
MGM
John McKlusky
Dave Newton
NV Uitgeverij Spaarnestad
Saito
Semic
Signet
Titan Books
TOPPS Comics
United Artists
World Distributors
ZigZag

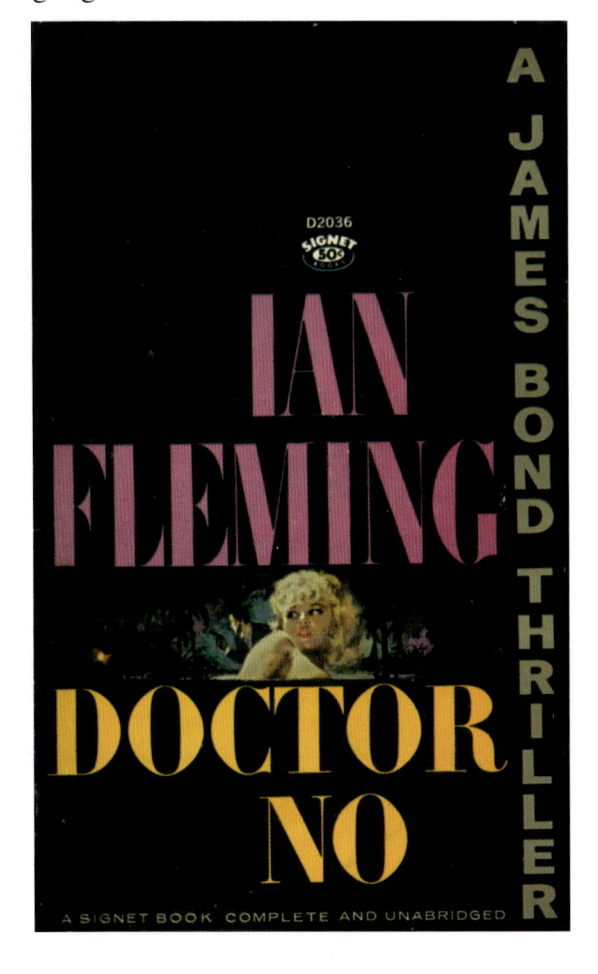

ABOUT THE COVER

In 1988 renowned movie poster artist Bob Peak, best known for his work on the *Star Trek* movie series posters, plus classics like *Camelot* and *My Fair Lady*, was commissioned to produce a sequence of teaser posters for the Timothy Dalton movie, *Licence To Kill*. He produced several using a combination of striking figure poses against a strong red background. In the end none were used by the studio-marketing department. The cover image for this book is a detail from one of those unused commission pieces and is from the original art which is now in the private collection of Hermes Press publisher Daniel Herman.

A further example of Peak's unused poster art can also be seen in the *Art of Bond* book published by Abrams in 2006.

Left: cover from the 1964 Signet pocket book version of *Dr. No*. **Right** cover from the 1964 Signet pocket book of *You Only Live Twice*.

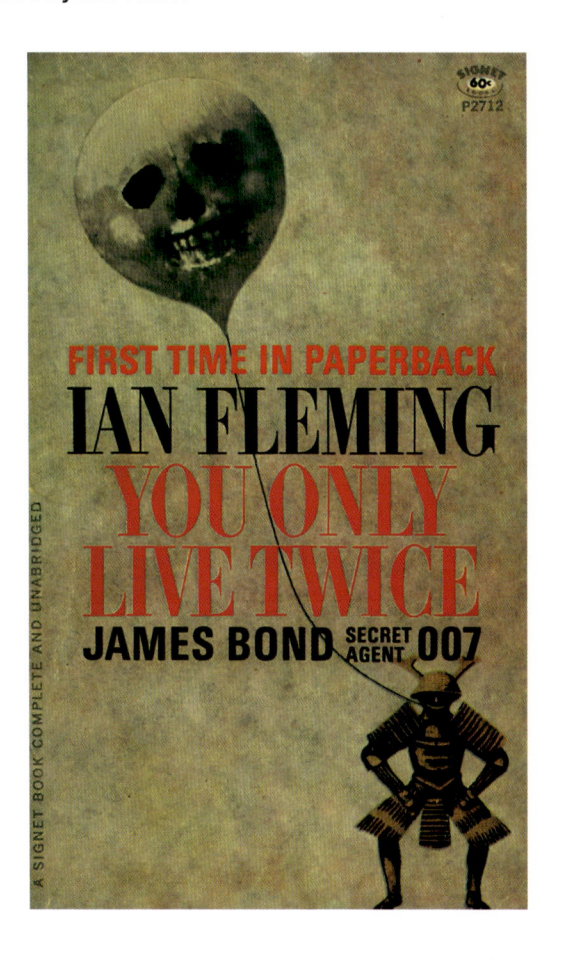

IAN FLEMING'S JAMES BOND 007
THE QUASIMODO GAMBIT

Dark Horse Comics / acme

JAMES BOND 1 OF 3

$3.95 US
$5.55 CAN

DON McGREGOR
GARY CALDWELL

Afterword

In 1994 I was hired by Dark Horse Comics as an associate editor to preside over several titles featuring licensed characters, one of which was Ian Fleming's James Bond 007. Dark Horse had already published a few miniseries featuring Bond including 1992's *Serpent's Tooth*, 1993's *A Silent Armageddon*, and 1994's *Shattered Helix*. "Light of My Death" and "Minute of Midnight" also appeared within the company's monthly anthology, Dark Horse Comics.

The next story to be published was entitled *The Quasimodo Gambit*. My colleague, Edward Martin III, whom had already secured the creative team of writer Don McGregor, interior artist Gary Caldwell and cover artist Christopher Moeller, called me into his office asking if I would be interested in taking over the responsibilities of editing this story. Edward's tenure at Dark Horse was coming to a close and he needed to pass this new series onto someone else. Being a Bond fan since 1981's film adaptation of *For Your Eyes Only*, I accepted this mission with high enthusiasm.

Cover from *The Quasimodo Gambit*, 1994, cover artwork by Christopher Moeller.

The Quasimodo Gambit certainly had its share of challenges. As with the previous 007 stories released through Dark Horse, this miniseries was actually a co-publication with Acme Comics, Ltd. and Glidrose Publications. Therefore, I was working with another editor, Dick Hansom, whom was based in the UK. Dick's primary role in co-editing this series was to secure the necessary publication approvals from the rights holders to 007. Obtaining these permissions proved laborious as it was not unusual to wait weeks to receive feedback from the Licensor. These frustrating delays ultimately resulted in the series being released significantly later than originally scheduled.

Although Don McGregor's original script was well written and certainly worthy of publication, formatting it to work within the comic-book medium was difficult. I was impressed by the amount of development Don had provided for Bond, Valentine Nebula, Quasimodo, and other characters. However, in order to adapt those character attributes properly for comics, I believed it was necessary to edit much of the back story. Many of the text captions featured monologues from specific characters and ultimately crowded the artwork. I had hoped to eliminate a lot of this text so the readers could focus on the illustrations and interpret the visual portion of the story for themselves. Unfortunately, Don didn't agree with me and the final printed result was less than what we and 007 fans had hoped for. Due to declining sales, extreme restrictions from the licensor and increased production costs, *James*

Below: photograph of Ian Fleming, circa 1962.

Bond 007: The Quasimodo Gambit was Dark Horse Comics' last publication featuring the character. Perhaps one day this story will be republished as a 007 novel; it's an excellent tale that deserves credit as one of the better non-Fleming works featuring the character.

– Robert V. Conte